The One

JM Dragon

Affinity
eBook Press
NZ

2014

The One
© 2014 by JM Dragon

Affinity E-Book Press NZ LTD.
Canterbury, New Zealand

1st Edition

ISBN: 978-1-927328-28-6

All rights reserved.

Editor: Nat Burns
Proof Editor: Alexis Smith
Cover Design: Irish Dragon Designs

Acknowledgments

Sometimes we take a different path to go back to the roots. This is my attempt to get back to what I love to do—write.

For this to happen I am inordinately grateful to Mel, my best friend. She cajoles me, listens, and even virtually kicks me from time to time to get back to writing.

Nancy, ah, what the hell the dragonfly loves you even when you mess with me mentally. I love the cover—you are ace.

Nat, as always you bring your best game to edit the story, it is so much better with your expertise, thank you.

I want to thank Rosa Moran for her investment in everything lesbian literature. If she can help, she will.

For all my readers, thank you for your support, and criticism—we all move forward because of you.

Notes:

I used a section of Peter Pan by J M Barrie under the public license copyright agreement.

A translator on the internet generated the Chinese featured in the story and I am unable to give 100 percent accuracy. I used the Chinese writing to add flavor to the storyline.

Dedication

For Mel

Who goes from one health issue to another, each one is challenging, some more than most. I cannot think of anyone better to dedicate this book to than her. Life is a trial and she certainly knows how to meet it with grace and a smile.

I could not wish for a finer best friend. I am honoured to have you in my life.

Table of Contents

Other JM Dragon Stories

Chapter One

In a dimly lit room, a tall figure stood at the window, watching shadows move on the rickety cane blind. Occasional bright light, from revelers in the procession going by on the street below, bounced off the dust-encrusted window dressing.

A woman lay indolently on the crumpled bed—the naked torso stretched to full length, conveying contentment. Black hair, as deeply dark as a raven's wing, moved over her thin shoulders. Almond-shaped eyes glanced at the naked form silhouetted against the window. She moved off the bed and padded silently to stand behind the person. Sure hands splayed over the enticing chest. A satisfied smile curved thin lips as the body under her touch reacted with a squirm and turned in her hands.

"Come back to bed. We have another hour before I have to go." Her voice had a delicate ring to it, the words spoken in broken, accented English.

There was a tensioning of cheekbones as if the comment had been abhorrent.

"You could stay with me and kick that son of a bitch out for good this time."

The slow deliberate movement on naked skin was working its magic. Lust, rather than anger, became the overriding emotion invading the air.

Dark brown eyes gazed up into flashing pools of steel blue. With a sigh that creased the otherwise flawless olive skin, the petite woman shook her head.

"You know it's impossible. My father chose him and I refuse to disobey his wishes. You understand what it means if I betray the bond."

A dainty hand snaked its way down the taunt belly of her prey and she felt the shiver reverberating in her ear as she nuzzled into the tanned neck.

"I can look after you. You don't need your father's money or his permission, Ming." There was a harsh laugh. "You're thirty years old. You can make your own decisions." A tanned hand stilled the questing one on its travels.

A tinkle of delicate laughter floated between them as the hand moved again, the restraint ignored. This time it moved to curly hair, the color of yellow cornflowers, and slithered fingers through the juices that flowed there.

"We've talked about this numerous times in the past year, Phil. You don't make enough money to give me what I need." Ming smiled. "Now please, let me make love to you and forget about words. Our time together is so short." Her hand moved insistently through the curls and found what she was looking for—the perky nub the evidence of a sexual response to her journey.

Phil groaned, then lifted Ming in strong muscular arms. Seconds later, they landed on the bed, minute particles of dust rising into the air around their bodies.

Discussion forgotten, the bodies intertwined and began a hurried, passionate lovemaking session.

✝

An hour later only one occupant remained in the dingy, back street hotel room. Phil once again took a stance to watch over the street below. People below, in a dragon train, continued their cruising through the street. Tonight had been the blessing of the virgin, or some other ridiculous ritualistic theme the people followed. Ming had been right; it was all about the money here in the city. With only a meagre commission flying cargo in a beat up, old cargo plane, her bank balance wouldn't be enough to keep someone like Ming in the luxurious life she was accustomed to.

Turning to survey the room, Philomena Casters decided that Ming was right, it was best to keep their relationship only in the lust category. She didn't have the money or the lifestyle to settle down—probably never would.

She grinned. God, but wouldn't Ming's pompous father and idiot husband be livid if they ever found out that their dutiful daughter and wife saved up all her passion for a woman? And a foreigner to boot.

She checked the clock and climbed back onto the bed. Her next flight out was in six hours, giving her enough time for a nap and a shower before she had to head off to the airstrip. She pulled the covers over her body, more out of habit then any need for the warmth. When she closed her eyes, however, a picture of Ming, nipples erect and body humming for what only she could provide, came to mind in glorious Technicolor. Sleep evaded her as she masturbated.

†

Hours later, she walked through the door of the reception area of Saunders Airlines.

3

"Phil, am I glad you're early. I have an emergency run for you." Blake Saunders, the owner of the airline, a pudgy man who resembled a monkey because of his profuse body hair, placed a map and a letter enclosed in a waterproof pouch in Phil's hands,

Phil took the pouch and gave it a cursory glance, then looked at the retreating back of the older man. He was wiping his hands to remove the sweat that profusely ran from him all day long. The humidity in this part of the world was horrendous. In the cities, in the hotels, it was tolerable, but venture outside the town boundaries and into the countryside and it was a completely different story. You had to be mad to work in it—especially a European. At least Saunders had opened his wallet and purchased a few fans to place around the major work areas.

"What about Jamie? I thought he had the early shift. Have we been inundated with work since I left yesterday?"

Blake stopped walking and turned around to face the woman. He scratched the side of his head before trailing sweat and oil over the rough stubble on what looked like a week old beard. "Jamie has a stomach bug."

"Again? I keep telling him he should stay away from the whore houses," Phil said.

"He's wet behind the ears. Too much, too soon." Saunders scratched his cheek.

Phil shook her head. He was a stupid fool, barely out of school. His Clark Gable looks had infatuated every girl who looked his way and he was naïve enough to think each one loved him. Silly boy. "I agree. This run, I guess it's the usual?"

"Read the letter while I check out the plane." Saunders turned away.

She slid a fingernail across the top of the envelope and retrieved the contents.

4

Mr. B Saunders
Saunders Airlines
Zongnan
China
May 12th, 1937
Dear Sir,
We require you to collect a package of delicate disposition, from Selah in the interior of the Rashid kingdom. Ask for Rosa Moran and give her the sealed envelope enclosed. When collected you must forthwith return to Zongnan and dutifully deposit the package to the British Consulate. They in turn will complete the final transaction and your ultimate negotiated fee.

In good faith, we deposit in your account the amount of a thousand pounds on the 23rd May.

The package must arrive within five days of this deposit or the deal is rescinded.
Joseph Bertram Ponsonby.
Solicitors of law
Ponsonby, Gold and Locke
23B Greyfriars Street
London
England.

Phil frowned as her eyebrows almost reached the top of her head. She whistled at the amount of the deposit and strode toward the supine figure of her employer who was under the Northrop.

"Boss, if the deposit is a thousand, what's the whole job worth?"

There was a curse under the fuselage as Saunders emerged. He was rubbing his head. "Now that's my business, Phil. Yours is to do the job."

"That's almost impossible." She frowned. "You know we have to give that area a ten day notice for fuel. We have exactly…." She glanced at the Bank of England calendar on the wall of the office area. "Four days."

"Almost, you said." He grinned. "Sure, if Jamie was on the run, or anyone else in these parts, it would be. You, Phil, are something else when it comes to breaking records in flight. I know we'll do it."

"Appealing to my pride right?"

"Works every time, I've found." He looked solemn. "Actually, I've used some of the retainer to pay four outstanding fuel and maintenance bills. I guess you understand that the pockets were empty. Tell you what, I'll make you a deal. If you pull this off, we could talk partnership."

"I didn't know you were in that much financial trouble." Phil looked at her short clipped nails then turned her eyes to the man who was waiting pensively. "Are we ready to go?" she said, idly flicking a speck of dust off her jacket.

"Yep, Gilda's ready and waiting." Saunders grinned and slapped her back. "See you in four days."

Phil nodded. She moved toward the ladder, climbed into the cockpit of the Northrop, and began her preflight checks. A few minutes later, she waved at Blake Saunders and took off.

Chapter Two

Rosa Moran watched the group of children laughing and playfully splashing water over one another. She so enjoyed watching them have fun.

"Missy, missy, you play?"

Rosa shook her head. "Not today, Bang. We have a lesson." She checked her grandfather's gold fob watch around her neck. "In ten minutes." She held up her hands and wiggled all her fingers.

"Be there."

"I know you will." She smiled as he headed back to his cohorts and held up his fingers as she had done. "I guess he just wanted to check on the timetable."

"Timetable, we have a timetable?"

Rosa spun around and faced the speaker. "We do, Prudence. At least I do."

"Hmm, it's the devil's work playing as they do. They should be in class now." She raised her eyes heavenward. "Do you approve this behavior?"

"Actually, yes I do." Rosa liked Prudence. Of all the Catholic missionaries, Prudence was the most practical.

"Harrumph, they need to be educated to support themselves, not fooling around. Especially orphans in this heathen country."

7

Prudence pulled at her coarse cotton blouse where light brown marks traced the normally pristine white fabric. It was a testament to the harsh and basic conditions where they lived. Starching clothes was easy but removing the dark stains of hard labor was another matter altogether, especially with the old, threadbare material.

"When is the next shipment of supplies due? I know I could certainly take advantage of some material to make another set of clothes. Mine are almost rags," Rosa said, glancing down at the pale blue cotton shirt that had once belonged to her mother. During the past few years, she had mended it in numerous places.

"Father Ralph hasn't seen fit to advise us. I will ask Charlotte if she knows more after dinner." Prudence sniffed the air, wriggling her nose.

"I must return to the classroom, or the children will be there before me." Rosa turned away as a wracking cough shook every bone in her body.

"You need to take a trip to the village and see the doctor," Prudence remarked.

Rosa noticed the look of concern and a gentling in the fierce expression.

"It's nothing. Besides, Anne has given me a poultice that she said will definitely work this time," Rosa managed to say before another cough shook her.

"God, give me strength. Anne is a novice in the medicine department. She barely made it out of nursing school."

Rosa bit her lip, wanting to laugh at the remark, but she schooled her features. "Don't you think that is a little uncharitable? Anne is doing her best."

"Do as you please, because we all know you will." Prudence turned away.

"Thank you," Rosa replied. She knew that the woman's gruff reply was from concern for her, not that she would ever openly say so.

"You are welcome. I have to go."

Rosa watched Prudence walk toward the walled entrance of the missionary. She coughed again, this time it was a little easier. Perhaps she did need to see a doctor. Maybe she would make that trip soon.

Her fob watch chimed softly. She smiled and with a brisk step, headed to the small bamboo and thatch building that was her classroom.

✝

"I'm an idiot, Gilda." Phil tapped the control console and scowled. Then she pulled back the throttle lever and settled back as the aircraft levelled out. She set the flight controls to the required coordinates.

She considered Blake's offer of a partnership and knew he must be desperate. Maybe he was and she hadn't been taking notice of anything other than Ming. Hmm, Ming. Maybe her turn of fortune would make Ming consider her proposition more viable. In the recesses of her mind, she could understand her lover's position. As much as that word was like soap in the mouth, money was everything to Ming, with position in society a close second. Money, as a pilot, was always touch and go but as a partner, well, the sky was the limit. Yes, she had a chance. With money came position. She knew that much about Chinese culture

Her stomach did a double twist as she considered the thought of seeing Ming's uptight husband take that on the chin. Phil's hand clutched the throttle tighter as a freak wind shunted the plane off course.

9

"Yep, how could that dick ever compete with me? Especially if I have money, along with Ming's beauty and sex."

She grinned and turned her attention to the worsening weather pattern that was seemingly trying to inhibit the progress toward her fortune, and ultimate goal—Ming.

"Let's get through this, Gilda, and I'll top up your engines myself." Droplets of rain hit the cockpit windshield.

†

"Bang, will you please read the first paragraph today."

Bang smiled. His round face appeared to glow as he stood up quickly. The rickety stool he sat upon danced on the ground.

"At once the lost boys—but where are they? They are no longer there. Rabbits could not have disappeared more quickly. I will tell you where they are. With the exception of Nibs, who has darted away to reconnoiter, they are already in their home under the ground, a very delightful residence of which we shall see a good deal presently. But, how have they reached it? For there is no entrance to be seen, not so much as a large stone, which if rolled away, would disclose the mouth of a cave. Look closely, however, and you may note that there are here seven large trees, each with a hole in its hollow trunk as large as a boy. These are the seven entrances to the home under the ground, for which Hook has been searching in vain these many moons. Will he find it tonight?'"

"Delightful, Bang. Well done." Rosa winked at the boy, who was the tallest in her class. He had a thirst for knowledge that out surpassed hers at that age.

"Who shall we ask next, I wonder?" Rosa smiled as her gaze caught the shy stare of the smallest child in the group—Tao.

"Tao, the next paragraph, please." There were sniggers in the room and Rosa gave the laughers a steely look. Tao might be small and a bit hesitant but she worked hard and deserved a voice.

Tao stood and her hands trembled as she clutched the book that Bang passed to her.

"As the pirates advanced, the quick eye of Starkey sighted Nibs disappearing through the wood, and at once his pistol flashed out. An iron claw gripped his shoulder.

"Captain, let go!" he cried, writhing.

Now for the first time we hear the voice of Hook. It was a black voice. "Put back that pistol first," it said threateningly.

"It was one of those boys you hate. I could have shot him dead."

"Aye, and the sound would have brought Tiger Lily's redskins upon us. Do you want to lose your scalp?"

"Shall I go after him, Captain?" asked pathetic Smee.

"And tickle him with Johnny Corkscrew?" Smee had pleasant names for everything, and his cutlass was Johnny Corkscrew, because he wiggled it in the wound. One could mention many lovable traits in Smee. For instance, after killing, it was his spectacles he wiped instead of his weapon.

"Johnny's a silent fellow," he reminded Hook.

"Not now, Smee," Hook said darkly. "He is only one, and I want to mischief all the seven. Scatter and look for them'."

Rosa smiled as Tao gave an almost perfect dictation of the book. Hesitantly, yes, but she had nailed the feel of the book. Rosa felt that Hook was Tao's favorite character by the inflection in her voice when she read about him.

"Thank you, Tao." Rosa glanced around the room at her fifteen students. Several were from wealthy families but the others were orphans. The only way the church could fund this mission was to offer education to the wealthier families.

"Showling, you can read the next chapter."

"No." The negative response was followed by a tirade of Chinese that even she had difficulty following.

"Why not?" Rosa frowned. "In English please, that is why your parents want you to be here."

Showling Chow scowled. "I will never follow a serf."

Rosa drew in a deep breath. There were times when she really wanted to smack a child. This one in particular as he was always disruptive. She briefly closed her eyes to allow the uncharitable thought to drift way. Showling's father was the local magistrate and you did not cross that family.

Rosa glanced in Tao's direction, her head held low. She chewed on her bottom lip. Then picked up her copy of the book and began to read the next couple of paragraphs.

"Showling, will you please read the rest of the chapter."

"No."

All eyes in the class were on her as she digested that word.

"Why?"

"Boring."

Rosa let loose a secret sigh of relief at the answer. "Okay, so what do you consider less boring?"

"We should be reading Chinese stories, not English propaganda," Showling declared.

Rosa drew in a deep breath at the child's anger. "We do, remember last month and *The Donkey of Guizhou*? The English stories are not propaganda, merely tales of bravery and life."

"How can a girl and her brothers believe in such a thing?"

"You don't believe in imagination?"

Showling snorted. "China grows with strength and truth."

"Life grows with enlightenment, which to me means accepting differences. Can you do that?"

"No! China is the whole."

Rosa passed a hand through her dark hair. "The whole? Can you explain?"

All eyes in the room turned to Showling who stood, his eyes wild. "You are beneath me. I do not explain to inferiors."

Rosa bit her lip holding back a retort. Her control of the class was slipping and she needed to reassert herself as the educator. "As you appear to have had enough of our classes, you are excused."

Showling frowned, picked up his school tablet and writing instruments, and stalked out of the room.

Rosa drew in a deep breath and wish she hadn't when a cough engulfed her. Sympathetic cries from the children filled the room. When she finally controlled the spasms, she smiled at the children. "How about today we have a short lesson."

There was a whoop of joy as chairs scraped the floor and children collected their belongings.

Rosa gave a smile as the majority left the room. Then she faced Bang and Tao still seated. "That meant everyone," she said gently.

"You ill, Missy?" Bang asked.

Rosa saw Tao nod and tears welled up in her eyes at their concern. "No. No, just a cold, nothing more. Now I know you two love to play and you have extra time, so go."

They both stood up and walked slowly out of the room, Tao giving her a shy smile as they left.

Rosa sat back in her chair and speculated on her position regarding Showling Chow. The child was beyond disruptive. She'd have to speak with Charlotte. Influential or not, Showling had to go.

The sound of a plane overhead diffused her thoughts away from the precocious child. She jumped out of the chair.

"At last, supplies," she said as she left the schoolroom.

Chapter Three

Charlotte narrowed her gaze at the cavalier jaunt of the pilot striding toward her. The plane wasn't the usual jalopy that brought supplies, nor did it seem that the pilot was one of Major Johnson's team. Very odd. Father Ralph had a habit of frugal communication at times. She surmised that this must be one such time. The pilot neared and she saw the familiar leather jacket and gray trousers most fliers wore. However, this one didn't have the decorations of war that the Major's people usually portrayed.

"Are you from Father Ralph?" Forthright was best, she had discovered in this infidel country.

"Nope."

"I see. And why would you land here then, young man?" Charlotte saw a faint smirk cross the smooth-skinned young pilot's lips and she held her tongue as uncharitable thoughts forced their way into her consciousness.

"You have a package for me."

Charlotte shook her head and her straw hat tipped precariously. "We are the ones waiting for a package, young man, more than one. I take it you are not here with our supplies. Don't answer that, it's obvious."

She turned and began to walk away.

"Rosa Moran?"

Charlotte switched back, her eyes narrowed almost to the point of closing. "Rosa, how do you know of her?"

The pilot withdrew a letter from the worn jacket. "I have a letter for her that indicates what package I need to take back with me. Sorry to be abrupt, but I do not have a great deal of time. If I can take off in the next hour, I will still meet my deadline. Is she here?"

"Yes, Rosa is here. May I ask who sent you?"

"I don't usually explain myself to anyone other than the name on the list but in the current circumstances, and to speed things up....My company was commissioned by solicitors of law, Ponsonby, Gold and Locke of London, to do exactly what I've told you. Contact this Rosa Moran woman, receive the package, and transport it back to Zongnan within four days. If I leave in the next hour with the package, the job will be on time "

Charlotte was dubious about this claim. "May I see the letter?"

"If you are Rosa Moran, sure. If not, pardon my manners—no."

"That's rather impertinent, young man. I am not Rosa. Do you know or care who I am?"

"Nope, but now I know who you are not."

"Stay here. I will find Rosa for you." Charlotte walked toward the mission and heard the pilot move in step with her. "I said stay here. Do you not understand a simple instruction?"

She saw the pilot lift up his hands in acknowledgement.

"I will stay exactly here. Is that fine with you?"

"Yes."

Charlotte shook her head as she headed for the schoolroom.

†

16

Phil scuffed the dry ground and wondered, not for the first time, if her role in life was to pick up non-descript packages of no interest to anyone but the eventual receiver. It did pay the bills, or at least she thought it did. A voice caught her attention and rippled through her body at a rather disconcerting speed.

"I don't understand, Charlotte. Why would they send me a letter and what package am I supposed to send?"

"The answers, my child, are with the young man. I'll be within earshot if something untoward takes place."

"Thank you."

Phil doused the need to laugh at the absurdity of what she'd blatantly heard. Her eyes focused on the young woman heading her way. Hmm, a nice piece of skirt and with a voice that would melt a thousand hearts. Maybe today wasn't so bad after all.

"I'm Rosa Moran. You have a letter for me."

Now, up close and personal, Phil was definitely interested. Flawless skin greeted her along with a body most would happily give up a year of ciggies just to look at for minutes. Fortune favored the brave and she hadn't had to part with anything for the privilege.

"Yes, I do." Phil reached inside her leather jacket and withdrew the letter given to her. "Whatever is in that letter, you need to understand that I'm on a deadline. If I don't take off in the next forty minutes the time span given will be a dead loss."

"I understand," Rosa remarked. She tore open the letter.

Phil enjoyed watching people. In fact, in another life, she was pretty darn sure she'd been a voyeur. These days they would call her a plain pervert. Which they already did for her sexual deviancy. She chuckled.

A deep frown was her reward. The Moran woman appeared none too happy about the contents of her letter, if the tremble of her full lips was anything to go by.

"Anything wrong?"

Rosa shook her head and then sighed. "Well, yes, actually."

There were a few moments of silence.

"Are you going to share? Remember I'm on a deadline." Phil clicked her fingers.

"Yes, yes." Rosa glanced at the aircraft. "My grandfather's …A family friend is ill. He wants me to travel home."

Phil shrugged. "Not an unusual request. If you like your family, that is."

There was a snort from behind.

"I have responsibilities here. I can't just go back with you."

Phil took a step backward as the implication permeated her brain.

"Hey, doll, wait a minute. I don't take passengers. All I want is the package they sent me for and I'll be off." She waved her fingers in the air as a gesture of a takeoff.

"I'm sorry to disappoint you, but it appears I'm the package," Rosa declared with hands on hips. "You can leave. I'm not going." Rosa turned away.

Phil bit her lip. *I hate you, Blake, I hate you, Rosa Moran, and I hate just about everything about this.* Saunders' predicament reared its ugly head. The company was broke and this woman, as abhorrent as the idea of taking a passenger was, was a means to an end and for her, a new life with Ming.

"Look, doll, why not check out Grandpa? You can come back after the visit. I'll fly you back here myself for free. Then we can all come out of this happy."

Phil ground her teeth. "My boss needs the commission or we will go broke," she admitted reluctantly.

Rosa spun around and faced Phil.

Beautiful, slate gray eyes glared at her and Phil caught her breath for a second.

"You changed your tune. I haven't. You may go...no, wait. Give me a little time and I will pen a reply."

Phil frowned. "Okay, maybe that will appease the old man and he will pay the fee."

Rosa screwed up her eyes and walked toward Charlotte.

"Well, they could have been more hospitable," Phil muttered as she trudged back to Gilda. As she did, a gaggle of children came toward her laughing and shyly pointing at her and the plane.

"Hey, kids, have you ever seen a plane before?"

They all stopped. Their faces became masks as their laughter stilled.

"Obviously not." Phil turned to the tallest of the group. "Want a look inside?"

They all nodded and smiled. Phil had to stifle her laughter. She waved the closest one forward. Within fifteen minutes, all the kids had looked inside and she was facing a beaming group. Hmm, what next, she wondered? Didn't they have homes to go to?

"Bang, please take the rest of the children to the refectory. Lottie has made another special treat for you." Rosa appeared as if from nowhere.

Phil watched as the tall kid that she had first noticed nodded. He spoke in rapid Chinese and had the group moving in the direction of the main building.

"I guess kids are the same everywhere."

Rosa, with her back turned to Phil, presumably watching the kids, didn't speak. When she turned, she handed Phil an envelope.

"For my grandfather's associates. I'm sorry I cannot travel with you," Rosa said.

Phil took the envelope and their hands touched briefly. A flutter of excitement began in Phil's belly and lingered after the connection severed. She must have been tired.

"Me too. I'll be off then."

"Yes, we wouldn't want you to miss your schedule."

"No, we wouldn't." Phil dismissed the sarcasm, climbed inside the cockpit, and was about to shut the door when Rosa spoke.

"Thank you for bringing me news of my family. It was not a total waste of a journey."

There was a marked sincerity in the voice and Phil smiled. "I guess we will see when I get back." She closed the door and began the procedure to take off.

When the engine revved into life, she looked to the side and saw Rosa Moran still watching her. She gave a saucy wink and the devil in her blew a kiss. She chuckled as she saw a red stain graze Rosa's pale skin.

Minutes later, she was in the air. "Hope Saunders hasn't spent all the advance or we really are in the crap."

✝

Rosa brushed aside the tears that trickled down her cheeks as she watched the plane climb high into the sky and eventually disappear behind billowing clouds. She really hoped grandfather and Alfred would understand. Right now just wasn't the time for a visit. She turned back and gazed at her surroundings. They were a missionary surrounded by mountains and a river that flooded every winter. It had been home for the first twelve years of her life and she suspected that, had it not been for a friend of her parents and her tenacity, in a nice way of course, she would never have known of her grandfather. When he had found her there, he shipped her to England and the best schools to learn etiquette. It had not resolved her need to come back here, however, for it was home—where her heart was. Until there was a time that her heart no longer belonged to this place, she would live here.

"You look pensive, child."

Rosa smiled weakly. Then she faced Prudence. "Not pensive exactly, more torn. A good friend of my grandfather's is gravely ill and I have declined his wishes that I visit them."

Prudence nodded. "Your grandfather may not understand you wanting to remain with us, child. He must have thought you would travel back to England, especially since the political climate is not conducive to happy times right now."

"You mean the Japanese and the rebellions?" Rosa frowned as Prudence nodded. "Surely they will not let happen what happened twenty years ago."

"Rosa, you know that there is a lot of animosity toward the Western cultural teachings. You must be prepared for more of the disruption such as Showling Chow causes."

"How did you know...?" Rosa smiled. "I forget, you know everything."

"Not everything." Prudence laughed harshly.

"You think I should have gone?"

"I think you should do what your heart tells you. I've known you for years and it has served you well. Besides, God is always guiding us."

Rosa smiled. "My heart tells me to stay."

Prudence grinned. "Then let's go and have dinner or Bang will be giving us that starving expression he has."

Rosa hooked her arm in Prudence's as they walked toward the main building.

Chapter Four

Six months later, hands on hips, Phil beamed at the new sign above the hanger.

"It has a ring to it, I'll grant you. You never did say how old Saunders made you a partner?" A slap on the back with as much force as a newborn accompanied the question.

"I didn't." Phil glanced at Jamie Sheppard, flicking him a wry smile.

"Phil, it's not like you to keep me in the dark." Jamie grinned. "Besides, I work for you and we keep it in the family."

Family. She hadn't had that kind of association since she was ten years old. Hmm, family didn't have a bad ring to it. Go figure.

"Please, Phil, maybe in the future I might be a partner too, if I know the right ropes to pull," Jamie pleaded.

"Money."

"Money? When did you have any money?"

Phil sucked in a deep breath. "That's for me to know and you to find out."

Jamie gently cuffed Phil on the cheek. "I will, you don't do secrets well. Are we going into town tonight?"

Phil looked up at the clear blue sky and frowned. "Yeah, nothing doing until mid-day tomorrow." She took a deep breath. "Don't forget you have the interior route tomorrow. Be sober when you turn up."

Phil knew Jamie would be lost, within a couple of hours once they reached town, in the abscess of whores that circled the bars that foreigners frequented.

Jamie saluted and grinned. "I'll be on the job, boss."

"Yeah, right." Phil showed him a derisive smile. "One day, you idiot, you will learn what reality is." Phil threw an arm around his shoulders as they headed to the jeep that would take them to town.

†

Donna's Bar didn't particularly distinguish itself from the numerous ones that lined Chang Street. Outside lights flickered and dazzled the eager young man and the old pro. This part of town suckered you out of your hard-earned cash like a gaping hole in the pocket.

Phil was familiar with the bar and the owner and she felt comfortable there. From her slouched position at the edge of the bar, she watched a female, barely an adult, sucker Jamie in. The exploitation of children here made her sick to the stomach. She steered clear from any attempt at fixing her up with one of those unfortunate children. She was here to fly and not become involved with the under-aged sex rings that seemed to be a staple in the larger towns and cities.

"Philly, my lovely, why the long face?"

Phil fingered the rim of her beer bottle and shrugged. "Do you ever check the ages of the girls?"

"Not on your life. If I did, there wouldn't be any business for me."

"What about making it harder for the rascals? Ask more for their services?" Phil stared at Donna, the only woman around these parts that she called friend.

"Same results. I'd be losing out. Anyway, what's with the philanthropic review? Had an epiphany since you became a partner with greasy Saunders?"

Phil laughed and drank from her beer. "Nope."

Donna leaned on the bar and touched Phil's arm. "Come back at three a.m. and we can talk."

Phil frowned. "Three a.m.?"

"Yeah, contrary to popular opinion, that's when we close up. I have something to show you."

"Really? By three a.m., I'll be less than sober."

"Be sober," Donna replied forcefully and moved away to serve another customer.

Phil slugged back another drink and considered Donna's request. She looked at the time on her wristwatch—nine. Crap, it was her day off tomorrow. Sober wasn't part of the plan.

✝

Donna popped her head out of the door and then rapidly shut and locked the door of the bar. She turned and gazed at Phil. If she had been twenty years younger, Phil wouldn't be looking at that piece of expensive crap, Ming Xian. Nope, in her heyday, Donna would have walked rings around the Chinese woman.

"So, I've given up a drunken, debauched evening for what?" Phil asked. "It had better be good."

Donna bit her lip and then clicked her fingers. The sound surprisingly reverberated around the room.

The door marked Private opened and two girls entered the bar.

"Phil, I want you to meet Mai and Ziong."

Phil moved toward them. "Hi, girls."

25

Donna placed an arm around the two girls and spoke to them in fluent Chinese.

They smiled at Phil and giggled.

Phil laughed. "Okay, Donna, what's the give?"

Donna moved to the bar, selected a couple of cokes, gave them to the girls, and indicated they sit at a table. Then she motioned to Phil to go to the other end of the bar.

"We've had some interesting conversations over the years," Donna said.

Phil laughed. "Sure, I'm usually half cut but yeah, I guess."

"I need your help. At least help in the transport department."

"Transport. Sure, I can do that."

"This is a little more difficult." Donna looked to the girls and then looked back at Phil.

"Crap, Donna, I'm not a human trafficker."

Donna shook her head. "It isn't like that. Those girls are sisters. Their parents are a very wealthy family who has fallen out of favor with the current regime."

"Doesn't that happen at least once a day? Hell, why aren't their heads chopped off?"

Donna flicked Phil a severe glance. "Uncalled for, Phil. You are beginning to sound like the government."

"Not quite." Phil shrugged. "What exactly do you want me to do?"

"There's a mission, at Selah in the interior of the Rashid kingdom. I know they will take them in."

Phil slipped off her stool. "Selah? In the interior of the Rashid kingdom?"

"Well, you didn't need to repeat it, but yeah, do you know it?"

"I went there once," Phil bit out.

"Great, I know it's an imposition, but will you take them there."

"I don't take passengers, you know that, so why should I do it for you?"

Donna bit her lip and drew up her shoulders. "I was, am, in love with their mother."

Silence shrouded the room for a short time.

"Okay." Phil chewed her lip and gazed at the children. "Jamie has the interior flight tomorrow. I guess I'm going to replace him." She sighed. "They'd best come with me now."

Donna's heart beat joyously. "Thank you, Phil, for not asking any more questions." She placed a hand on the sinuous forearm of her friend. "I will get you some money for the trip."

Phil shrugged. "Forget it. You can owe me a few beers when I next come by."

"Thank you. This is a good thing, Phil. I know it."

Phil rolled her eyes. "We will see."

Donna leaned across the bar and placed a light kiss on Phil's lips. "Thank you."

She turned to the girls and motioned them forward.

†

Phil had wondered what she'd say to Rosa Moran if she ever came across her again. She still wondered and hoped that she could avoid the woman. What can you say to a person that can possibly convey how an act of kindness to a stranger had changed her life? Thank you, maybe, but those words really couldn't cover what she felt.

There was a commotion in the back of the plane and she swiveled around to look at the two Chinese kids Donna had foisted on her. She decided the noise must have been from

Gilda's creaky wings because the children were sleeping. What could she have said to Donna…no? Hardly. When things had been tough in the beginning, Donna had been a good friend. Now it was repayment time. One thing she knew for sure was how to repay her debts.

She throttled back the wheel and began her descent into an area that she had a gut feeling was going to be trouble.

Chapter Five

Rosa grasped her diary, which she religiously scribbled an entry into every day, to her chest. She sighed heavily. Why hadn't God answered her prayers? It wasn't as if she was asking anything for herself. Her eyes strayed to the courtyard and children squealing in play. She smiled. Ah, to be so young and not know the workings of things you can do nothing about. Perhaps that was her folly—wanting to do something about the harshness in the country she called home. Being born in China did not bring with it the status of being Chinese—her designation was foreigner.

She turned her attention back to her diary, placed it on her lap, and began to write.

I do not ask for a miracle. No. I ask for hope and compassion. I believe it will come our way soon. If it does not, then I will pray for those who look to their own ends and not to others'.

She closed the volume and placed it on the plain wooden bedside table next to a faded, silver-framed picture of her parents.

Rosa left her room and headed toward the courtyard, only to be stopped by the boom of a familiar voice.

"Rosa, we have news from Father Ralph. Come to my office, my dear, we need to talk."

The dark expression on Charlotte's lined face was not a good sign. With a smile, she followed the rotund figure.

Charlotte, instead of settling into her comfortable leather chair at her desk, stood at the window looking out. She sighed.

Rosa raised her eyebrows. This really didn't look good. "Surely it can't be that bad, can it?" Rosa asked.

"I'm afraid it can, my dear Rosa." Charlotte turned to face Rosa.

Rosa frowned and bit down on her lip. "What did Father Ralph say?"

There were a few moments of silence.

"You know, my dear, that we try to keep the governmental workings of those around us out of our lives."

Rosa frowned. "Yes, but that isn't always...."

"No more, I'm afraid." Charlotte gave her a grave expression.

"I don't understand. What did the Father say?" Rosa shuffled her feet.

"Disruptive pupils should be dismissed from class and removed from the program."

Rosa grinned. "Oh, that isn't bad news. Finally, we can teach properly, without the distress of children like Showling."

"You don't understand, Rosa. Showling is welcome. It is those that create problems for him—such as Bang—that will be removed."

"That's ridiculous." Rosa leapt to her feet at the news.

"Calm yourself, my dear. Bang is a favorite of not just you but all of us here at the missionary."

Rosa watched Charlotte pace a tiny area near the window. She turned and gave Rosa an intense look.

"Things are changing in China due to the Japanese invasion of the continent. We have to be grateful for the patronage of the Chinese in power."

Rosa shook her head. "If that means children like Bang become victims then I say *no*."

"We do too, my dear."

Rosa frowned. "And that means what, exactly?"

"We need to find a safe haven for our so called *disruptive* children."

"Not all the children?"

"No, not all."

"I don't understand?"

Charlotte smiled and placed a hand on Rosa's shoulder.

"I have been in touch with a friend. She is English by birth but has been adopted by the Chinese for her devotion to the Chinese people, you might say."

Rosa balled her fists. "What does that mean for Bang?"

Charlotte stood next to Rosa. Placing a hand on her shoulder, she smiled.

"We need you to take Bang and Tao on a journey, one that will take them from this province and find shelter in another missionary. There are several who are willing to take them in, and you, if you choose."

"I'm puzzled. What has your friend to do with this?"

Charlotte shrugged. "She has agreed to take all our orphans, except ones with a potential to have the authorities come looking for them."

Rosa shook her head. "I don't understand. You said Bang was disruptive and not Tao. How could anyone think such a shy, sweet child could be so? Why isn't she allowed to remain with the other children?"

"Showling doesn't like her."

Rosa closed her eyes and shook her head. The cruelty of the young.

A furrow ran from Charlotte's left brow to her right in a deep straight line.

"The missionary is to be closed within the year, Rosa. We are all being sent to other missions or out of the country altogether. I will be going to France."

Rosa cried out and barely suppressed tears. "Why are we closing? This mission has been here more than a hundred years. It doesn't make sense."

"Father Ralph is reluctant to grant me that information. However, I suspect I know the answer. I've lived here for thirty years and understand these people well enough."

"Are you going to permit me to share your suspicions?" Rosa wiped away a trickle of tears.

Charlotte nodded.

"For several years now, there have been rumblings of rebellion against the power brokers of provincial government. Their scapegoat, shall we say, is Westerners. Many now do not tolerate western influence, perhaps they never did. That aside, we have been fortunate in the patronage of the Chow family, in particular, during the past decades. Now we can no longer count on it."

Rosa sighed. "Showling's grandfather's passing two years ago was the catalyst, I suspect. I guess that explains his attitude."

"Perhaps. The Chows own much of the nearby land and with it the influence to change the minds of others. We have no one else with half the influence to turn to for financial and security help. We are on our own unless we do what the Chow family wants."

"Isn't it enough that Bang and Tao have no family, that they are to be the ones to leave the only home and friends they have ever known? It isn't fair."

"Fairness, my dear Rosa, has never been a part of political machinations." Charlotte moved the few feet to Rosa's side and stroked her hair. "I believe that you and they will find a better life."

"Oh, how can you say that? We have a better life here with you all," Rosa cried out.

"Our beautiful, Rosa, who has a gentle way and a hardy spirit. We know in our hearts that this sacrifice will be beneficial. Now, I'm afraid, my dear, I have to make travel plans for the other children. Father Ralph is arranging for Major Jones to make a few unscheduled trips to take the children away safely. By the time the Chows find out, there will be only a few of us remaining."

Rosa reached out and laid a hand on Charlotte's forearm. "Nothing will happen to you when they find all the children gone?"

"We might be old, but have you ever met a missionary from here that couldn't hold her own against a set of bullies."

So true, especially Prudence. "I was wondering…no, that's okay." Rosa turned to leave.

"Prudence is going to be my right hand woman at the new position. I can't have her wandering into another mission—think of the commotion she would cause."

Rosa grinned. "I'm glad, not because you are both leaving but that at least you will be together."

"Yes. Rosa, you need to leave by mid-day tomorrow. I'm sorry it's short notice."

"That's okay, it will be another life adventure, and at least I won't be alone."

"You are never alone, Rosa. God is with you always."

✝

Phil throttled back the engine and began her descent close to the mission. The recent unexpected heavy rains of the winter months hadn't wiped out the sketchy runway, which surprised her. "Must have lots of aviation visitors. What do you think, Gilda?"

Phil switched her attention to the sleeping twins. "Time to get up, kids."

There was no response other than the taller of the twins, Mai, snuggling closer to her sister.

"Crap, heavy sleepers. That's all I need." Phil frowned as she engaged the wheels, no matter what, it would be bumpy and scary if you didn't know what to expect.

"孩子现在" (Children up now) Phil spoke harshly and was pleasantly pleased when two sets of dark brown eyes blinked at her. She wasn't sure if it was the tone of voice she used or the less than perfect Chinese. Either way, it worked.

"按住到面,我们都了解" (Hold on to the sides. We are going down)

The twins nodded and grasped the metal handholds on the side of the plane and gave Phil a frightened look.

"像你爸爸在操场摆在你身边" (Think of your dad swinging you in the air) Well, maybe not their dad swinging them in the air, but it was the only thing she could think of. It seemed to work as they gave her a wobbly smile.

Phil concentrated on landing the plane safely and a few minutes later they landed and she suppressed a laugh as the kids gave a whoop of joy.

Taxiing along the rough ground for a few hundred yards, she came to a dead stop. The plane lurched and the girls groaned.

Phil smirked, glad she hadn't offered them breakfast before landing. She cut the engine and shutdown the equipment.

"现在在这里,先生?"(Here, Mr.?)Ziong's timid question had Phil frowning.

Why did everyone think she was a guy? Must be the damned short haircut Ming insisted she have since they'd become lovers.

"Yes, we are here now, Ziong, and you can call me Phil." The blank looks on their faces had Phil rolling her eyes.

She pressed a finger to her chest, "My name is Phil."

Mai's pert nose crinkled and Ziong narrowed her eyes.

"我的名字是菲尔." Phil said it again in Chinese.

The girls nodded and grinned.

A commotion outside the plane caused Phil to gaze out of the small cockpit window.

"I've seen that tall kid before," she muttered.

Opening the door from the cockpit, she climbed down the ladder and jumped the last foot onto the brown, dry ground. A cloud of gray dust rose into the air.

"Hey, how you doing, kid?"

The boy, showing crooked teeth, grinned.

Scratching her head, Phil tried to recall if she had ever heard the boy's name. If she had, she couldn't remember to save her life. Then a shiver went down her spine as a voice she recognized spoke.

"This is a surprise. Do you have another message from my grandfather?"

Phil switched her gaze to Rosa and gave her attention to the seemingly breathless young woman who had been her lifesaver. She sounded out of breath and her cheeks had a rosy glow as if she'd been running.

"I'm sorry, not this time."

"Oh."

Phil wasn't sure if that was a disappointed or a curious answer. Perhaps it was both.

"I do have a package of sorts to deliver though." Phil rummaged in the pocket of her leather jacket. She retrieved the envelope Donna had given to her which explained the predicament of the twins. Addressed to Charlotte Spicer. Phil handed her the envelope.

"It's for Charlotte?"

Phil shrugged.

There was shuffling in the plane and Mai and Ziong's heads appeared out of the side of the door.

"I see you have brought company this trip."

Phil watched, fascinated, as a delighted smile crossed Rosa's lips. It transcended an average looking woman, in comparison to the exotic looks of the Asian women. It was right what they said about beauty transcending the outer shell. Rosa had that in spades, along with gorgeous black hair that went to her shoulders....

"Are you going to introduce us?"

Phil's cheeks grew warm as she had probably been caught staring." Sure, Mai and Ziong. It's all in the letter."

"很好地满足您小." (Good to meet you, little ones) Rosa smiled at the children and motioned for them to leave the plane.

The twins gave a pensive look at the steep ladder on the side of the cockpit.

Phil shook her head, and then climbed up the ladder and one by one took each girl on her back and settled them on the ground. It was quicker than trying to find the passenger ladder, which was gathering dust under tarpaulins in the rear of the cargo area.

Rosa nodded at the children and stroked their hair in a gentle manner. She turned to Phil.

"We had better see Charlotte in haste." Rosa turned and spoke to the boy as she walked away. "Bang, we have visitors, Take Mai and Ziong to the refectory and give them something to eat." She spoke swiftly in Chinese to the twins who nodded as they took Bang's hands and walked toward a walled section to their left.

Phil glanced at her plane. Normally she wouldn't leave Gilda unsecured

"Are you coming or just going to stand there?"

"I'm coming." Damn this woman was bossy. She liked it. She grinned and caught up to Rosa.

✝

Charlotte gazed at the young man who had been here before and though he had not caused any trouble, there was just something not quite right about him.

"This person who has sent the message and the children to us, expressly indicated our mission?"

"Yes, explicitly. Isn't it in the letter?"

Charlotte fingered the unopened letter. "I prefer to make an initial judgment on situations as they appear to me."

"That helps me how? I need to return or I'm in big trouble. Are you going to take the twins?"

There was an arrogance in the tone and a false sense that it really didn't matter to him what happened to the unfortunate children. They were unnecessary baggage. In most circumstances, Charlotte would have given this man short shrift. However, she realized he might be in a position to help with their current predicament.

"I'm afraid not."

"You have to take them. What kind of missionary are you that you ignore the plight of children in need."

Charlotte stood. Her wooden spindle chair creaked, much like her old bones. She moved around her desk and came within inches of the man. She stared into unflinching blue eyes. She waved the letter in front of her.

"It is the plight of the children that we hold sacred. We are closing the mission and our flock is moving on. We cannot take them. I'm sorry."

The pilot pierced Charlotte with a gaze that would have made many a person move to the other side of the room at the rage held there.

I'm made of sturdier stuff, young man. You cannot intimidate me.

"You haven't even read the letter! What will happen to them now?"

Charlotte looked down at the letter. "That is true. Even if I did, I cannot help. We have more than forty children to find homes for, and soon. Time is running out for us here."

"Time is running out. What does that mean? I thought all you pious types had all the time in the world to take up charitable causes."

The young man turned away and headed for the door.

"What will you do?" Rosa asked.

"What I should have done in the beginning—declined to help. Now you see what charitable notions have done for me and those children—nothing," Phil snarled.

Charlotte sympathized with the predicament. "There may be another way. You would be required to help."

The young man stopped as he reached the door, spun round, and glared at her. "I think I've done my civic duty. Not a chance."

Charlotte clucked at the rejection. "Young man, civic duty has nothing to do with this. Charity is our weapon against the violence toward peace."

"I don't understand," Phil said.

Charlotte walked back to her desk and regained her seat. "Violent acts are often carried out by some in the name of peace. China is a melting pot of such an ethos at this time. We have the Japanese invasions, the usurpers to the current government and their relationship with the West. Also, there is the ignorance of the general populace about what is happening to their country. Courage, strength, and charity will be the only things that prevent this country from breaking apart. Alas, I think we have found this out too late. I suspect your child refugees are a product of this. Am I right?"

"I guess. You could read the letter and find out for sure."

Charlotte placed the unopened letter on her desk. "You say Donna Poillucci sent you?"

"Yes."

"Then I know your mission is just, but I cannot help. I'm sorry."

"Do you know Donna well?"

"Our paths crossed, many years ago. She is a friend to us here."

"Then why can't you take in the children as a mark of respect for that friendship."

Charlotte looked down at the bold lettering knowing that it was from Donna. They had corresponded every few months for many years now. "If I did, the children would be in more danger here and Donna would not want that."

There was silence in the room.

"You said there might be a solution that I can help with. How can I help?"

Charlotte grinned. She was right. It was a false sense of bravado this young man gave, as if he wasn't interested in the outcome of the twins.

"Give this letter to Rosa and she will make the final decision. When she does, she will need you to take her to a place of safety. Will you do that?"

The young man shuffled on the spot and then nodded. "What if she says *no*?"

Not a chance. Rosa would never say no to anything that could help another. It wasn't in her nature. "We both know the answer to that."

The young man frowned then walked back into the room and collected the letter, "I guess this is goodbye."

"Yes, safe journey wherever you travel, young man. May God be with you."

He left the room.

Charlotte leaned back in her chair, "We will protect them, my good friend." She picked up her pen and began to write.

Dear Donna,

It is with sadness that I write this letter....

†

"What does it say?" Phil asked.

Rosa raised her eyebrows. "Let me finish and then you can read it for yourself."

Moments later, Rosa passed him the letter, frowning as she contemplated the contents.

"Holy crap!"

"That's not suitable language," Rosa said.

"Sorry. I forgot I was in a pious place."

"There is no place suitable for that language." At the man's shrug, Rosa figured that in the man's circle of friends, it might be acceptable language.

"I do not know your name?"

"Phil, Phil Casters."

Rosa liked the sound of the name—it suited him. "Mr. Casters, you indicated that if I help the twins you will help to take us to a safe place. Is that still the case in light of the information in the letter?"

The morning sun now shone brightly into the schoolroom where she had been packing away her books. She had chosen to take her favorite children's novel, Peter Pan, for the trip with Bang and Tao. They still had to finish it and where better than on a long journey.

"If I'm not to be seen as a blackguard, do I have any choice?"

Rosa smiled. "We all have choices, Mr. Casters. I would not hold you to something that might place you in danger."

"Danger? What about you and the children? Believe me, I can take care of myself."

"Does that mean you plan to help us?" Rosa watched the smooth skin of Mr. Casters forehead crease. It looked like the fate of the world had been assigned to him. Perhaps in a small way it had.

"I'm not letting you go alone with two fugitive kids."

"Well, actually it won't just be two. Bang and Tao will accompany us also."

Rosa gave her attention to the book she held in her hands. Sure that she was being scrutinized by the cool blue orbs of the man who was to help her leave this place she called home, the hairs on the back of her neck stood up.

41

"Anything else I need to know before we embark on this epic journey?"

Rosa shook her head. "I believe you and I, Mr. Casters, will do very well together. We need to leave by early afternoon. Is that good for you?"

"I'll be ready. For the record just where is this journey taking us?"

Rosa moved toward her desk and felt tears forming as she moved a hand across the gnarled surface. *I'm going to miss this so very much.* She sucked in a deep breath and turned back to the man.

"Langshow, Mr. Casters. Langshow."

†

Phil dragged out every map she had collected during the years. Langshow wasn't on any of them.

She rubbed her eyes and wondered how to tell Rosa Moran that she had no clue how to fly them to this Langshow. Pride asserted itself –she wasn't telling anyone she didn't know the route. She took out the newest regional map she had and searched for any mention of a place called Langshow.

There was a clattering of feet on the ladder and the tall kid, Bang's head popped inside the plane.

"Missy Moran ready now, sir."

Phil bit her lip. She still needed to check a few things before take-off. "Sure thing, Bang. I need ten minutes."

Bang smiled and clambered down the steps.

"Crap." She checked the time and frowned. Where had the past three hours gone? Not only was she unprepared for take-off, but her stomach was growling like a bear. Scrambling out of the plane, she did a hurried check of the tires, fuselage, and the propeller. That would have to do until they landed for fuel. Damn, Blake would be furious with her. She was furious with herself.

Unlocking the side of the plane, she frantically shifted empty boxes and personal gear around to make space for her cargo. Tucked away under a heavily stained tarp was the passenger ladder. She hauled it out and secured it to the side of the plane.

When Phil completed the task, a voice cleared in the background. She looked at Rosa Moran with the four children and marveled at their meagre belongings—she was expecting a lot more baggage. They had no more than a knapsack each between them. And, God, they looked so forlorn. How could anyone, with a heart, not help them?

"Great, you travel light," she quipped.

"It's out of necessity," Rosa replied softly.

"Found that works for me, too." Phil looked around and frowned. "No goodbye party?"

Rosa appeared visibly shaken at her comment. "We have said our goodbyes. Now we need to leave. It's important," Rosa answered huskily.

Phil shrugged, skidded down the ladder, and landed in front of Rosa. "I'll take the bags. You get the children comfortable."

They looked at one another and Rosa handed Phil her bag. Phil's heart beat faster at the touch.

"Thank you, Mr. Casters." Rosa hurried the children up the ladder and they all disappeared into the plane.

Phil stood there for a few seconds and allowed the quietly spoken words of gratitude run through her body. There was something decidedly enticing about Rosa Moran and it worried her. She didn't need the distraction of a missionary who thought she was a man clouding her already complicated life. The devil in her head spoke. *"Tell her you are a woman. What does it matter to you?"*

I will, when the time is right. Now wasn't. Rosa and the kids need to think they are in capable hands and if that means taking on the persona of a man—so much the better. She smirked.

"You are welcome, Miss Moran." Phil saluted the empty space and climbed abroad the aircraft.

Chapter Six

Rosa peered out of the grimy window she'd tried hard to clear, and then realized the grime was on the outside and she could do nothing about that. What she could see fascinated her. Land as far as the eye could see, circumvented by paddy fields, and the odd settlement. Her heart swelled at the sheer enormity of what she was doing. Would her grandfather be happy? No. Her parents would though, thinking it the adventure of a lifetime. She removed a small volume from her breast pocket and flicked several pages until she came to the entry she recalled by heart.

Arrived at Shanghai. What a thriving metropolis of foreign people. I thought I knew the language however rudimentary. I do not. There are so many dialects. Quite reminds me of home. How funny that might sound, but to hear a Scots person and an English person converse, my, it could be difficult at times, and we are all supposed to speak the same language. I think I am going to like this country. In fact, I shall call it my great adventure. Perhaps I will find the peace my heart is looking for here.

Rosa smiled. "You did, Mama, you certainly did."

45

"What was that?"

Rosa guiltily replaced the diary back into her hiding place. "Nothing, nothing at all, Mr. Casters. We are heading the right direction I see."

There was a marked silence.

"Any chance you can come up here and do a little navigating. I'm not entirely familiar with Langshow province," Phil said.

Rosa laughed. "Hardly a province, Mr. Casters, Langshow is a village in the Yunnan province. I'll gladly navigate if you believe I can."

"Sure you can."

Rosa glanced at the children who were talking together animatedly. Happy to leave their sides for a short while, she ventured forward.

"Good to have you aboard, Miss Moran."

Rosa knew she blushed at the remark from the pilot and felt her heart race a little at the words. "How do I help you navigate?"

"Map, in the seat pocket."

Rosa looked around her and spied the map. "Ah, excellent. I did a little ordnance survey in my schooling in England. Though only of England."

"Same principles apply."

Rosa looked at the map and frowned. How did one find a small town in such a vast area?

"Mr. Casters, perhaps Langshow might not be on the map." Rosa's brow narrowed. "We need to be in the Yunnan province."

"Then take us as near into the province as you believe Langshow will be. Do they have any defining factors?"

Rosa drew on her minuscule knowledge of the village that she had visited once as a child.

"To be frank, I'm not sure. It's a village. Hardly a spec on the landscape."

Rosa was sure she heard Mr. Casters curse but let it go. After all, she felt like doing a little cursing herself at this juncture.

Think, girl, think. What do you remember of your last visit? She clenched her hands. Of course. Silly me, how could I forget such a marvelous vista.

"Mountains as close as you can get to them and there is a pass in the middle. With only one village of a reasonable size nestled inside." Rosa recalled the mountainous region remembering the name of the mountain. "The Black Dragon Mountain. Do you know it?"

Rosa was surprised by the look of shock on the pilot's face. "Is something wrong?"

"Hell, I don't have fuel for a journey that far. It's close to the border of Burma. We will need to refuel."

Rosa glanced at the children who were still happily engaged in conversation. "Is that a problem?"

The plane shuddered.

If Rosa didn't know any better, she'd have thought it was in reaction to her question.

"Oh, of course not! I'm going a thousand miles away from my base of operation, with two political refugees and…. Well, I think that says it all really," Phil spit out.

Rosa bit her top lip. She had no clue as to where the man had originated. In fact, there had been no reason to ask this time or the last. They had used the man for their own means—blackmail was probably the correct term in the circumstances. It had been less than charitable and guilt weighed heavily upon her.

"I'm sorry, Mr. Casters, perhaps we should turn back."

"Turn back? Are you crazy? I don't know about you, but having the deaths of two kids on my conscience isn't something I want to live with. Particularly if we can save them."

"I had to ask."

Rosa grinned. *I like you, Mr. Casters. That's exactly what I would have said.*

She contemplated the map and wondered if there was a way to do this and give Mr. Casters a free conscience. "You can leave us at the refueling station. You will have done your duty and can go home."

Blue eyes pierced gray, Rosa found herself caught in a strong connection to the man, with her heart racing and blood throbbing through her veins.

"Duty be damned. I will take you to your destination."

The man's determination made Rosa smile. "Spoken like a gentleman. Thank you."

"You are welcome."

†

Phil glanced into the back of the plane and saw her passengers sleeping. She figured that they cocooned next to one another for warmth. It wasn't exactly a luxury accommodation in the cargo hold. Rosa was scrunched up at the foot of the children and by the looks of her position, she had been watchful until exhaustion finally overcame her. The picture had Phil smiling as she turned her attention to the clouds ahead.

The gas stop in Cheghzu had been thankfully uneventful. Saunders must have finally paid the bill and they were very helpful, rather than the usual morose haggling sessions that normally took place in order to secure more fuel.

She'd told Rosa to keep the children out of sight. It was best that way should the authorities drop by asking about the twins. It was going to happen soon from the information she garnered in the letter from Donna. Damn, why hadn't Donna confided in her about the kids? She rolled her eyes. Fat chance she would have accepted the job if she had. But she was here now and would keep the promise to take the children to safety. It was the perfect way to pay Rosa back for her generosity months before.

Phil checked the altimeter and throttled the plane higher. The mountain range ahead wasn't going to be easy to negotiate. Not to mention finding a suitable landing spot. Soggy rice fields were not her idea of an ideal landing, especially with passengers aboard.

She settled back in her seat and gripped the wheel as they cruised along. The next ten minutes would be a bumpy ride.

A jolt rattled the plane and groans from the children echoed off the steel shell.

"Sorry folks, it's going to be a little choppy." Phil called back, her attention on what she was doing rather than the politeness of facing her fellow passengers.

There was a giggle among the children and Phil frowned. She didn't think she'd told a joke.

"Not choppy like chopsticks." Bang chuckled before repeating himself in Chinese.

There was a burst of laughter from the children.

"Nope, no chopsticks flying today, Bang." Phil gave the boy a wink and turned back to the gigantic vista of a mountain range ahead of her.

The children laughed as Bang interpreted.

"Mr. Casters."

Hmm, I'm going to have to burst that Mr. Casters bubble sometime soon, it's damn irritating. That and I don't want a lie like that to take root.

"Yes, Miss Moran."

The plane lurched and Rosa shot forward. Phil caught her elbow and prevented her head hitting the cockpit windscreen.

"Thank you," Rosa said and Phil noted the high color in her cheeks.

"You are very welcome. How can I help you?" Phil replied.

Rosa wobbled precariously beside Phil.

"I'd take the seat if I was you, definitely safer."

Phil discreetly watched Rosa smooth down her skirt before taking the seat.

"Are we near our destination?"

"Once we navigate across the mountain range...."

"Over it?"

"Yep, over. Can't see a magical entrance opening up to allow us to go right through, can you?" Phil smirked, wondering how she thought they'd get to Langshow—the mountain range surrounded it on three sides. At Cheghzu, Phil had shown the map to a fellow aviator who was about to fly to Laos and then Vietnam. She asked if he could provide her with a route that had no trail for anyone who might come looking for them. Jasper Richards, a First World War pilot, happily pinpointed the route.

"I...I thought perhaps that we went around. This is very dangerous, what if the aircraft cannot maintain the height?" Rosa asked. Her eyes were like saucers as she gazed at the mountain.

Phil had already considered that. In a nutshell, they would probably crash and the chances of survival would be minimal.

"She'll make it. Gilda might not be the most polished plane around, but her maintenance record is impeccable. If I thought there was a chance it would be a problem, I would have landed and we would have gone on foot."

Rosa stared at Phil. "You would have come with us?"

Phil nodded.

"I see."

The plane lurched again.

"Perhaps I will go back to calm the children." Rosa stood and turned away

"If you think the kids are scared, get them to take turns to look out the window for a secret entrance into the mountain. They say the Black Dragon lives there."

Rosa looked surprised and left.

Moments later, Phil heard Rosa begin the I Spy game. She chuckled softly and then drew in a deep breath.

Let's hope my brash confidence doesn't let me down. Now, Gilda, it's up to you, my princess.

She caressed the wheel much as she would a woman's skin and concentrated on the task ahead.

Fifteen minutes later, Phil let out a relieved sigh, spying the entrance to the valley. It was just as Jasper Richards had indicated. There had been a few difficult twists and turns that had made the little girls scream, and Phil was sure that Rosa had a tremble in her voice as she soothed the frightened children. Who wouldn't have been a tad frightened under the circumstances? She had almost lost her stomach contents at least twice with an unexpected drop in altitude, when ferocious wind currents had challenged the strength of the engine and the aviator controlling the aircraft. They fortunately had both been up to the task.

"Everyone take hold of something. We are about to go in to land." Phil said, and then heard Rosa repeat the instruction in Chinese. Rosa's translation is far superior to anything she could have said. *I wonder how many dialects she understands.*

The plane gently dropped altitude then flew very low. Phil saw field after field of rice and workers who stopped to watch their approach. She noticed a large field on the outskirts of the village. Minutes later, the wheels touched the ground and the plane skidded a few yards before it came to rest.

Phil rested her head on the wheel and closed her eyes. She was dog-tired and hungry as a bear. Drawing on the final reserves she had, she turned with a half-smile to her passengers. They looked tired and drawn, especially Rosa. A spirited flight would do that to people.

"We are here," Phil stated unnecessarily.

Rosa gave her a weak smile and spoke in Chinese to the children. The language was definitely a natural talent. It flowed from her like a torrent of water over a waterfall.

The children chorused. "感谢您."

Phil grinned, she was sure that thank you was the furthest from their minds with that flight but the enthusiasm was there.

"欢迎您" (You are welcome)

The children frowned then nodded.

"I'll check outside before I extend the ladder, won't be long." Phil jauntily opened the door and slid down the small ladder attached to the cockpit area. She sprung off onto the damp ground and it gave way like a sponge.

Before she could do her preliminary checks in her side view, she saw several people moving toward them. "Welcome party, I hope," she muttered. Securing the fuel line, she whistled off key while waiting for them to get closer.

A wizened man moved ahead of the contingent—Phil counted six men in all.

"欢迎陌生人" (Welcome)

Welcome is good, Phil decided. She smiled and made a small bow. Not sure if that was the custom here but it wouldn't hurt she figured.

"感谢您." (Thank you)

The old man's white beard, touching his chest, twitched.

Phil wondered if something lived in the thicket.

He motioned, with a finger that would have given a long carrot a run for its money, to one of his comrades, a much younger man. At least that's what Phil deduced by his clean-shaven face with barely a wrinkle showing. He also had a short, muscled body and his chest muscles flexed when he moved forward.

"Westerner, what brings you to Langshow?"

The stilted English was very good, considering they were in a village that time had probably forgotten, from the fashions the people wore. Still this was a good sign—it meant the crap going around China right now hadn't yet touched this place.

"My name is Casters. I'm looking for a safe haven for my passengers."

The man spoke in rapid Chinese that Phil didn't have the chance to decipher. He then gave Phil a look that made her jaw torque and her chin raise.

"Why Langshow?"

Before Phil could answer, Rosa, from the plane's door, did.

"Chang, how good to see you."

The younger man, obviously called Chang, beamed a smile that Phil decided was a magic potion. It made his dour expression disappear and miraculously left in its place a handsome, if you liked men, profile. The fact that Rosa appeared pleased to see the man, gave Phil a kick in the gut.

"I'll fetch the ladder." Phil murmured and hauled herself back into the plane.

"You know him?"

Rosa grinned. "Yes, we had schooling at the missionary together when we were very young. Chang is a friend. He's one of the reasons I chose this place."

"How close a friend then?" Phil bit her lip and busied herself with the ladder. What kind of question was that? It sounded like she was a jealous lover.

"Not as close now, of course. Chang left for his ancestral home in Langshow when my grandfather took me back to England. We were both teenagers at the time."

Phil was thankful that Rosa hadn't seemed bothered by her question. "A few years then." She laid the ladder down the side of the aircraft and secured it to the hinges.

A few minutes later, Phil watched as Rosa quickly stepped down from the plane and Chang crushed her in a hug. Chang introduced her to the others in the party.

Okay, so they all knew one another. Figures. She searched Rosa's face and found nothing but joy there. It looked like the perfect place for her and the kids.

Within ten minutes after introductions, an entourage removed the children and their belongings from the plane. Phil watched as the group began walking away.

"Aren't you coming, Mr. Casters? Rosa asked. "They have offered us a meal and a bed for the night."

"Just for the night?" Phil narrowed her eyes.

Rosa smiled. "It's customary to ask the Grand Master his permission to stay. Unfortunately he is meditating and I will go there tomorrow and ask to see him."

"Sounds like a plan. What if he says no? What do you do then?"

Rosa gazed at her—the intensity seared her soul.

"I have faith."

"As simple as that, huh," Phil scoffed.

"Yes, Mr. Casters, as simple as that. It will be rude if you do not eat with the village elders and their families. Are you coming?"

Phil nodded. "I need to secure the plane. It will take me about half an hour. Tomorrow I'll move on...after you've seen the guy in charge."

Rosa's eyes seemed to sparkle but it could have been the sun.

"Thank you again, Mr. Casters."

"You are welcome, Miss Moran."

Rosa rushed back to the gathering and Phil watched for a few moments. Then, with a heavy heart, she began securing the aircraft.

Chapter Seven

Rosa's hands formed a steeple as she pressed them to her lips. She was watching the four refugee children mingling with Chang's family, particularly the children of their own age—they were numerous. She closed her eyes and sent up a silent prayer to God for his benevolence in getting them here.

"Penny for your thoughts?"

Rosa opened her eyes and stared into the electric blue gaze of Mr. Casters. How extraordinary were those eyes. They were very beautiful. In the right light, she could imagine a bolt of lightning streaking through them.

"Okay, maybe a pound then."

Rosa shook her head and smiled. "Alas, Mr. Casters, that would be very generous in the circumstances."

"May I be the judge of that, Miss Moran?"

The smile, one that had a little boy essence of mischief, captivated Rosa. She would now think of Mr. Casters as incorrigible.

"You may. I was thanking our Lord for His efforts in bringing us safely here."

Mr. Casters laughed a particularly jolly laugh.

What was so funny? "You find that funny, Mr. Casters. Do you not believe in the benevolence of our Lord?" Rosa saw the lips twitch in a tic like motion and then a frown appeared on the olive-skinned forehead.

"A long time ago I might have. Now I prefer to believe in the effort of those around me and in myself for reaching my goals. It's simpler that way, I've found."

The words resonated in Rosa's head. To her it was incredible that one would not have conviction in God and all that was offered under his protection.

"Are you shocked, Miss Moran?"

Rosa frowned. "No. Surprised perhaps, but then I have been taught to be tolerant. China is very much a mixed cultural society."

"Very liberal of you, I might say. I prefer to thank the weather and Gilda for getting us here safely. God, as far as I'm concerned, didn't have a hand in it."

His eyes grew hooded and a thin line stretched across his lips. Rosa speculated that anger or perhaps frustration might be the cause.

"I didn't have time to ask before, but you named your plane Gilda? A very unusual name."

"Not really. My mother's name was Gilda."

The stilted way the explanation was spoken made Rosa wonder about that particular relationship. *I'd better not pry, it isn't my business*, she thought.

"You could say it was God who provided the right conditions for us to travel." At the sharp pierce of those incredible eyes, Rosa backed off. "We will be eating soon, don't you find this village wonderful."

The eyes never wavered but their expression softened considerably into candlelight intensity.

"I must make time to return here one day and enjoy the tranquility, especially if all hell lets loose everywhere else."

"Ah, you feel that way too." The man drew Rosa in, in a way she had yet to fathom. The only thing she knew was that being with him made her heart flutter.

Mr. Casters chuckled and stared over Rosa's shoulder. "Look at that vista."

Rosa turned and gazed at the scenery. A snow topped mountain seemed to enclose the village in its arms as protection. Orange blossom trees flanked the lower level of the mountain and a body of water, covered in the petals of the trees, ran steadily through the village. It was a picture of perfection. Peaceful was the perfect word to describe Langshow. Its beauty had already captured her heart. Tomorrow she hoped to convince the Grand Master that it was the right choice as well."

"You look pensive. Surely it can't be the surroundings?"

"No, definitely not the view. Until I speak with the Grand Master, this is still but a dream." Rosa placed her fingers to her lips as she looked at what could be her new home.

Phil nodded.

"Rosa, I'm here to take you to the feast."

Rosa giggled and turned to the voice. "Chang, a feast for us? I don't think…."

Chang's eyebrows narrowed.

"I think it's wonderful. We are ready are we not, Mr. Casters?"

"Absolutely, Miss Moran."

Chang bowed and motioned for them to follow him.

Rosa's eyes flared as she saw the enormous table. It could, she was sure, seat at least twenty people. Chang pointed to a place for her to sit and she dutifully did so. A toothless matron and the old man who Chang introduced as Qua Lowshan flanked her on either side. She bowed to each of them and they grinned at her. She watched Mr. Casters take a proffered seat at the other end of the table next to Chang. Then the smell of garlic and the sound of sizzling platters drew her attention.

Chang was right. This was a feast. The servers placed several dishes, including beans, chicken, vegetables, and rice in front of them.

"吃了,感谢"

Rosa grinned. *Eat and give thanks, works for me.* She picked up her chopsticks and with deference to Qua, they began the feast.

†

Phil drew on a cigarette, the ember at the tip attracting insect life. She flicked the tip and stomped on the gray ash that fell. Her belly was full. If anyone asked her, she'd say it was the best meal she'd ever had in China.

Chang was a boring companion. He talked incessantly about Rosa. The boy was smitten, that was for sure. That fact alone made him someone she didn't want to continue an association with. Boy, what was she thinking? He was a young man of Rosa's age. His yellowish skin glowed and the brown eyes that appeared permanently narrowed had blatantly scrutinized her on several occasions during the meal.

It irked her that everyone here, including Rosa, thought she was a man. How had that happened? She ran a hand through her short hair and rolled her eyes. Perhaps the bigger question is why she hadn't nipped it in the bud? There had been opportunities. "Yeah, why didn't I?"

"Why didn't you what, Mr. Casters?"

Phil rolled her eyes, took a deep drag of her cigarette, and exhaled through her nose watching the gray smoke spiral into the air.

"I wasn't aware you smoked. You do know that it is bad for your lungs?"

"I do, Miss Moran, I surely do. I guess we all have vices. What about you? What would you consider your vice?" Phil stared at Rosa and felt a warmth in the pit of her stomach she'd only felt when in the throes of lovemaking.

Wow. What hold does this woman have over me? I barely know her.

"Vice?" Rosa glanced around, then walked to a wooden bench opposite the house they were staying at and sat.

Phil regarded Rosa for a few moments. She stubbed out her cigarette underfoot, and walked to the bench. She placed one booted foot on the three-foot wall behind the bench. "You don't have vices?"

"I...I would imagine so. No one is perfect in this world. I do not smoke however. For a man I suspect that is not a vice."

Phil twisted her lips at the naive comment. "I guess you've never seen a movie recently. Women smoke as much as men these days."

"The last movie I saw before I came back here was *Dracula*. I have to say, Mr. Casters, it was a very scary movie."

Phil chuckled. "That was a while back. I think you would find some of the new movies a little less frightening. I saw *Mr. Deeds Goes to Town* a couple of months ago. It was a great feel good movie. Kind of reminds me of you."

Rosa looked up at Mr. Casters. She noted that his eyes seemed to shimmer, not with tears but something else...amusement? No. There was definitely something there though.

"Then, Mr. Casters, I will take you at your word and if ever I have the opportunity to view Mr. Deeds, I will think of you."

Phil drew in a breath of fresh air and it made her lungs sting for a second. "It is a recommendation I will stand by."

Rosa nodded. "You never answered my original question."

"That was?" Phil said, totally forgetting the original question.

"Why didn't you what, Mr. Casters?"

Phil laughed. "Ah, that question."

She stepped away from the wall and gazed at the incredible snow-capped mountain that enveloped Langshow.

Shangri-la. Yep this place reminded her of a book she'd once read. She wondered if the author had ever visited this place. A dreamy world long divorced from reality. Could this be why she was having feelings toward a woman who was a stranger?

Rosa stood. "It is fine, Mr. Casters, not to answer my question. It was very personal."

Phil reached out and touched Rosa's forearm. "I wanted to come clean about a misunderstanding, but somehow it has taken a life of its own, and I don't know how to change that."

Rosa smiled. "The truth perhaps will set you free, Mr. Casters."

"The truth you say? How do we know that one person's truth may be another's lie?" Phil sighed, withdrew a packet from her breast pocket, and pulled out another cigarette.

"We don't, Mr. Casters, we don't. It is the character of a man, or, a woman, that defines the truth. Only you can decide if the truth for you is everyone else's lie. Good night, Mr. Casters."

Phil nodded and watched as Rosa walked toward the residence.

Rosa turned. "Life is a long road, Mr. Casters, with many pitfalls and as many joys, if you allow. I do not believe a man like you will have a secret that everyone else sees as a lie. It is not your character." Rosa turned away and entered the building.

Phil didn't move. *You may not think that when you know I'm a woman.*

She struck a match and placed it to the tip of the cigarette.

Perhaps thinking I'm a man, she feels safer. Oh, what the hell, that's what I'll convince myself of.

Chapter Eight

Untold secrets are the mystery of the morning when one wakes. Life itself, perhaps even death, has its game to play.

Phil threw back the blanket that had kept her warm during the chilly early morning and stood. Their hosts had given her an alcove screened off from Rosa and the children, none of whom stirred early, it would seem. At least that is what she assumed since there wasn't any noise from that part of the room.

She sniffed the air and grimaced.

The air was pure but she wasn't. She needed to bathe. A canal ran through the village, quite sophisticated for a backward part of the country and the perfect impromptu bathing area.

Stretching, she heard the crack of a few bones protesting the position she must have slept in.

"Ah well, no one gets any younger once they are born." She softly chuckled.

As silently as possible, Phil exited the building, took a huge breath of fresh air, and smiled. Then she placed a booted foot on the wooden railing of the balcony that led to the four steps to the ground. She marveled at the view.

"Absolutely spectacular," she whispered. Her eyes roamed across the snow-capped mountain directly in front of her and shaking her head, she smirked. Flying through that valley between the mountains wasn't for the faint of heart. Something no one could ever call her after that trip yesterday. To her face at least.

Descending the steps, she strode toward the canal and once there, was amazed that the water was clear—very much like a constantly running stream. She also saw several people bathing, the men stripped of their shirts.

Can't do that in broad daylight. Not without giving them a cheap thrill, she thought.

Wiping her jaw with her hand, Phil wondered if she could discreetly leave the area when a familiar voice called to her. "Darn. It would have to be him," she muttered under her breath. "Morning, Chang, it's a beautiful sunrise."

"Yes, Mr. Casters, I'm surprised you are up at dawn since you had such a long trip to get here. No one would have said anything if you had slept all day. The rest would have been beneficial."

Phil noted the rather supercilious tone, along with a faint twist of the thin lips, which seemed less than friendly.

"I'm sure it would but I'm used to late nights and early starts in my line of work. What about you, what do you do around here?" Phil waved her hand in a circular motion.

Phil would swear that Chang gave her a challenging look.

"My father is the senior elder, you met him yesterday. I will one day take up that role. I'm currently working as a teacher of my people."

Phil nodded. "Very laudable, I'm sure. Can't say I took after my old man, but then I'm not into all this family togetherness."

Chang's expression changed. It became dourer, if that were possible.

Phil frowned.

"Family is the most important, Mr. Casters. To not acknowledge such is a mark of disrespect."

Phil looked down at her boots, which needed shining, and then back at the man. "What if you don't have family? Surely there's no disrespect then."

Chang gave her a pitying look. "It is not all about the family that lives, but also those that have passed. We have to make our ancestors proud. It is a sign of respect."

"Yeah, well, I prefer to give respect to the living, not the dead. I wondered if it was okay to bathe in the canal."

"There is a communal area for bathing, Mr. Casters. If you would follow me, I shall show you."

Phil bit her lip. Crap, not what she wanted. "Hey that's fine. I wouldn't want to take you from your work. Point me in the right direction and I will...."

Chang shook his head. His dark blue-black hair never moved.

"You are a guest in our village. It would be bad manners for me to not show you around." Chang turned away and began to walk.

Phil hesitated and looked down at the clothes she was dressed in. It was true she looked like a man by what she wore. Her gaze took in her flat chest. Only when she was freezing did her nipples ever show through and then that was only when she wore flimsy fabrics. Her beige trousers were slim fitting and specially made for her in one of the sweatshops on the strip in Zongnan. Her well-worn leather flying jacket made it difficult to distinguish her gender. Maybe she should grow her hair again. She shook her head. Nope, not going to happen. Ming liked the sleek look.

"Are you coming, Mr. Casters?"

"Absolutely." Phil stepped lively forward and was soon walking side by side with Chang.

They negotiated several well-built houses, which would look perfectly respectable in one of the larger cities. Phil was amazed at the large, ornate architecture for such a small village. She noted that the buildings were mainly two-stories. The wood-beamed frames walled with adobe on the ground floor appeared to have planks on the upper floors. The exteriors of the walls were plastered and lime-washed. The houses had tiled roofs with verandas. What she noticed most was the intricate carving on the arches as they passed each house.

"I have to say, you have a beautiful village here. How come?" Phil saw Chang grimace. "I meant no disrespect, Chang. It is merely that most villages in the provinces are less luxurious than yours."

Chang appeared mollified by her explanation. "Our ancestors used their talents wisely. We are very fortunate with nature's bountiful gifts in this area."

"I guess you'd have to be mad to want to leave here. It must have been hard when you were away at the mission?" Phil looked up at a particularly startling dragon figure that looked like it was about to rain fire on her head as they walked past.

"It was hard to leave my family, but exciting too. I meet many different people and I'm very grateful for their influence on my life." Chang pointed to a larger building standing alone. "That is the bathing house. At this time, few will be there. Most houses have their own washing facilities."

Phil drew in a silent breath of relief. Someone was watching out for her it would seem. "Thanks." She began to walk away and Chang spoke in a whisper.

"How well do you know Miss Moran?"

Phil almost laughed aloud but refrained from doing so. She knew that a question like that from a proud man was difficult for him to ask. She figured mocking him with her laugh would have been less than beneficial.

"Not well at all. She needed help to travel here. I had the fastest available transport at the time."

"Good, good. I will leave you to your morning bathing. Please accept my invitation to breakfast in an hour. We will eat at the same place as last evening."

Chang's expression was inscrutable—the one description for almost every Chinese person she'd come across. Definitely unreadable.

Phil smiled. "Sure, I'd love to accept. I will be there on time."

Chang nodded and walked away.

Phil scratched the back of her neck and wondered if Rosa knew she had a would-be suitor. Once again, the thought that someone was interested in Rosa churned her belly. Damn, she needed to get back to civilization sooner rather than later.

She mounted the four steps to the front door and grinned at the swan that watched her every movement. Maybe these ancestors still live in the monuments. She entered the dimly lit building.

†

Rosa rubbed her eyes and glanced around. Tension began to build, for she didn't recognize her surroundings. Then, just as quickly, her mind filled in the blanks. She was in Langshow. She stretched and the woolen blanket dropped away from her shoulders. The chill of the early morning breeze coming through the slightly opened window had her huddling back under the fabric.

"Brr, that's cold. Must be the mountain wind stream."

A commotion from the thin panel that separated her from the children had her wrapping the blanket around her shoulders as she left her bed and popped her head around the intricately decorated panel. Her fingers traced the outline of a flock of birds on the panel in front of her. "Children, did you sleep well?" she said in English then repeated it in Chinese for the twins.

She smiled as the four children gave her a startled glance. The noise hadn't been very loud but they had obviously been talking.

Bang grinned. "Yes, Missy Moran."

Tao gave her shy glance and nodded.

The twins nodded vigorously, their smiles lighting up the room.

How could people be so cruel as to want to harm the innocent, Rosa wondered as she walked around the screen. "I will find us a place to wash and then search out breakfast. Has anyone seen Mr. Casters?" Rosa looked in the direction of the area their pilot had been given.

"He left, early," Bang announced.

"Ah, he left. I see," Rosa murmured. "Right. Let's find the bathroom and then some food I don't know about you but I'm hungry."

The children squealed in delight as Bang pointed to the corridor that they had not explored the night before.

"Kitchen, Missy."

Rosa shook her head. The children had been up a while if they had already explored, just as, it would seem, had Mr. Casters. "Then let's go." She shepherded the children along the corridor. Before they entered the door that Bang indicated was the kitchen, she opened the door immediately preceding it only to discover a bath and sink. "Ah, we can wash children."

Rosa chuckled at the groans from the children. "We all know, my dears, that cleanliness is next to Godliness, right?"

Bang and Tao nodded. The twins looked confused.

"Come, let's clean up." Rosa opened the door, cajoling the children to wash their hands and face, particularly the twins. She doused water on her face and washed her hands. She would take care of her other needs after she found something for the children to eat.

Then she heard footsteps on the veranda. "We have a visitor, children." She was fully expecting it to be Mr. Casters and she felt her heart skip a beat.

Rosa opened the door and was disappointed when she saw Chang in the doorway. She gave him a forced smile.

"Chang, good morning."

Chang bowed and gave a smile. Though his thin lips barely moved, his eyes opened wider. Rosa saw genuine joy in his expression.

"Good morning, Rosa."

Rosa had liked Chang from almost the first moment they had met as children. They had spent many hours either studying or playing together in the early days. Then studying became the focus for them both as they grew. She had appreciated his quiet intense ways, sprinkled with gentleness to those he cared for. When he departed for home a month before she left, she missed him sorely. Now as she faced the grown man, she felt the childhood affection return.

"We all slept well, Chang. Thank you for the hospitality in our time of need." Rosa waved him inside.

Chang hesitated and she frowned. "Is something wrong?"

Chang shook his head. "I came to invite you for breakfast. We will eat at my family home like last evening, in about fifteen minutes."

Given no other option, Rosa bristled inside, but remained outwardly calm.

"I was wondering if you had seen…."

Chang held up a hand, his previous sunny expression replaced by a more serious one. "If you are talking about Mr. Casters, he and I have already conversed and he will be there."

"Excellent," Rosa said. She looked around at the children behind her. "May the children go with you now, I need to bathe."

Chang nodded. He motioned for the children to come forward and they did so shyly. Even Bang was wary, which wasn't like him.

"儿童" (Follow me.)

The children did so and as Tao moved by Rosa, the tiny girl grasped the side of her skirt.

Rosa smiled down at Tao.

"我很快就将他们Tao,我承诺." (I will be there very soon, Tao, I promise.)

She placed a hand on the head of the child and stroked her light brown hair.

Tao gave a tremulous smile and walked up to Bang. She placed her hand in his. A lump formed in Rosa's throat at the action. The two reminded her very much of her early days with Chang.

"Thank you, Chang, I will see you all soon."

She watched them leave. The children, at least Bang and Tao, went reluctantly but the twins seemed to be less afraid.

Closing the door, she lay back against it hoping that things would simplify when she saw the Grand Master later in the day.

†

Phil quietly re-entered the house, trying not to wake Rosa or the children. It was still early but people were beginning to start their day as she'd headed back from her clean up session. She sniffed the air around her and grinned when all she could smell was freshness. As she'd exited the bathing house, an ancient looking woman had stopped her and pointed at her clothes. She was the local laundry woman. Not having planned to spend as many days away as she had, her clothes were dirty and the thought of fresh garments next to her clean skin was too good to resist.

Negotiating the use of a Chinese tunic and trousers, she now looked more like a resident of Langshow than a pilot. Still her clothes would be clean and the valise she'd brought with her from the plane had two shirts in and some underwear. Phil was glad she wore boxer shorts or the gossip would be rife. She went into the room she had slept in and saw the beat-up leather satchel she used for longer trips right where she'd left it.

Then she heard water running and frowned. Surely, they didn't have bathing facilities there. If they did, why didn't Chang tell her so? *Damn him.* Although, it could be just the kitchen. She'd find out.

Turning back to the corridor, she ventured down it quietly figuring that either the kids were asleep or someone had gagged them. No kids that she had come across were ever this quiet.

Intriguing.

The sound of water was coming from the second door to the left before the end of the corridor and the final door. Fully expecting it to be the kitchen, she threw open the door and held her breath.

The sight that met her eyes dazzled her. The naked body of Rosa Moran greeted her and she stared. She should have apologized and run out of the room as fast as her legs would carry her but she didn't.

Rosa, who was singing, apparently hadn't heard her enter and didn't turn around and scream in horror.

What was she singing? Phil hadn't heard it before.

Phil smiled. Rosa couldn't carry a tune in a bucket that was for sure, but it didn't matter. Rosa was enjoying herself and that made everything all right.

Phil swallowed as her gaze took in alabaster skin, curves that screamed to be touched, and the tightest bottom she had ever seen on a woman. God, the temptation to go and run her fingers across the sleek lines was making her wet.

Phil sucked in a silent breath, turned, and left the room.

She leaned against the door and closed her eyes. Rosa's perfect lines had her heart racing. She thought Ming was the only one who could stimulate her libido like this—obviously not. There was only one thing she had to do. Leave now, before Rosa became a problem she couldn't overcome. Except she'd made a promise to make sure they were safe here and she would see that commitment out.

As quietly as she had arrived, she retreated to her room and collected her clothes. She was hoping to leave the house before Rosa emerged from the bathroom.

Moments later, Rosa paused outside Phil's sleeping area.

"Mr. Casters, I wasn't...at least I supposed I was alone." Rosa said, frowning.

Phil smiled, as she looked at Rosa who was covered from shoulder to toe in an oversized peasant smock. Highly unfashionable but on Rosa somehow it had its merits.

"I went out early, didn't realize there were bathing facilities here. I have to say this is some village. Did all the rich in China move to Langshow?" Phil grinned. "I tell you

72

this place makes some of the main cities in China look like hovels. A rare find. A rare find indeed."

Rosa chuckled. "I'm sure there are other villages like this, you just haven't found them yet."

"Perhaps." Phil smiled.

Rosa walked closer and was in touching distance. "You look like a Chinaman in those clothes."

Phil considered what to say. She wanted to say that she'd prefer Rosa be naked as she had been a few minutes ago and not covering her attributes with an ugly peasant outfit.

"It was better than wearing dirty clothes when my body smells so good. The water here seems to have a wonderful aroma to it."

"Of course, Mr. Casters. It is fresh and natural. If you could bottle it, I'm sure there is a market." Rosa tugged at her robe.

"I'm sure there is." Phil caught Rosa's gaze and smiled.

"You are smiling, Mr. Casters. It is a little disconcerting."

Phil hadn't even realized she was smiling. It appeared, like the pervasive smell of the water, to be a natural occurrence around this woman. *Damn, I'm thinking like a philosopher.*

"I'm sorry. We have breakfast in…." She consulted her fob watch. "Five minutes. I have a feeling Chang might be upset if we were late. Particularly you."

Rosa frowned. "I will see you at breakfast, Mr. Casters and…good morning."

"Good morning to you too, Miss Moran." Phil watched as Rosa disappeared behind the screen that separated the large room.

Phil shrugged and left the building, she still had a few minutes to take her other laundry to the old woman and arrive at breakfast. She might even be late.

"I doubt they would even miss me." She scowled and increased her pace toward the home of the laundry woman.

Chapter Nine

"You are late, Mr. Casters." Rosa pursed her lips in irritation. She ignored the raised, perfectly shaped eyebrows.

They look very feminine. *I wonder if he knows that. I should be so lucky to have a thin line. Mine are like a bush.* She raised a hand and stroked her eyebrows.

"I'm sorry. The old lady who is doing my laundry was very chatty. What was I to do?" Phil raised her hands.

Rosa shrugged. "Nothing that would have been impolite. Then again, not arriving on time for breakfast was, too."

Rosa watched the pilot stroke a hand across his jaw. His jaw wasn't that manly looking either, no stubble. Ah, but perhaps he had shaved in the bathing area. That would explain it. What did it matter anyway? At that moment, they were heading for a bridge surrounded by perpendicular rocks, rising like a barrier between them and the temple where the Grand Master was meditating.

"You didn't have to come with me. Chang is a satisfactory escort. You could have been on your way." She looked ahead and saw Chang striding away toward their destination.

"Not until I know you and the children are safe here." Phil took a swig from the earthenware jug of water she carried.

Rosa stilled at the answer. "Why, of course we are safe, Mr. Casters. It is just a question of formality. I'm sure that we will be welcome here."

"Yep, formality is the great hidden weapon of the Chinese. I have found that to my detriment in the past. Even when you think they are upfront and honest, they stick a knife in your back."

The words were uttered harshly. It was clear to Rosa that Mr. Casters had been through some bad experiences in China.

"Did you expect something from someone that was rescinded?"

Phil gave a hollow laugh. "That's a fair assumption. But make it more than once and you'd be on the right track. Women—can't live with them sometimes and can't live without. Right?"

He was definitely bitter. Rosa wondered which woman had broken his heart? It was such a shame he was a very....

"You are falling behind. Is there a problem, Rosa?" Chang shouted.

"No. No, Chang, just a water stop. The air is much lighter here. How much farther is it to the temple? It looks so close from the village." Rosa smiled at her old friend.

Chang stopped and shuffled his backpack around and turned his head to one side, peering at the rocks ahead of them.

They arrived at his position.

"There is a little more to go. When we reach the pass and cross the bridge, the Temple of Zingling will be mere minutes' walk away," Chang said.

Rosa smiled. "Excellent. Mr. Casters is eager to be on his way home, I'm sure."

Phil walked ahead of Rosa. Her booted feet were scrunching on the gravel path leading to the entrance of the pass, as Chang called it.

"Then we must proceed with haste," Chang replied. He began to walk forward again.

Rosa stood and watched the two men. How different they were in physique. Hadn't Prudence once indicated that all men were alike inside if not out? She picked up her pace and followed them.

Five minutes later, they reached the formidable rocks and a small wooden bridge that appeared to Rosa to swing rather precariously from side to side. It was eminently dangerous from her viewpoint.

Chang, without hesitation, stepped onto the bridge and strode across it.

Startled by the hand that reached out and took hers, Rosa gulped down a moment of fear.

"Don't worry. I'll see you safely across, Miss Moran. After all, that is my purpose on this journey."

Rosa's heart swelled and she thought it would pound out of her chest at the welcome support. "You are very kind, Mr. Casters. It does look rather intimidating." She grasped the slightly larger hand tight. "I do not want you to think that I have a fear of bridges, it is just…." She trailed off.

"Not fear. I'm making sure you are safe, Miss Moran. I would be remiss if I did not. You are still in my charge until this Grand Master guy decrees you can stay." He bowed his head gallantly.

"Thank you, Mr. Casters." Rosa's smile widened when she received a friendly wink in response. "Let us go, shall we?"

"Absolutely."

Phil walked ahead, loosely holding Rosa's hand as she followed as close as possible on the narrow bridge.

When they crossed the bridge, the angry expression on Chang's face puzzled Rosa. She switched her head around to check the bridge wondering if marauders were following them.

"Is everything all right, Chang? You look a little put out," Rosa said.

Chang's lips tightened and then he shook his head as his eyes moved to her hands. Then Rosa realized that she still held onto Mr. Casters hand—she dropped it like a hot coal.

"Okay, Chang, let's go. We don't want to be late for our audience," Phil said.

Rosa was pleased that Mr. Casters had spoken. Darn, that was embarrassing. Not that she should feel embarrassed. It was after all, for safety.

Chang muttered something she was unable to decipher as he gave Mr. Casters a violent look. Now why would that be? Prudence was right, men are very strange creatures and not to be taken at face value.

They moved forward and quickly arrived at the steps of a beautiful pagoda styled temple. It's glowing red roof and gilded carvings made it a work of art. Rosa sighed in appreciation.

"It is very beautiful, Chang. Do you have a resident monk?

Chang stared at her with what she thought was an expression of annoyance.

"Perhaps you did not understand. The priest here is also our Grand Master."

"Oh," Rosa said. Perhaps this wasn't a foregone conclusion after all. They were not of the Taoist religion. She, Bang, and Tao were all Catholics. Perhaps the twins might be.

"This way," Chang walked up the seven steps and opened the enormous door.

Rosa was amazed that Chang had the strength to open such a mammoth door. It appeared to open easily and she thought he must have hidden talents.

Inside the temple were wooden benches on each side of the vestibule that would have accommodated a hundred people with ease. A simple stone plinth at the end of the room indicated an altar, at least what Rosa thought was an altar. The murals along the walls danced with color. Pictures of dragons in all shapes and sizes appeared to gyrate before her eyes. It was spectacular.

"I'm impressed."

Rosa grinned. "Indeed, Mr. Casters."

"I've been in a few Taoist temples in my time here and this beats them all. Did you see that flying dragon with the orange wings widespread? It is magnificent."

"It is indeed a sight to see. I am a catholic of course but I do appreciate the other religions around me. I feel that education is inspiring," Rosa gushed.

"I guess. I've got to admit that the Taoist religion, if I was going to choose one, works for me. With the colors anyway."

Rosa was surprised at the admission. "You do not believe, Mr. Casters?"

Phil laughed loudly and the sound bounced off the walls.

Chang glared at them.

"Yeah, I believe, but not in the traditional crap."

Rosa grimaced.

"Sorry, in my lifetime religious groups and what I believe in to be able to live don't usually work out."

"What do you…?"

"I will announce you to the Grand Master. Please wait here." Chang said. He immediately retreated through a door Rosa hadn't even seen.

Rosa frowned as he trounced off. She thought from his aggressive pronunciation and disappearance that he was angry again.

There was silence for a few moments.

"Right, we have time to kill, I guess. Let's check out the pictures, shall we?"

Rosa drew in her brows and thought about that. "What do you mean, time to kill?"

"Hey, you heard, the guy's a Grand Master. Sounds important to me, so I figure you might have to wait a while for that audience."

"That's true. Perhaps you might want to go now, Mr. Casters. This could take some time." Rosa bit down on her lip.

"Naw. Come on, let's check out these murals." Phil grabbed her hand.

Mr. Caster's hand pulled Rosa toward the right hand side of the room and she welcomed the familiarity and security of his touch. She would be sorry to see Mr. Casters leave. Very sorry indeed. No matter the warnings Prudence had given her about the men she might encounter, he was different. Just so…caring.

†

Phil twiddled her thumbs for the umpteenth time as she sat with Chang in silence. The melancholy expression plastered on his sallow complexion didn't bode well in her opinion.

"Is the Grand Master a relative of yours?"

Chang remained motionless and didn't appear to hear her. She was about to ask again when his deep voice moved the still air around them.

"Yes, my uncle."

Phil considered the measured answer. Giving nothing away. That was standard for most Chinese folk she'd met. Scratching her eyebrow, she nodded.

"You must be proud. A Grand Master must be quite the achievement."

Chang appeared to re-animate his features as he turned to face Phil.

"Yes, we are blessed and my uncle deserves the accolade. He worked hard for the *achievement* as you call it." Chang clasped his hands together and turned away.

"Can't say I have such exalted folks. My dad was a wastrel and my mother died when I was ten. I did have an uncle who took me under his wing. That's how I learned to fly. At least he paid for the lessons." Phil chuckled, recalling the first bill to hit her uncle's desk for her lessons. And hadn't he been mad at Jack Merrylee for ripping him off. He'd kept on paying though. A kernel of sadness touched her heart as she realized that she still missed the old goat.

"That makes you happy that he had to pay for you?" Chang asked. His face remained stoic.

"I was a kid earning a few bucks a week at the local store. Flying lessons cost a little more than that."

"Was he proud of you when you reached your goal?"

Phil grinned. "Ecstatic. It wasn't easy to be a ...."

"To be what?" Chang asked. He appeared to be interested.

Phil was sure he wouldn't be if he found out that a woman pilot was almost unheard of unless you were in the wealthy crowd. "Poor. I was going to say poor and achieve something usually only the rich did."

Phil would give herself an extra drink at Donna's bar when she arrived home for that catch.

"I, too, did something that only the rich do," Chang replied.

"Yeah?"

Chang's expression became serious." I went to live in a Western mission to learn English and...your culture."

Phil wasn't sure that it was something Chang had wanted to do from his tone. Family she knew was everything with the vast majority of Chinese and to live away from them must have been hard.

"Rosa helped you get past your homesickness, so that was a good thing. She appears to be a good person," Phil said.

Chang nodded.

Quiet, not what she was expecting but that was okay. Phil looked at the plain door that Rosa had entered more than an hour ago and wondered what was taking so long to say yay or nay that the kids could stay.

"Do you think they will be much longer?"

Chang shrugged. "It takes as long as it takes. I have known some decisions to take some time."

Phil frowned. "When you say some time what do you mean? A couple of hours, half a day, a day?"

Chang's face was bland as he replied, "I have known some decisions to take more than a year."

"A year!" Phil sucked in a breath. "Okay, a year, sure that works."

"When it is important, the right decision must be made and that cannot be rushed."

Phil gave a tight smile and began twiddling her thumbs at twice the pace she had in the beginning.

82

†

Rosa's face was white as she returned to the main room of the temple. Phil stood and took her hands.

"Hey, what did he say? You look terrible."

"Thank you, Mr. Casters. I'm sorry I look less than at my best." Rosa sat at the nearest bench disentangling her hands as she did so.

"Chang, the Grand Master wants to speak with you," Rosa said.

Chang nodded and quickly entered the door Rosa had exited.

Phil pouted. Hmm, was this going to be one of those decisions that Chang says takes a little more than three hours? "I didn't mean it like that." Phil wiped her hands across her face and sat next to Rosa.

"I'm sure."

"How can I help?" Phil asked.

Rosa remained silent.

"Mr. Casters, I'm sorry."

Perplexed Phil frowned. "Sorry? Why are you sorry?"

"For bringing you into this and delaying you. It was not my intention." Rosa sighed heavily.

"Hey, I'm delayed because I choose to be. What did the Grand Master say?" Phil took Rosa's hand, not sure, if the tactile touch was more for her benefit than Rosa's.

"That the children can stay and they will be welcome."

"Hey, that's great, right?"

Rosa gave a half smile. "Yes."

"There's something more?" Phil stroked Rosa's hand and felt her gently clutch the fingers into her palm.

"He is unsure about me staying."

Phil frowned. What the hell. This woman was perfect for this community. She was good, intelligent, and cared about people. Why was it so difficult to let her stay? "Did he give a reason?"

Rosa shook her head and Phil assumed it meant that she didn't know. The door to the room Chang had entered opened and Chang stepped back into the main room.

"The Grand Master wishes to see you, Mr. Casters."

"Me? Why? I don't want to stay here," Phil said.

Chang shrugged. "Apparently, you are important. Please, the Grand Master is waiting."

"Let him wait a minute more." Phil turned to Rosa. "I'm going to fix this okay, don't worry."

She strode to the door and entered the inner sanctum of the Grand Master.

✝

Phil had to look hard to find the Grand Master. He sat in the furthest corner of the room, which remarkably lacked light. She moved closer to the priest, unsure what to do next. Her limited experience of the Taoist religion could be tattooed on her palm.

"You wanted to see me," she said, after clearing her throat. Hell, what else could she say? She had no idea how to address the man. It was better for protocol if she didn't talk much, then she could offend less.

There was a scraping of a chair and a tiny man, barely touching her shoulder in height, stood in front of her. His hair was as white as summer clouds, his face weathered by life, and his eyes were cloudy. He wore a plain gray tunic, which she figured was not very befitting to his position.

"我没有" (I did)

His voice was gentle, almost feminine, and Phil was surprised.

"我怎样才能帮助大吗?" (How can I help, Grand Master?)

The old man gazed at her intently and she almost drew her gaze away. Deciding it was better to take the scrutiny. Maybe he'd see through her disguise—not that she had one, really. The thought alone made her suddenly nervous.

"I speak English. My grandnephew Chang has taught many of us your language. We are grateful."

Phil was surprised at that, pleased nonetheless. Her Chinese was reasonable but each province had a dialect all their own and speaking Chinese could be tricky.

"How can I help you, Grand Master?" she reiterated.

"Sit, sit. I have heard much of you from Chang and Miss Moran."

The comment took Phil aback. Rosa probably hadn't said anything derogatory—but Chang—what had he been saying? Probably nothing good by his expression every time they met. She sat in the nearest chair, which was a rickety stool that wobbled precariously as she held onto it. As she did, the Grand Master remained standing. Towering over her was a misstatement.

"Hopefully, all good." Phil clutched the stool that rocked even more as she spoke. They had all the modern conveniences in the town, a beautiful temple, and crappy stools to sit on—go figure.

The old man chuckled. Waved a hand in the air and smiled at her.

Well, I guess I can take that anyway I want. "Are you going to allow Miss Moran and the children sanctuary?"

Those cloudy eyes peered at Phil and she was pretty darn sure he couldn't see much—probably he was half-blind.

"Sanctuary is always open to those that need."

Phil gave a sigh, thankful for that. *Because sure as hell those kids needed sanctuary.* "Then it's a done deal?"

"I do not understand?"

Phil shrugged. "That you've granted them sanctuary."

"Perhaps."

"Great, that means I can leave." Phil stood.

The old man stared his mesmerizing cloudy orbs at her. "It takes a strong person to do what you have done for…strangers. Perhaps it is your penance."

What the hell? Penance? "I don't understand, Grand Master."

"Do you understand the Tao faith?"

Phil frowned. "Not really."

"As I thought."

"Pardon me, but you have never met me before. How do you know?"

The elderly man chuckled again.

This was getting old. "I think it's time I left. I don't need sanctuary." Phil stood, towering taller than the old man.

A frail hand touched her forearm. "Secrets can be the death of us."

Phil bit her lip. Is this what she thought? He knew she wasn't a man. Damn, someone must have seen her at the bathhouse. "Do you want to tell me more? I haven't lied to you."

"No, but to others, the most important one, an innocent and that isn't right."

"Hey, look, old man. I did the mission a favor. Everything I've done is above board. I'm going to leave now, okay?" Phil said.

"Taoism believes the female is equal. We don't have to hide behind masculinity. It is in our teachings that we follow the female doctrine."

Phil swallowed hard. What did this mean? Why doesn't he just say? "Is there such a thing?"

"Oh, yes. Perhaps if you believe in your self-worth, your life would be different."

Phil watched the old man carefully. Why would he think she wanted anything to be different? He knew nothing about her, nothing at all, unless he could read minds. "What exactly do you want of me?"

"Your fellow traveler has doubts. As well she might. It is a big step to remain here. We have a simple yet fulfilling life."

"Rosa said she had doubts?" Phil didn't believe that for one second.

The old man smiled and his teeth showed as much age as the man himself.

"Not in words. When I said that it may be a day or two before I reach a decision, she sounded upset."

Phil frowned. "Upset, well, I guess she hoped that a swift decision could be made. Why wouldn't you want them here?"

The old man moved his gaze away from Phil to the small window, barely a foot square.

Phil followed suit. The mountain dominated the view as the sun streamed in, giving what light there was in the room.

"The children will be most welcome, more so those that have a death sentence on them."

Okay, so the bug in the decision must be Rosa. Phil couldn't believe it. "Is there a problem with Miss Moran? Maybe because she's a westerner?"

The Grand Master shot her a serious look.

Phil felt as though she needed to dodge sparks she knew were heading toward her.

"We have no such bigotry, unlike your civilization. It is more that Miss Moran hesitates in her wish to stay here."

"It can't be. She was the one who mentioned this place as the perfect spot for them. I hesitate to say this, but maybe you judged too hastily." Phil had half an eye on the exit just in case those sparks actually did hit her this time. She heard, instead, a rumble of laughter.

The old man laughed for some time.

Phil waited.

"You would make a very good Tao priest. You are not afraid," the Grand Master said.

Phil ran a hand along her jaw and wondered when this audience would be finished. She wanted nothing more than to pick up her stuff and fly away. This guy was needling her something rotten and she need a drink—preferably a stiff one.

"That's debatable and I couldn't be a priest, I can promise you that. I'm not perfect enough for that kind of vocation."

Once more, the rumble of laughter filled the room. "I like you, *Mr.* Casters."

Mister. The emphasis on the mister was not lost on Phil. "I guess I like you, Grand Master. So is there a reason you needed me? Maybe to fly you somewhere?"

The old man shook his head vigorously. "No. No! Nature would have given me wings if I were to fly."

Phil grinned and nodded. "It kind of feels like nature gave me wings. I'm happiest in the clouds. Closer to …well, closer."

"The universe is the term you were looking for."

"Yeah, the universe." Phil smiled. "One day they are going to fly into space, even closer to the universe."

"You will return to The One, when it is your time."

"The one?" Phil asked.

"It is The One we return to in the end. If you stay, I can show you in the night sky."

In the night sky. What was that all about? Phil shrugged, "I'm leaving when we get back to the village."

There was a marked silence in the room.

"Pity, you could learn much and save yourself."

"From what?" Phil was annoyed again. It was all a crock.

"Yourself."

"Oh, I think I lost myself years ago. If it isn't a flight out of here, what do you need from me, Grand Master?"

The old man touched her arm and smiled slowly. "I need you to be true to those that matter. Now, I'm tired, please send me Chang."

Oh, great, they ended on a cryptic message and she was dismissed. Phil stood.

"Thank you for the audience, Grand Master."

There was no reply and she left the room.

†

Phil wandered to Rosa and Chang, who stood when they realized she was in the room.

"How did it go?" Rosa asked breathlessly.

Phil shrugged. "Chang, the Grand Master wants to see you."

Chang nodded and left the room within seconds.

"You look perplexed, Mr. Casters?"

Perplexed—sure and more than that. All this Mr. Casters crap had to stop. That's the least she could do —not lie to this woman any longer. Not that she had really. People just assumed.

"You know, I was going to mention that Mr. Casters title, well, it isn't Mr...." Phil blew out a breath.

"I'm sorry for being so formal after all you have done for us. Please, call me Rosa and your first name?" Rosa smiled.

Damn, she was cute when she smiled.

"Phil, they call me Phil."

Rosa nodded. "In that case, Phil, you still look perplexed."

"Much as you did, I suspect. The Grand Master is somewhat cryptic in his manner. I'm not sure what to make of it." Phil scratched the side of her temple.

Rosa sucked in a breath and as she exhaled—the air spiraled upward. "I felt much the same. Did he mention if we are to be allowed to stay?"

"The children look a safe bet, as much as I could make out." Phil hesitated. "He wasn't sure that this is the place where you want to spend the rest of your life."

Rosa frowned, then stared ahead and remained silent.

Phil placed a hand on her arm. "I'm not so sure he's wrong."

Rosa gave Phil a sharp glance. "Why do you say that, Mr. Casters?"

There was that Mister tag again. She dropped her hand. "You are a young woman with lots of potential. To remain here in this small village, as lovely as it is...." Phil smiled. "Well, I think it's a waste."

"There would be no waste!" Rosa shook her head. Phil could see that she was angry.

"Hey, look, I wasn't being derogatory. I just meant that maybe you might get bored." Phil shook her head. "Look, it really doesn't matter. I'll be out of here in a few hours."

"You are leaving?"

"That was the plan. I figure that if you convince the old man of your genuine need to stay here and help out, he'll come around."

"What if he doesn't, Mr. Casters? What then?" Rosa walked away. Phil watched her stride toward the altar surrounded by two golden dragons.

Phil shook her head. What was it with this woman being contrary today? Did it have something to do with being in a religious temple? That was probably why Phil avoided them like a bad cold.

Making her way to Rosa, Phil stopped a few feet short, giving the woman some personal space.

"I'm sorry."

Phil's lips tugged into a half smile at the words. "So am I. If I offended you in any way, it wasn't my intention."

Rosa pointed to a figure of a bird to the left of the altar. "Do you know what that symbolizes?"

"Can't say as I do. Exactly what kind of bird is it? A flamingo?" Phil peered at the long legged creature.

Rosa chuckled. "No, a crane. They are a symbol of immortality. It is much of what the Taoist religion believes."

"Yeah, the old man said they go back to *the one*. I haven't a clue what he meant but it was important to him. He even said he'd show me where in the night sky." Phil grinned. "Can't say I've seen any flying Grand Masters shooting upward on my way here."

Rosa chuckled. "Perhaps not, but the faith is very interesting. If I wasn't a catholic, I might turn to this religion. There is more equality."

Phil was certain she heard a wistful note in Rosa's voice.

"I guess being a catholic with its many, interesting, shall we say, rules, I'd be inclined to toss my hat in the ring of something like immortality."

They both turned as Chang reappeared.

"The Grand Master must rest now. He will give his final judgment in three days. We can leave now."

"But, Chang…" Rosa shook her head.

Phil knew this must be a worry waiting three more days without a conclusion, especially in a place many miles from what Rosa was familiar with. And the closed expression Chang gave her didn't help her any.

"Chang, from your knowledge of the Grand Master, does Rosa and the children's situation look promising?" Phil decided it was a worth a try to get some kind of positive answer.

Chang cast her a withering glance. "There are no promises. It is the Grand Master's decision. Now we must leave." The sound swept by her ears like the swish of a sword. They collected their belongings and left the temple.

Chapter Ten

Rosa watched pensively as Phil Casters collected his belongings from the house that they were temporarily living in. She stood just inside the door and leaned against the wooden structure, her arms folded.

"Hey, if you want to get something off your chest, Rosa, go right ahead."

Caught unaware by the suggestion, Rosa straightened and drew in a shallow breath. "I have nothing to get off my chest."

"Really? Could have fooled me. You are standing there as if I'm committing a crime." Phil drew the strings closed on the duffel bag and then stared at Rosa.

"No, I'm not." Rosa pouted.

Am I? Rosa wondered. The man owed her nothing and in fact, had done far more than anyone could expect of a stranger.

Yet, right now at this moment, I deny that he is a stranger. The only strange thing is the rapport I have with Phil. I always had a sense that he was important. That's probably why I wrote that letter to my grandfather. What were the odds that he would be my savior in our time of need?

"Okay, have it your way. You know that you and the kids are going to be just fine here. There is no way the Grand

Master won't let you stay. You'd be an asset to any community," Phil said before he smiled.

I like that smile, it makes my insides turn to jelly every time he flashes that quirky smile at me, Rosa thought. She placed her hand to her belly, hoping to stop its riotous movement. "Perhaps. Will you wait for Chang to bring the children to say goodbye to you. I think the twins would like that. They might seem ambivalent about their situation but...."

Rosa recalled the previous evening when she'd heard the children talking. They all had good things to say about Phil. The twins especially had waxed lyrical about him saving them from their fate. As to what fate that might have been...thankfully, the children had not known when Bang had asked them.

"Sure. I'll miss the rug rats."

"Rug rats?" Rosa frowned.

"Just a whimsical expression. My uncle used to call me his favorite rug rat."

Rosa smiled at the affectionate tone in Phil's voice as he mentioned his uncle.

"You had a happy childhood, Phil?" Rosa asked.

Phil gave her a long stare and then nodded.

"Sure, in a way. My folks died when I was young and my Uncle Joe took me under his wing. He was a pilot in the First World War, injured in the last few months so he couldn't fly again. When I wanted to be just like him, he had someone teach me how to fly."

Rosa saw Phil's eyes fill with tears. Her heart jumped at the sensitivity of the man before her. "You must love your uncle very much."

Phil shrugged. "I did. The old goat is dead now but I sometimes think that he comes around to check on me from time to time."

Rosa chuckled at the term *old goat*. It was so loving. "I'm sorry. I wasn't laughing at your loss."

"Hey, the old goat would have loved you if you had. He had a weird sense of humor. In fact, if you had met him, he'd have been trying to court you with stories of his war triumphs."

Rosa giggled. "I'm sure you would have prevented that."

Surprised at the frown that crossed Phil's face Rosa was perplexed. She felt her throat constrict and didn't know why.

"You are too classy for the old goat. He would have tried anyway, especially with what you do. I guess you would have something in common."

"What do you mean?"

"He took pity on me and brought up an orphan. You do that for so many. He definitely would have had you there for dinner." Phil shrugged.

"You were family, Phil. It makes a difference. You don't abandon your own."

"Yep, I was family," Phil said. "What is your excuse?"

Rosa's stomach did a triple somersault. "I...I care."

Phil came to the door. He touched a finger to her cheek and nodded. "You sure do."

Rosa was mesmerized and impulsively reached out and took the hand that had touched her and kissed the palm.

Phil stared at her and then bent his head and seconds later, their lips locked.

Rosa was lost in the sensations that cursed through her blood, heating every surface they touched. She didn't want it to end then, abruptly, it did.

"I'm sorry." Phil said. He shoved her away and retreated into the room.

Rosa felt the world was tumbling repeatedly and she wasn't able to do anything but remain motionless. She then lifted a hand to her lips and marveled at the sensations she was still feeling.

Phil picked up the rucksack, rushed forward, and gently pushed her aside as he left the room.

Before she had a chance to catch her breath, Phil was gone. The outer wooden door was still swinging on its hinges from his speed.

"He kissed me," Rosa exclaimed.

Then as the action and the reaction sank in—she slipped to the floor and wept.

✝

Chang gazed at the four children that had been the prerequisite of him being in the company of the only woman he had ever loved. *I can come to like them in time. Our children will be the priority of course, but these ...orphans...could go to families in due course. Especially ones that required extra help in their households.*

He glanced at the rice fields and the workers toiling there then back to the room.

It will be good to have a wife and keep the baying wolves at bay. Too many questions about my lack of a wife and celibacy have been irritating. Not that I am. There have been liaisons that might have worked. Except, no one touches the feverish senses that invade my body when Rosa Moran is in the vicinity. She defines love for me. Once my uncle agrees to her staying, then we will be together forever.

"Do you want anything, Chang?"

Chang looked long and hard at the woman, Meihui, who had spoken to him. She was beautiful in the eyes of many but was not his type.

"Meihui, the foreign pilot is leaving. The children need to say goodbye." Chang crossed his arms and stood feet apart as he instructed the children to follow him.

The older boy gave him a scrutiny fitting of a much older person. He liked that. Maybe he would take this boy into his family. He looked strong and able.

"Mr. Casters leave now?" Bang asked.

Chang inclined his head slightly.

"Missy Rosa not go with him."

To Chang, there seemed desperation in the voice. He could understand that. "No, Miss Rosa will stay."

There was a marked brightening of the boy's profile as he spoke in a whisper to the other children and they all smiled.

"Let us go. We do not want to delay Mr. Casters." He turned then swiveled around "Thank you, Meihui. I'm sure the children will return when they have said goodbye."

Meihui nodded.

†

Phil dumped the duffel on the passenger seat and cursed. She then leaned heavily against the side of the plane.

Damn, I shouldn't have kissed her. What an idiot I am. For God's sake, she thinks I'm a man. Now I will be in even more trouble if she finds out I'm a woman.

Lifting her head from the cool metal, she glanced toward the village. The afternoon sun shone brightly overhead and the tallest buildings with their ornate decorations beamed a welcome. It looked idyllic. She fervently hoped that Rosa had found what she was looking for and wished her a happy and safe life. Yeah, right.

"Damn her! She makes me want to stick around and ensure she's safe and happy," Phil spoke aloud before chastising herself for her stupid notion. Rosa wasn't likely to want anything to do with her. Especially now. Get yourself together, Casters. It's time to go home.

Phil drew in a deep breath and began her take off the wheel chocks. A few minutes later, she was about to climb aboard when she saw Chang and the four children heading her way. Her heart dropped when she didn't see Rosa. She now knew for sure that the woman didn't want anything to do with her.

She waved and waited as they approached—well, Chang approached at a sedate pace. The children broke into a run. She figured they must have a competition on who got to her first. Bang did and she ruffled the jet-black, short-cropped hair.

He giggled.

"Good to see you, Bang."

"Say goodbye, Mr. Casters," Bang said with a smile that showed off his crooked teeth.

Then the twins barreled into her and hugged a leg each.

"Hey, kids, how have you been?" It wasn't a question. She knew someone would take good care of them.

Mai grinned and Ziong gave a shy smile and gripped her leg tighter. *Anyone would think that they didn't want me to leave.*

She knelt as best she could and, as she came face to face with the twins, she touched their cheeks.

"要是正常" (You are going to be just fine.)

The twins narrowed their eyes simultaneously and then nodded.

"你会给妈妈一个消息?" (Will you give Mama a message from us?)

That was a toughie. She had no idea who their mother was or if she was still alive, but guessed Donna might still have contact.

"确保小" (Sure little ones.)

First Mai and then Ziong wrapped their thin arms around her neck and hugged her before kissing her cheek.

"我们爱你妈妈," they both whispered in Phil's ears. (We love you, Mama.)

Phil straightened and peered around Bang and saw Tao hiding behind him.

"I was sure that I brought four children, where is little Tao?" Phil looked at each child exaggeratedly, with a wink, then touched a finger to her lips.

Seconds later, the shy Tao stepped from behind Bang with a tentative smile on her lips.

Phil walked toward her and lifted the tiny girl in her arms before hugging her close.

"每个人都照顾的陶,这是你的工作现在." (Take care of everyone, Tao, it's your job now.)

Tao seemed to grow in her arms at the responsibility—or at least that was what Phil hoped.

"我一定会看一看. 蚱蜢罗莎?" (I will. Missy Rosa, as well?)

Phil felt her heart swell at the kindness of the child. Perhaps this episode in her life would teach her to be less selfish.

"Absolutely, Missy Rosa." Phil kissed the child on the cheek, placed her back on the ground and Tao ran to Bang and held his hand.

They were going to be okay. They had to be. If she heard anything different, she'd be back in a shot.

"Chang, it was good to meet you." Phil held out her hand and was surprised at the hesitation of the man.

He eventually shook her hand and stepped back.

"Good journey, Mr. Casters," Chang said solemnly. "Time to leave."

He motioned for the children to go with him as he turned back toward the village.

Phil felt her stomach twist at his cold attitude with the kids. They needed warmth and love, not matter-of-fact care. She closed her eyes as the tug of leaving the children behind tore into her. Worse thing was, if Rosa came running now and asked her to stay until the Grand Master had made a decision, she would in a heartbeat. She scanned the direction Chang was taking the children but there was no sign of anyone else.

She glanced back at her plane and shrugged. "Just you and me again, Gild. It's time to go home."

Phil climbed aboard and started the engine.

✝

Rosa held her head and allowed herself to cry. After several minutes of self-pity, she stopped.

She couldn't wallow in this...pity party. The children needed her.

It made little difference—the depression she felt at Phil Casters leaving continued to hit hard. It wasn't the kiss—it was more than that. Since the moment she'd first met the man, he had called to a part of her soul and right now, that part bled profusely. Why was life being so unfair to her? Wasn't it enough that she'd given up all her friends and the people she called family to bring the children to safety. Why did God want to punish her? Had she not given up enough? Now to lose someone who she was sure that, if given time, she could develop a friendship with…perhaps more. The thought of sharing something more with Phil resonated in her body. It made her feel happy, even while she wasn't sure if they would ever meet again.

Perhaps this was what the Grand Master meant.

The sound of a plane's engine had her rushing to the door and opening it. She walked to the veranda, looked into the distance, and saw Chang and the children heading back to the village.

Rosa sped down the steps and briskly caught up to them. "Chang?"

Chang gave her a smile.

It didn't light a flame in her the way Phil's had. Why should that be?

"As agreed, Mr. Casters is leaving. The children have said goodbye."

Rosa glanced at the children and they all looked sad, particularly Tao. She walked to the child and knelt down.

"Tao, it isn't so bad. Mr. Casters was very good to bring us here but he needs to go home now." She hugged the frail child close.

Tao's expressive face began to tear up.

"他说要照顾的每一个,尤其是您蚱蜢罗莎" (He said to take care of every one, particularly you, Missy Rosa.), Tao whispered into Rosa's ear.

Rosa closed her eyes and her heart did a triple somersault. She smiled at Tao. "Thank you, Tao." She straightened.

Without a word, she picked up the folds of the extra-long trousers she wore and ignoring Chang's words, she raced in the direction of the aircraft. The sound of a plane in the air had her cradling her hand over her eyes to see the take-off. She was too late.

She stopped and watched as the plane gained altitude and turned away. Moments later, it was gone from her sight.

"Goodbye, Mr. Casters," Rosa whispered brokenly. "May God keep you safe."

She waited a few more minutes, then turned back to the village, wiping away fresh tears. When her vision cleared, she saw Chang waiting for her alone.

Chapter Eleven

Rosa sat on the veranda of the home of Chang's parents and stared out onto the paddy fields where several people, mainly women, hoed the fields. She could hear them faintly singing a song. It had been several hours since Phil had left and the hole that it had made in her heart was indescribable. How could one become so enamored of another in such a short space of time? It didn't make sense.

Her attention turned to a woman who was carrying a child in a basket cradle mounted on her back. She, too, was working in the fields with a long, hoe-like tool. Rosa doubted that many of the women in the circles she traveled while in London with her grandfather would do as much, especially with a smile. It was a hard life in the countryside, but here, at least, there were compensations. The marvelous view, for instance.

The mountain that enclosed the valley appeared daunting and yet once inside the community, they gave a sense of security.

"You admire the mountain?"

Rosa glanced at Chang and nodded.

"Majestic is a good word, I think," Rosa said.

Chang stood at her side but did not sit. He stood like a statue, with his hands behind his back, his legs slightly apart.

It reminded Rosa of her grandfather standing at the fireplace, stiff and formal.

"Yes."

"You look pensive, Chang, is there a problem?"

Chang shook his head. "No, everything is perfect now."

"Why not sit and we can talk. We haven't had much time to do that without other people being around and I want to know how things have been with you since you left the missionary. Prudence, in particular, mentioned you before I left," Rosa said.

I hope he doesn't ask any questions. Prudence had mentioned Chang, but not in a nice way. She said he was such a rigid boy that he would probably turn out to be a cold, heartless man.

"She was always fair." Chang made no move to sit.

"Yes, yes, of course she was. Thank you for your kindness and that of your family. I didn't know where else to turn, particularly with the twins."

Rosa wished she hadn't said anything about the two girls when Chang pierced her with a stark gaze.

"Why those children in particular?" Chang moved to her.

Rosa felt intimidated by his towering stance. "Why nothing really. It's just that Bang, and Tao have been with me for years. The twins are new."

"How new?"

Rosa ran her tongue over her front teeth as she considered what to say. "Mr. Casters—"

"Him again! He's gone now. We will have no more dwelling on that man." Chang's lips curled into a snarl.

This time Rosa stood and was thankful that she was the same height. "I don't understand your animosity. Mr. Casters, other than being late for breakfast this morning, has been a perfect gentleman." Rosa declared. "Unless you know something I don't?"

Chang gave her a tiny bow. "I'm sorry I meant no ill will. Will you join me, and my parents, for dinner this evening? I have taken the liberty of asking Meihui to make the children an earlier meal. Then we can do as you ask and talk."

The arrogance of the man to do that with the children without asking her first—damn him.

"As you have already made the arrangements, thank you for the invitation." Rosa half smiled but knew the emotion wasn't heartfelt.

They both turned with different degrees of surprise as the familiar sound of an aircraft in the distance met their ears.

"He's back!" Rosa grinned and rushed to the veranda to watch the empty sky. A minute or two later the tiny spot between the valley got bigger and bigger just as her heart did. She was darned sure that her heart had taken wings and was soaring to greet the pilot.

As Rosa glanced at Chang, she was surprised at the thundercloud of an expression he wore. It didn't matter, not a jot. She scrambled down the steps and headed to the field where Phil had previously taken off.

"Are you coming, Chang?" She threw the words into the wind as she ran toward the plane that was descending steadily.

†

"You came back?" Rosa said breathlessly as Phil's feet hit the ground.

Phil turned to her and gave her a slow appraisal. "Yes, wasn't sure it was the right thing to do in the circumstances but...." Phil shrugged.

Rosa didn't need to be hit over the head to understand what Phil meant—it was the kiss.

"I think we need to talk about what happened, don't you?" Rosa held her breath.

"It was an impulsive kiss and I apologize. I promise it will never happen again." Phil's hands dived into the pockets of the leather jacket.

That wasn't exactly what Rosa wanted, but he was back and that gave her time. Time to do what was another matter. A relationship of that magnitude was not part of her knowledge.

"Why did you come back? Surely not to apologize to me?"

Phil smiled.

There it is again. That smile and my heart is melting again. Rosa mentally shook her head.

"Well, that was partly why I came back. I don't usually take a hike when I kiss a girl." Phil gave Rosa a tight smile.

She forgave him instantly.

"I figured I promised to make sure you were safe and we don't know that yet."

"That is very gallant of you, Mr. Casters." Rosa smiled.

"I thought we had worked that Mr. Casters cr… nonsense out. Phil is so much friendlier."

"Yes, sorry."

"I'm a bit surprised that you are the only one here to greet me. Where are the kids?" Phil's gaze moved to the village and the empty distance between them.

Rosa looked in the same direction and let out an audible groan.

"Oh, I don't like the sound of that. What's happened? I've only been gone a short time. I doubt even you can get into trouble in that time." Phil winked at her.

"Really? I'm not trouble." Rosa frowned. Was she trouble for this man? Oh, she hoped not.

"Bad choice of words. So what made you sigh so heavily?"

"Chang has made it his mission, I believe, to take charge of the children." Rosa frowned. "Of me, too," she said flippantly.

Phil's mouth matched her frown and she was glad. At least he wasn't immune to her. He couldn't be if he had kissed her. Then again, he might have many liaisons. Prudence said men of a particular kind had lady friends everywhere and she knew so little of him.

"Well, he has competition now, doesn't he? Until the Grand Master gives you the green light, you and the kids are my responsibility if that's okay with you."

Rosa resisted the temptation to wrap her arms around Phil and hug him. "Thank you," she replied demurely.

"You are very welcome. Right. Let's go and find the kids. I have a notion that Chang's idea of fun is not so fun. Besides, I promised to teach the twins catch and I haven't done that yet. Do you know how to play catch, Rosa?"

Rosa shook her head. "Then catch it shall be before they have dinner. Which reminds me, Chang has invited me to dinner with his parents. Now, I extend that invitation to you."

Phil laughed. "Can you do that? I figure straitlaced Chang won't take kindly to me being a tag along."

"He may not but he gave me no choice. If he dislikes it, will you have dinner with me, Phil?" Rosa liked that idea so much more than spending her evening with Chang's family. As uncharitable as that sounded. Her heart was pulling the strings right now and she had little option but to go along.

"Hey, I'm all for dinner with you, Rosa. Chaperoned or not, it will be my pleasure." Phil held out an arm.

Rosa gazed at it, unsure if it was ladylike to take it. Then she threw caution to the wind and slipped her arm inside his. She wasn't in stuffy England any longer. "Mine, too. The children will be happy to see you."

They headed toward the village and saw four small figures running in their direction.

"Ah, there they are. Let's go teach our kids how to play catch," Phil said and grinned.

Rosa's blood surged at the genuine sentiment in Phil's tone. Perhaps miracles do happen. She hoped so, she really did.

✝

The catch session had been entertaining for them all. The laughter they shared had resonated with the other village children who had joined them. Before Phil knew it, she was coaching twenty kids. Rosa had been somewhat helpful, but not much. She had as much control of the ball as a two-year-old. It didn't matter though since it made the session even more fun and Rosa was happy to take the teasing on the chin.

When they finished, Phil saw Chang watching from his home. He stood like a sentinel ready for action. There was now no doubt in her mind that Chang considered Rosa his property. It was perhaps draconian but from the little Rosa had said, it fit the man perfectly.

Tonight, as she wrestled into a clean blue cotton shirt and buttoned it up, she looked remarkably respectable. Her hair was slicked back and yes, now as she gazed at her reflection, she did look masculine—at least her hair did.

"I'm going to have to tell her tonight. It isn't right that she has a misunderstanding about my gender. I like her and she deserves the truth," Phil said to the tiny mirror in the room. She pulled on a gray coat that had been given to her by the laundry woman who'd told her that it was a better look than the leather jacket she'd had with her. Yeah, like it was so nondescript. She laughed as she wondered what Ming would make of her appearance right now. The thought of Ming had her stare directly into the mirror.

Was she that shallow that she could forget her lover so easily? Ming was a pale comparison to Rosa Moran and she didn't even know why. Rosa wasn't exactly in Ming's league when it came to sheer beauty. Not that any of it mattered in the big picture. She thought Phil was a man and that gave off its own death knell.

"It's just payback for her helping me in the past. Anything else is just...a dream. Yep, a dream of what might have been but never can be. Crap, I'm beginning to sound like the Grand Master." Phil chuckled and gave the mirror one more look and then left the room.

✝

The meal was sumptuous. There was no other word for it. Phil salivated at the spread on the round table. The aroma of ginger, garlic, and chili invaded her nostrils. If the food tasted as good as the smell, she was in heaven.

"Please be seated, Mr. Casters." Chang waved her to a cushion at the far end of the table.

Dutifully Phil made her way there and sat. Within seconds, several people sat around her and then she spied Rosa who was sitting opposite her. Rosa grinned and meekly remained silent. The seating surely wasn't Chang's idea.

Amid the volume of conversation, which was typically Chinese, everyone wanted a word.

"Smells great," Phil said.

"Yes it does. Hope you like chicken, because it's chicken with everything tonight. I saw the preparations." Rosa grinned.

"I love chicken." Phil winked.

Silence ensued.

Phil turned her attention to the entrance. "The Grand Master," she whispered. She watched as the old man moved through the Chang family, heading toward her.

"The One called you, after all. I'm happy." He gave a toothless grin and sat at the head of the table, nodding in Rosa's direction.

Phil glanced at Rosa and they smiled. They both had their stories about the old man and maybe one day they would share.

Phil was fascinated by the family, parents, siblings, and Chang himself, who sat next to Rosa. It was much to Phil's annoyance but there were pluses. She could look into her eyes. It worked for her.

The room filled with the scent of steamed dumplings and several plates on the table were in easy reach of the dinner guests. Two large ornate bowls were at each end of the table and the red inky substance had the pungent aroma of chili and ginger.

All eyes turned to the Grand Master who smiled and began to pray. Phil watched as everyone closed their eyes and bent their heads, except her.

She clasped her hands together in a minor show of support. They would call her a heathen. Her gaze rested on the bent dark head of Rosa and a trickle of warmth flowed in her chest. Damn, there was something about this girl....

"Eat, everyone, enjoy," the Grand Master insisted with a clap of his hands.

Phil had to mask her amusement at the voracious way the family attacked the food as she waited.

"It's safe for you to take food, Mr. Casters," Rosa said quietly. She then reached for a dumpling with her chopsticks. She drizzled sauce from the large bowl over the steaming item.

Phil was starving and quickly followed Rosa's lead. When she placed the dumpling with a dollop of sauce into her mouth and bit into the dough, the burst of the hot chili and ginger sauce burnt her tongue, and she heard Rosa giggle. Now she knew why she only drizzled the sauce. It was like having a firebox in your mouth. With a narrowing of her eyes, she chewed and had to admit that, the actual dish filled with minced chicken was delicious.

She reached for the glass of water placed at her side and drank thirstily. "Wonderful." She finally allowed herself to speak hoping she didn't sound hoarse. "Next time I'll ease up on the sauce."

Rosa chuckled. "Good idea."

There was little conversation. Phil's eyes bulged as she watched everyone devouring the dumplings at a speed she had never seen before.

Once the servers removed the plates, conversation filled the room once again.

"Did you enjoy the chicken dumplings, Rosa?" Chang asked.

"As Mr. Casters said, they were wonderful. Your mother makes excellent dumplings. Perhaps she will show me the recipe one day."

Phil watched Chang's expression. His face was so expressive that it was as if winter and summer existed at the same time.

"Perhaps, one day," Chang replied, with a smile.

"Mr. Casters, I'm glad you returned."

Phil's attention diverted to the old man at the head of the table.

"Thank you. I owed it to Rosa. Her safety and that of the children were my responsibility. Until you make a final decision, I need to be here with them."

Phil traded gazes with the Grand Master. His watery pale eyes seemed to delve into her soul and she wasn't sure how she would fare under such introspection.

"After dinner I will show you the star system we talked about."

"You are interested in our religion?" Chang asked.

Phil moved her glance to the younger man. "Sure, knowledge is king. When you ignore the chance to learn, you are on a slippery slope."

Chang frowned. "Slippery slope?"

"Sorry, it's just an expression. It means a dangerous course of action."

"Perfect explanation, Mr. Casters. I couldn't have come up with anything better. Now, who is the teacher, I wonder," Rosa said.

"Thanks, but I'll keep to flying, I'm so much better at that. Besides, I think you are a great teacher."

Rosa tipped her head to one side.

"Now how would you know anything about my talents as a teacher? You have never seen me teach."

"Don't need too. The fact the kids love you says it all." Phil grinned. "Can't say I loved my grade school teacher. She was akin to the wicked witch of the west from the Wizard of Oz. Between you and me, I think Baum based that character on her."

Rosa laughed before turning with what looked like apologetic eyes to the Grand Master. "I'm sorry, Grand Master."

"No, go on. It is fascinating. What is a wicked witch?" The old man gave them both a serious face.

Rosa scratched her neck.

Phil figured she was stuck for an answer. "Ever had a female in your life that you really wished you'd never met, Grand Master?" Phil grinned at the man.

He nodded vigorously.

"That's your wicked witch for you. She gets everywhere." Phil settled back in her chair and hoped the man didn't want further explanation, as she really didn't have more to say.

"I understand. Yes, I understand very well." There was a faint twist of the thin lips and he continued to nod. "Chang, what of you, who is your wicked witch?"

Chang looked positively shocked at the question, cleared his throat, and looked toward the closed door of the room.

Probably hoping for the next course. Phil suppressed a chuckle.

"Come, boy, this is interesting conversation," the Grand Master insisted.

"I...." He frowned. "I do not think, perhaps Prudence."

"Chang!" Rosa glared at him.

Phil pursed her lips at Rosa's reaction. Not a good way to win a girl.

"Let the boy say what he thinks, Miss Rosa. It is best to be honest at the beginning of a relationship. Don't you think, *Mr.* Casters?" the Grand Master pierced Phil with a hard glance.

The door opened and the next course arrived. Saved by the bell.

Dishes of colorful adzuki beans, loaded with mushrooms and fresh peppers, appeared. Then sizzling strips of chicken, dressed with chilies and prickly ash, looked marvelous.

Phil's mouth watered at the feast before her and she picked up her chopsticks and was about to reach for the food when Rosa spoke.

"Phil, there is another prayer."

"Ah...right." Phil shrugged and dropped her chopsticks beside of her plate.

The Grand Master once more began to pray.

Phil closed her eyes this time and was lost in the aroma of the food. The smell was better than anything she had come across in all her time on the continent.

"You may stop praying now, Mr. Casters," the Grand Master said.

Phil opened her eyes amidst laughter and saw amusement in the old man's eyes. "Oh, I figured a little more prayer wouldn't hurt," Phil said to disguise her embarrassment.

She looked at Rosa who had a smirk on her face. *Yeah, and I fooled her, Right.*

"Prayer is good for the soul." The Grand Master waved at the food and they all tucked in again.

†

"You don't pray, do you, Phil?" Rosa sat on the steps of the house they were living in.

Phil pulled a cigarette out of her pocket and tapped the end on the box. "Nope."

"Have you become a new recruit to Taoism after the Grand Master regaled you with the stories of The One? I personally found it fascinating." Rosa looked up at the sky.

"No, however it was interesting. Do you suppose they think me immortal since I can fly?" Phil grinned and struck a match.

The glow flickered for a second over Rosa's averted profile.

Rosa turned and their eyes met. She shook her head. "If you wore a pearl on the top of your head and were flanked by dragons, perhaps." Rosa chuckled.

The sound made Phil's heart race.

"Around the neck maybe," Phil replied. "The dragons might be a bit trickier." She blew out a swirl of smoke. "The Grand Master seemed amiable. I think he will let you stay."

Rosa turned her gaze back to the stars. It was a clear night and the Great Dipper was unmistakable.

"Is this a place you would consider spending your life, Phil?"

Where did that come from? Phil frowned. "I like to travel, that's why I'm a pilot. Maybe when my wandering days are done, I might consider a place like this." It wasn't strictly true since a vibrant city was more her choice.

Rosa leaned her chin on her upturned hands. "I have often wondered what it would be like to travel the world. I've been to England, of course."

The musing made Phil smile as she sucked in cigarette smoke and the nicotine coursed through her blood. "There's nothing stopping you now, is there. The children will be well-looked after here."

Phil gazed at the pensive expression on Rosa's face and she stomped on her barely used cigarette and sat next to the woman. "You could come back with me."

Rosa smiled and gazed at Phil.

Her gray eyes held a sparkle that would live in Phil's mind forever.

"It is never that simple."

Phil impulsively reached out and took Rosa's hand. "Why?"

"I could never impinge on your good nature, Phil. You have done so much for the children and me already. To be honest, I do wonder why you have been so generous."

Phil shrugged. "That's easy. Do you remember the first time we met?"

"Of course. You brought a message from my grandfather."

"You could so easily have told me to leave without a tangible message to your family and the lawyers. Instead, you took the time to write and ask them to pay for our services even though we had not completed the task to their satisfaction."

Rosa frowned. "Of course I did. It wasn't your fault that I wouldn't leave. Any reasonable person would have done the same."

Phil shook her head. "I'm afraid there are many who would not. Anyway, the upshot was my boss made me a partner in the business." Phil saw Rosa raise her eyebrows. "It's a long story but it changed my life. I owe you, Rosa Moran, big time."

Rosa squeezed Phil's hand gently.

"Then I'm very glad that I took the time to do such a small kindness. Perhaps it was unconsciously leading to this." Rosa shivered.

Phil moved and threw her arm around the thin shoulders of the woman at her side. "Do you mind?"

Rosa smiled and rested her head into the crook of Phil's neck. "This is perfect, thank you."

Phil drew in a steadying breath as her heart did a triple jump. "Want me to point out the pole star where the Grand Master said The One lives and where we all return to at the end." Phil almost lost it as Rosa's warm breath flickered along her neck.

"I would love that," Rosa said softly.

Phil pointed to a far off star and began telling Rosa stories of shooting stars and the magnificence of flying in the expanse of the sky.

Chapter Twelve

Rosa clasped her hands on her hot cheeks. It was a beautiful night and had been a lovely evening. Phil had left for a bathroom break, allowing her the time to dwell on Chang's dominance of her immediately after dinner. It had been a tad annoying. Still she had mentioned they needed to talk and talk he did.

"Did you enjoy the dinner, Rosa?"

"Yes, your family should be proud."

Rosa watched Chang's expression change from mild interest to slight animation. He never was one to show feelings. She remembered that even as a boy he'd rarely smiled.

"The Grand Master was present. It is only right that we honor him. It is the closest to The One we can ever hope to achieve in this lifetime." Chang replied solemnly.

"I was listening to the Grand Master speak to Mr. Casters about your religion. It was fascinating."

"Fascinating enough to consider a change, Rosa?" Chang's expression was bland.

"Oh, I wouldn't say that, Chang. I was brought up a Catholic. Can you imagine Charlotte and Prudence's face if I said I was leaving the faith?" Rosa bit down on her lip. "I didn't realize that you had problems with Prudence, Chang. I always thought you liked her."

Chang's cheeks took on a pink hue. "I cannot disrespect my family. I'm sorry. I have no issues and never have had with her." He gave her a curious look. "Does that make me a lesser man in your eyes?"

Rosa was surprised at the question. "No, of course not. We all say and do things to prevent others from being hurt. I'm sure I have and will in the future."

Chang pointed to the woman she knew as Meihui. "My family believes that I should marry Meihui. We have known one another since birth."

Rosa had to think what to say next. This wasn't the usual type of conversation she engaged in. "Do you love her?"

"No."

The word pinged off the wall like a death knell.

"She's very accomplished and pretty." Rosa felt sorry for the woman. She was kind and intelligent. Certainly not worthy of being written off like garbage as Chang had done.

"Accomplished, yes, though Meihui is a mere shadow of the one I admire."

Chang caught her gaze. Her reaction was so different from the reaction she had to Phil's gaze—actually no reaction whatsoever.

Rosa knew enough about Chinese protocol not to ask *that* direct question. "Life can be a mystery, can't it, Chang? We do not know who we are to encounter. Some will be good, others not so much. Then there is that special someone who changes the way we think in the blink of an eye."

Chang nodded. "Exactly. Do you think you have found that someone, Rosa?"

Rosa smiled. "I'm not sure yet." Her gaze traveled to Phil. "It is too soon to say."

Chang left her soon after with his expression sour.

She sighed. Now here I am with someone who might, just might, be my One.

"Hey, did you miss me?" Phil grinned and plonked down next to her.

"Of course. I was getting cold."

Phil laughed. "Can't have that."

Rosa snuggled into the offered shoulder. "No, we cannot. Now you were explaining how you navigated in the dark." A word tumbled around in her head—an unsaid word—*always*.

✝

Phil kicked the wheel on the left hand side of her plane and sighed heavily. The last three days had been the happiest she had ever known. She and Rosa, along with the children, were just simply having fun. Chang was a bit of a nightmare but the compensations were magnificent. Today was the day the Grand Master would give his answer. So she was preparing the plane for departure.

"I have to tell Rosa the truth about me before it's too late, Gilda." Her head slid against the cold gray metal. "What the hell is happening to me? I never thought I'd feel this way about a woman. Hell, I'm in love with Ming…at least I thought I was. Right now, I'm not sure of anything anymore. Except you, old girl." Phil kissed the cold surface.

She wasn't sure what highlighted the fact that she wasn't alone. She lifted her head and saw sandals on large feet. Her gaze moved up, encountering black leggings and a brown tunic, then the sardonic expression of Chang. "Oh, great," she muttered.

"Hi, Chang, what brings you here this early?"

Chang appeared to sniff the air. "The Grand Master has made a decision. Rosa is waiting," Chang said in a clipped voice.

Phil frowned. "I didn't think it was anything to do with me. Can't the Grand Master just tell Rosa his decision?"

Chang shuffled his feet. "The Grand Master insisted on your presence."

"I see." She didn't but if that were what it took to hear the final verdict, she would go. "Give me a minute. I need to stow my stuff away. As soon as the Grand Master has spoken, I'll be leaving."

"You said that before," Chang replied drolly.

Phil threw her bag into the cockpit. "I guess I did. Still I have no interest in staying here for any length of time, which should make you happy, Chang."

Chang's brown eyes pierced her and she felt the ice wash over her.

"It does."

Short and to the point, No love lost between them. Phil smiled.

"You're going to have to lighten up if you want to have a chance with Rosa." Phil climbed the ladder and locked the cockpit door. The silence following her last words made her smirk. Bet he wasn't expecting her to say that. She turned to face Chang—his face was a fiery picture of red. *Oops, maybe that wasn't a good thing to say.*

"Mr. Casters, for that slight you owe me recompense."

"Oh, come on, buddy, it wasn't a slight. You need to laugh more." Phil bit down on her lip. She knew a few guys who had taken a swing at her for her less than this in polite conversation. It looked like this minor infraction might cost her.

121

"I am not your…buddy." Chang puffed out his chest.

Phil drew a hand across her mouth effectively stifling the laugh. He was like a darn peacock preening.

"After the audience with the Grand Master, we will settle this." Chang turned on his heel and left her.

Dragging a hand through her hair, Phil shook her head. "I didn't say anything bad. It was a joke. Talk about overreaction. I wonder what he means by recompense, Gilda."

She gave the man a rueful look and slowly headed after him.

†

Rosa walked up and down the interior of the small temple where Chang had deposited her before setting off to find Phil. When she woke, she was expecting to see Phil for breakfast. Disappointment had surged through her when she realized he wasn't there. Chang's appearance at her door, along with his expression when she had immediately asked if he had seen Phil, had been sour to say the least.

A girl similar in age to Tao smiled at her before she ran to the altar and knelt there to pray.

Perhaps that was what she needed to do. Pray for guidance in her emotions regarding Phil. Perhaps it was her naiveté, or that she was alone without the stability she had known and Phil was a link to that old life in a small way. Whatever it was, last evening had been the best time she had ever had in a man's company—anyone's if she was being honest with herself.

The door to the temple opened and she glanced up expectantly. It was an old man, his body stooped, with his cane clicking on the floor as he walked by. He knelt awkwardly to pray.

122

Rosa went outside to take in the fresh and cleansing morning air. The cough that had irritated her for several months now seemed to have disappeared like magic.

Strange I hadn't realized it was gone until this moment. In fact, I haven't coughed since Phil turned up. How odd is that? He must be the cure for all that ails me. She giggled.

She watched several people walk past her. They smiled and waved and she returned the gestures.

It wouldn't be so bad living here. In fact, it's what she wanted...perhaps had wanted, because she didn't know any other option. Not to hear Phil's quiet voice, see his infectious smile, and simply be in his company made her incredibly sad. Life could be so contrary at times.

She lifted her hand and peered into the distance. Two familiar figures, distinctly apart, headed toward the village perimeter.

Chang arrived first. He gave a curt nod and entered the temple without a word.

Rosa frowned.

A minute later, Phil arrived. The pilot tipped a hand to his forehead and gave that quirky grin she was beginning to become accustomed to. "I hear that you need me as a chaperon?"

Rosa smiled and shook her head. "I think not, Phil. Perhaps the Grand Master thinks so. It was at his insistence."

Phil climbed the steps and stood beside Rosa.

"What's wrong with Chang? His face looks like a thundercloud."

"Can't say I noticed any difference to his usual demeanor." Phil shrugged.

Rosa laid a hand on Phil's arm. The leather of the jacket he wore was supple to the touch. "Did something happen between you and Chang, Phil?"

Phil drew in a deep breath. "He took a few of my words out of context. It's nothing to worry about. Shall we go inside? Otherwise Chang might actually send a thunderbolt our way." Phil winked.

"Yes, perhaps he might." Rosa chuckled.

They entered the building and Chang stood in the middle of the room like a statue.

Walking up to him, Rosa gave Chang a smile. "I guess we are ready for our audience now, Chang. We need to know whatever the answer might be."

Chang looked first at Phil and sneered, then slowly smiled at Rosa. "The Grand Master is wise. I'm sure whatever decision is made it will be the right one."

"Yes, I agree." Rosa hooked her arm in Chang's. "Shall we proceed?"

Chang smiled and nodded. Then Rosa looked at Phil who was behind her and winked.

Phil winked back as they entered the inner sanctum of the Grand Master.

As they walked into the dimly lit room, it was reminiscent of the last audience Rosa had with the man.

"You may leave, Chang."

Chang nodded and left the room.

"Sit, children, sit. How have the last few days been?" the Grand Master asked with a smile.

"Wonderful. Thank you, Grand Master." Rosa answered breathlessly. Her heart pounded in anticipation.

"And you, Mr. Casters?"

"Great. Your stories were very enlightening and you almost had me convinced to try your way," Phil responded.

"Excellent. Enlightenment is a much quicker path to The One." The old man lifted a plain kettle and poured steaming water into three tiny cups.

Rosa watched his action. The hands were frail and barely able to steady the kettle, however he never spilled a drop. She was impressed.

"Green tea. My favorite." Rosa accepted the cup the old man handed her.

"A good choice, my child. My parents harvested tea when I was very young. I have more than one favorite." The old man picked up the other vessel. "Mr. Casters, do you enjoy green tea?"

"Sure, I guess." Phil accepted the tiny cup.

"Excellent." The Grand Master settled back in his chair.

They drank for a few moments and Rosa saw Phil grimace from the corner of her eye. She stifled a laugh.

The Grand Master spoke. "I met a special emissary last evening. In fact it helped me make up my mind on what I'm to do about your situation, Miss Moran."

"Oh." Rosa frowned.

"I heard some of the others at dinner indicate that an emissary, and an important one, arrived for an audience with you," Phil said.

"You listen well to gossip, Mr. Casters. Indeed, it was."

Rosa frowned. Phil hadn't mentioned anything last night after dinner. "I know it may not be my business except if it influenced your decision, then it must be. What did the emissary say?"

The Grand Master gave her a withering glance.

Rosa saw Phil move forward in his seat.

"From anyone in particular? Perhaps from my mission?" Rosa asked.

The old man shook his head. "I wish it were that. This envoy was from a fraction of the old royal house."

"Oh, crap. How did they know we came here? I was careful," Phil declared before standing.

"Sit, Mr. Casters, sit. This envoy is not from the side that wants to harm the children. Quite the contrary. Their mother has gained an ally, who is more powerful than her husband and his friends."

Rosa considered the statement. From the look on Phil's face, he didn't believe a word and perhaps he was right. How had they caught up to them so quickly?

"Exactly what did the envoy ask, Grand Master?" Rosa asked.

"He asked that you consider taking the children back to a place called..." The old man frowned, smiled, and nodded. "Yes, yes, Donna's bar."

Phil laughed. "Yep, Donna's bar. How apt."

"It doesn't sound like a very good place to take children. I don't understand," Rosa said.

"If we take them back, what else did he say?" Phil said.

"That the children's mother will be there and she will explain everything."

Rosa knew what Phil had told her of the circumstances about the twins and of course, she had seen the contents of the letter. "How can we guarantee their safety? It might be a ruse, Grand Master."

"It may be, except for one thing. It is also the reason I asked Mr. Casters to be here." He fished out a letter from his tunic and handed it to Phil. "I'm told you will know the handwriting."

Perplexed, Rosa watched as, Phil, took the envelope, and gazed at it. "Do you know the person who wrote this?"

Phil nodded and ripped open the seal.

There was an expectant silence in the room as Phil read the letter.

"I'm taking them back today," Phil said.

Rosa saw the taut jaw and the serious concentration on his face as he clutched the letter.

"Actually, Mr. Casters, *we* are taking them back—all of us," Rosa announced.

Phil gazed at Rosa.

His expression told Rosa that she might have two heads. Nevertheless, she was certain this was the right path for her and the children.

"Why take Bang and Tao? They could be happy here. You, as well. I'm not sure what will happen when we get back to the city." Phil gave Rosa a pained expression.

Rosa stood and folded her arms across her chest. "It's all of us or none of us."

"But I...." Phil turned to the Grand Master. "You haven't made your decision. It's better they stay behind and I take the twins. It might not go the way the envoy expects and there could be trouble. Don't you think that's the wisest move, Grand Master?"

The Grand Master stood—his small frame dwarfed by Rosa and Phil. "Sometimes, events take place that remove my intervention. This is such a case. You have your choice, Mr. Casters, make it." The old man moved a few steps to a door that Rosa hadn't noticed before. "From our village's point of view, Miss Moran, you, and your children are welcome at any time."

"See, you don't need to come back with me. I can take it from here," Phil decreed.

"And I will not allow it. Let me know when you have decided. Thank you, Grand Master." Rosa stomped out of the room.

†

Phil looked at the Grand Master and at the closed door. "I guess she is determined."

There was a low chuckle and the Grand Master motioned for Phil to retake his chair.

"I have found that women are strong-minded creatures and you would know, *Mr.* Casters."

Phil's fingers tangled with the short hair at the back of her neck. "Yeah, I would." She looked at the man who stared at her. Damn, he knew. "How do you know?"

"Taking a bath in a public building, no matter how alone you think you are, there are always people around."

"Shit, sorry. How many others know?" Phil dropped her head into her hands. Life was becoming complicated again.

"Your secret is yours to tell. I think it wise you do tell, at least Miss Moran, of your subterfuge."

"I never meant to deceive her. It was an accident and as time has gone on…" Phil looked into the watery eyes of the man opposite her. "I think she would be better off staying here with you."

"Yet you believe that the letter you received is evidence enough that the envoy was genuine."

Phil nodded. "I do, want to read it?" She offered the man the letter.

"No. That is for you to deem the truth, not me. Would it be so wrong to have Miss Moran accompany you? Should things become difficult, I guarantee she has a home here for the rest of her life." The Grand Master poured more tea.

"Will it help me make my decision?" Phil grinned and took the cup.

The old man chuckled. "Alas, that is for you alone to make. Miss Moran has brought you happiness."

"How did you…." Phil frowned. "Yes."

"The truth will set you free—both of you."

Phil drank the liquid and it was refreshing for all of the few seconds before she felt like she had tea leaves on her tongue again. Gross.

"You promise me that, if things don't work out, Rosa and the children will have a home here?"

The old man scribbled on a parchment in front of him, rolled it up, and handed it to her.

"This is my decree. Even after my death, it will be valid." Phil accepted the parchment and placed it on the inside of her jacket.

"I guess the decision is made. Thank you, Grand Master. I hope one day we will meet again."

The old man nodded. "Look to the stars, my soul will be soaring to The One in the not too distant future."

Phil stood, and with a quiet goodbye, left the room. *Damn, I hope I'm as cool about dying as he is,* she thought.

†

"And?" Rosa gave Phil a stern glance.

"Get the kids and pack. I want to be out of here in two hours max." Phil felt vindicated for her decision when Rosa grinned and wrapped her arms around her.

"Thank you, thank you, Phil. You won't be disappointed." Rosa then sped off toward the house they had been using.

"I won't but you probably will." Her eyes cast around and she saw Chang who looked much bigger in silhouette. "What the hell. He is just one more problem to run away from."

Phil walked up to the man.

"I'm leaving in two hours. Whatever you want as retribution will have to wait."

Chang didn't say anything. He never moved.

"Look, let's just say it was a misunderstanding and leave it like that." Phil held out her hand.

"You are going alone?" Chang's expression remained dour.

"I have to take the twins back. However you will be pleased to know that the Grand Master has approved Rosa to stay here."

"As it should be." Chang turned away and then switched back. "Do not come back, Mr. Casters, you are not welcome here."

Phil shrugged and watched as the man left.

She scratched the back of her ear and she couldn't help laughing aloud. "Little does he know?" Phil drew in a deep breath and smiled. Life wasn't so bad after all. She scrunched up the letter from Donna and placed it in her pocket. "Sometimes, Donna, I wish we hadn't met."

†

Phil gave the village a thoughtful look. It was idyllic. Maybe too much so. Times were changing fast, especially with the Japanese invasion. Maybe she might come back here, even as remote as it was. Who knew what the future could bring.

Within a few minutes, she was back with Gilda and grinned at the machine. "Looks like we are going home, Gilda, with return passengers. What do you make of that?"

She grinned and climbed the ladder, unlocking the cockpit, retrieving the service manual Blake insisted she follow on take-off. He was sensitive about the machines under his maintenance. One of the reasons she flew with him in the first place was that he didn't take safety for granted. Nor did she.

Even though she had thoroughly done so earlier, Phil checked the tires. She opened the fuel manifold. Her earlier trip and return had been beneficial. There was a staging post two hours away and they had provided her with enough fuel for the journey home. She'd have to make another pit stop there after the deviation of coming back to Langshow. She figured it would be safer to stop there to refuel than closer to home. That letter might indicate the twins were safe but sometimes messages don't get to all the places as speedily as the envoy had. Another interesting thought was just how quickly the letter arrived. She'd find out that answer when she saw Donna in person.

Ticking off the various maintenance checks, she was ready to leave within an hour. "Darn, I wish I'd said an hour." Phil grumbled and fiddled around with several dials in the cockpit.

Stretching back in the seat, she lifted her legs and rested them on the co-pilot's seat arm then closed her eyes. A catnap would be good before they set off.

Chapter Thirteen

The remarkably quiet drone of the engines made Rosa smile. She glanced into the cargo bay, which was once more strewn with children. They were playing a game and it warmed her heart to see the simple, honest camaraderie that had developed between them in such a short time.

"How good it must be to make friends so easily."

Rosa was startled when Phil spoke.

"Not easy, just less cynical than adults." Phil smiled.

Rosa watched the pilot turn his attention back to the glorious blue sky ahead. Even the clouds were in short supply today.

"I think I prefer innocent," Rosa said ruefully.

"Okay, I can go with that. Although you make friends easily, don't you?"

Rosa considered the question and gazed at the averted profile of the pilot. He definitely knew how to shave since there wasn't a sign of stubble on his cheeks. Maybe he had a magic elixir. She automatically pulled at the tiny hair above her lip that grew back quickly no matter how many times she plucked it out.

"I suppose I do. It is the nature of a missionary."

Phil nodded. "How come someone like you became a missionary?"

Rosa figured that was a reasonable question. "I could ask why you become a pilot."

"Didn't I tell you? I'm sure I did. You answer mine and I'll answer yours. It will while away a little time."

Rosa watched as Phil's competent hands clasped the wheel. "My parents died when I was a baby."

"Sorry," Phil murmured.

"I never knew them, only of them. They were dedicated missionaries. I think a child was a burden in their work," Rosa said, narrowing her eyes.

Phil swiveled to look into Rosa's eyes. He reached a hand out and stroked away a line at the side of her eyes.

The touch sent heady signals of pleasure through Rosa's veins.

"They wanted you. Who wouldn't? I bet you were a good kid growing up?"

Rosa was bereft when Phil moved his hand away. "I...not really...just a normal child, I suspect," she said stumbling over the words.

"This Prudence woman. I like the sound of her."

"That's because Chang doesn't I suspect." Rosa shook her head. "Prudence was fair, strong when she needed to be, and loved me...all of the orphans."

"Bet she had a soft spot for you." Phil chuckled. "I don't bet. I guarantee it."

"I will miss her. It was hard when I went back to England for my education and what grandfather called the proper bringing up of a young lady. I wanted to stay with my family in China." Rosa's eyes misted as she recalled the loneliness of those years.

"You came back to your family. I'm sorry you had to leave them again. Maybe you can follow them to their new home once this business with the twins is done," Phil said.

"Perhaps," Rosa replied softly.

The plane shifted to one side and the children screamed with excitement. Rosa turned a fearful face to Phil. "Is there a problem?"

"Nope, weather is changing. We might get a bit bumpy. I think you need to strap down the children for their safety."

Rosa noted that Phil didn't look at her as he held tightly onto the wheel. "I will." Rosa climbed gingerly out of the co-pilot seat and moved into the cargo area.

"儿童,我们需要安静,带我们到自己的位置."(Quiet children, we need to hold onto the straps.)

Rosa helped each child then settled next to them and did the same with the strap next to her.

Tao reached out and took her hand.

Rosa grinned. "It's going to be fine, Tao. Mr. Casters is a very good pilot." She squeezed the tiny hand gently.

"We glad Mr. Casters is here with us. Will he always be?" Tao asked haltingly.

Rosa had to admit that was something she wanted but hadn't dared admit until this very moment. Phil was like family—more than family. It would break her heart to see him go and go she was sure he must. What on earth could she offer such a man?

Tao tugged at her hand and stared at her.

Ah, yes that question. "Mr. Casters has family and friends that need him too, Tao. I'm sure he will keep in touch with us." She fervently hoped he would keep in touch. Her heart demanded nothing less.

†

Phil walked to the only building in the vicinity. It was made of rough wood and a quirky slate roof. The door was cloth rather than wooden and billowed in the breeze.

She glanced back to the plane. There was no sign of activity. Great, Rosa had listened for once. Chuckling, she moved closer to the building.

"您会丢失?" (Are you lost?)

Phil shook her head and turned to the familiar voice.

"I never get lost, Carrington. What's your excuse?" She grinned at the man as his handlebar moustache twitched.

"Plane lost altitude over the mountains. The old girl isn't as reliable as she used to be. Waiting for spares to be brought in." Carrington grinned. "They told me you were here a few days ago, thought you'd be back in Zongnan by now?"

Phil shook the proffered hand from the Englishman. It was firm and cool to the touch. "A slight change of plans. I'm heading there now once I refuel. Any news from the city about the Japanese invasion?"

Carrington stroked the ends of his moustache. "The Japs are closing in. The Major will be moving the base of ops to Hong Kong. It's safer under the protectorate of the British. Can't see the Japs taking on our chaps."

Phil smiled. Carrington obviously thought there was no one on the planet who could oust the British. Generally, they had proven to be a force to contend with, that was true. Well, except for the US in her eyes.

"Strange times, Carrington, I thought China would be safe and look at her, besieged."

"Strange indeed, my friend. Which brings me to a little titbit I heard a month or so ago. I heard that you were serious about a pretty little thing. Heard she is married to the Chang Dynasty. It is not a nice family to get on the wrong side of. I hope you know what you're doing, Philomena." Carrington winked at her.

Phil ground her teeth. "Yeah, well, they can keep their noses out of my business."

Carrington chuckled, which sounded like a strangled chicken and would have been comic if she was in the mood, especially as his moustache twitched like a ferret. But she wasn't.

"That it is, my friend. The Major said if ever you wanted to join up with us, he's still got a job for you. Hong Kong, my friend, would love you."

Phil closed her eyes. Why did she think that was obnoxious? A week ago, she'd probably have considered the move but now.... Her gaze moved to Gilda.

"He's asked me many times since I turned up on this continent. The answer is still the same. Besides, I'm a partner in Saunders Freight. Doesn't he know that?"

Phil frowned, this encounter was slowing her down and Rosa might decide to come looking for her. She didn't want to deal with Carrington's insistent questions if that happened. The British might be proud but they are darn nosey in a discreet way.

"Blake Saunders is no fool, but he doesn't have much collateral and you need it in this business. Hope he's paid his bill here. They have been jumpy about people not paying on time. Must be the unrest rumbling around. You know they should never have kicked the British out...."

Phil nodded. "Sorry, Carrington, I need to go or my shipment will be late. Good to see you and when I see you next at Donna's, the round's on you." She cuffed the man on the shoulder and he nodded in agreement.

Two Chinese men had appeared during her conversation with Carrington and stood watching them.

She swallowed hard, the chance of Blake having paid for her fuel from the previous visit would be a miracle. Producing her best winning smile, she headed toward them with her hand outstretched.

†

"You were a long time, Phil. Anything wrong?" Rosa asked when Phil climbed back into the plane.

Phil didn't reply at first. She'd had a long run in with the guy in charge of the refueling station and had almost come to blows. Carrington had stepped in and written a promissory note for the fuel she needed. Thank God for Carrington, or they'd still be there.

"There is something wrong. I can feel it. Is it the children?"

Phil heard the fear in Rosa's voice and she shook her head. "No, not at all. Paperwork glitch. They almost wanted the greenback." Phil grinned.

"I have money, if you need...." Rosa scrambled to find her suitcase.

"No, it's fine. Everything worked out."

"You shouldn't have to pay for this trip. After all it was my idea to come here, and...I blame myself, for keeping you from your friends and family," Rosa insisted.

"My friends understand or will. I have no family. Well, I'll rephrase that...I do now." Phil winked at the children who gazed at her with rapt attention. She wasn't sure if they understood the conversation but they certainly smiled at the end. It was good, it was all good.

"You don't have any family?"

Phil smiled. "I guess I might have a long lost cousin but if you mean someone who knows me and wants me in their life, that would be a resounding *no*."

Rosa straightened as far as she could in the bulkhead.

"I'm sure you must be wrong. And if you are not, then we, the children and I, would very much like to be your family."

Phil wasn't sure if she wanted to laugh or cry at the statement. It was ridiculous and yet she loved the thought. How much of a sap was she becoming? It was time she reverted to normal and ditched this broad with the kids in Zongnan. Donna would take care of the rest—her friend owed her that much.

"In my line of work, family would be a hindrance. Right, let's get moving. I want to be in the city by early morning." Phil regretted every syllable as it left her mouth but it was too late for the damage to be undone.

It's for the best, she told herself. Yes, you remember that when you cry yourself to sleep tonight because of the loss.

"Family is everything to the Chinese. I think I understand that now...yes, I particularly understand that now." Totally, unlike the usual Rosa, she drew out the syllables.

"Understand what?"

There was the sound of someone mounting the ladder and Carrington's head popped into view. Phil closed her eyes and hoped it was going to be the usual British reserved wave and cheerio.

"My gosh, you never said you had company. When do you travel with company? And beautiful company, I might add."

Phil glanced at Rosa and frowned. *Jesus, what to say now.*

"Extenuating circumstances. What can I do for you, Carrington?"

Carrington grinned. "Why you can introduce me to this lovely lady to begin with."

"Now's not the time…"

"Hello, Mr. Carrington, I'm Rosa Moran. It's a pleasure to meet you."

"Why a lady from my homeland. It most definitely is a pleasure to meet you."

That damn moustache irritated Phil as it twitched into a smile. "Look, Carrington, we are on a schedule. We need to go. Like now."

Carrington seemed to ogle Rosa and that had her hackles up even more. He was like a damned limpet.

"Well, it was a pleasure to meet you, Miss Moran. If you are in the city when I return, I hope that this scoundrel will allow us to meet again."

"Yeah, right, all of that." Phil engaged the engine.

Carrington winked. Tipped a hand to his head in Rosa's direction and moved down the ladder.

Phil revved up the engine.

"I'm sure Mr. Casters will make the necessary arrangements," Rosa said.

Phil choked on the breath she gulped when she saw Carrington's eyes bulge. Shit.

He re-entered the cockpit.

"Going, Carrington, I will explain later." Phil said. Her eyes moved to the ground.

"Right, right. Donna's bar next Sunday and the drinks are definitely on you." Carrington slid down the ladder.

Phil ensured he was clear of the plane when she set it in motion, but an evil part of her almost wished he'd gone under the wheels. As soon as the thought came, she wished it away.

When they landed at the airfield, she'd tell Rosa the truth—no matter how much it would hurt.

†

Bang didn't fidget. He was like a stone and Phil's lips twitched in merriment. Rosa had asked Bang if he might like to sit up front and Phil was happy to have his company. Her stomach churned incessantly as she thought of all the ways to tell Rosa that she was under a misconception.

"What do you think, Bang?"

Bang turned his attention to Phil. He had an awestruck expression that she'd seen on other kid's faces and adults too, as they came face-to-face, or as close as you could, to the sky. Clouds floated by and sparks of sunshine glittered and glowed around them. Then there was the incredible scenery of mountain ranges seen from a different view. It was awe-inspiring and she should know since it had taken hold of her dreams as a youngster.

"When I was your age, a friend of my uncle's took me up in his crop duster." At the boy's frown, she had to think of another expression. "A small plane more like a kite."

Bang nodded vigorously.

"I loved every second. That's why I became a pilot." Phil grinned at Bang.

"I want to be a pilot," Bang replied quietly.

"Well, if you play your cards right, Bang, I might give you a lesson or two. In fact...." Phil placed the boy's hands on the co-pilot's wheel

"Take the wheel in front of you."

Bang shook his head. "No, not ready."

"Ah, but Bang, we are never ready for that first step. We have to take it to move forward, right?" Phil reached a hand out and placed Bang's shaking hands on the wheel again.

"I promise it's safe, Bang. Trust me." She stared into the frightened features.

A tiny smile creased Bang's thin lips and he nodded and clutched the wheel tightly.

"Wonderful, Bang. How about you do everything I do. Watch." Phil slowly moved the wheel a few degrees but there was virtually no direction change noticeable.

Bang grinned as he moved the wheel, only he jerked the object and the plane shuddered.

"Is there another weather problem?" Rosa asked from the back of the plane.

Phil didn't take her eyes from the view in front of her. "Nope, just a little cloud hopping."

"Oh, well, you know what you're doing."

"Sure do." Phil grinned at Bang. "Right, Bang. Try it a little more gently this time. Ready?"

Bang nodded.

Phil moved the wheel a fraction to the left and watched as Bang mimicked her action. It was a lot smoother this time.

Five minutes later, Phil winked at Bang. "I need to negotiate the mountain range you see in the distance. One day when you are more experienced, you can do this yourself."

Bang took his hands immediately from the wheel. "You promise?"

Phil smiled at the serious face turned to her. "I promise."

Bang climbed out of the co-pilot seat, his face wreathed in smiles, leaving her alone in the cockpit.

She concentrated on the range ahead of her. It was always a tough spot but there was light and that helped a lot.

"Why did you promise such a thing?" Rosa hissed as she dropped into the seat next to Phil.

"What are you talking about?" Phil frowned, mainly because of her loss of concentration.

"Bang. He thinks you are going to be around to teach him how to fly. He said you promised. How could you do that?" Rosa glared at Phil.

"I never said that in so many words. I need to concentrate right now."

"Do not fob me off with a silly excuse," Rosa demanded.

Phil pursed her lips. "I'm not fobbing you off, as you call it. If you were thinking calmly you would see a damn gigantic mountain range that we need to fly over."

Phil saw Rosa glance out the window. "Oh."

"Yep." Phil grasped the wheel tightly and ignored everything but the practice of flying. The potency of Rosa sitting next to her made her senses rivet to her nether region and she found that difficult to ignore.

Once the range was past them, Phil drew in a deep breath. She was ready for Rosa's verbal slashing.

"That was…incredible," Rosa whispered.

Okay, not what Phil had expected. Rosa sounded impressed.

"Yes, going across something as dramatic as the Felix range is quite the experience."

Rosa shifted and stared at Phil. "It wasn't just that. *You* were incredible."

Phil tried to move her eyes away but couldn't. Her cheeks grew warm at the unexpected praise. "All part of the training," she murmured.

"I'm sorry about flying off the handle before. If Bang is fortunate to have you impart any of your skill, he will be a very fortunate boy indeed." Rosa diverted her gaze to the view.

"Did he tell you that he flew the plane for a few minutes?"

At Rosa's widening eyelids, she took that as a no.

Phil laughed. "Don't worry I had my hand on the wheel all the time. You and the children were in no danger." Phil checked the altitude and then glanced at the map on the clipboard hanging close. "We'll be in Zongnan in three hours."

Rosa didn't reply.

"You still want to go right?"

"Yes, Phil, I still want to go. If the twins can be reunited safely with family, then that's the most important thing," Rosa said. "I'd better feed the children. Would you like something? Chang's mother gave me rice and some sweet dumplings."

Phil's stomach at that moment growled loud enough for Rosa to hear.

"I guess we have the answer to that." Rosa chuckled as she left Phil alone.

How did she make every single one of Phil's nerve endings tingle? Amazing.

Chapter Fourteen

Blake Saunders unconsciously streaked a line of grease down his left cheek as he looked in astonishment at the plane taxiing up the runway. "That woman never ceases to amaze me." He scratched the side of cheek again and then picked up a rag and wiped his hands.

Ten minutes later he was even more flabbergasted as Phil alighted the plane, quickly followed by a young woman and four children.

"What the hell happened to Phil? She never takes passengers." Blake shook his head and walked to greet his errant business partner.

"Before you say it, I should have told you," Phil said.

Blake took in her appearance, neat as a pin and she smelled clean, too. Then he gazed at her face—drawn and tired. "Yes, you should. Is this going to be common occurrence, disappearing for days without notice?"

Phil shuffled her feet. "I hope not, Blake."

"Me, too. I had to send young Jamie to the Xiango province yesterday. I couldn't wait any longer since we needed the money."

Phil shook her head. *Damn, they will eat him alive at the poker table.* "Sorry, Blake."

Blake nodded and then looked over Phil's shoulder to the young woman who had shepherded the children close to her. "Are you going to introduce me?"

"Sure." Phil turned and smiled at Rosa. "Rosa Moran, meet my partner, Blake Saunders."

Rosa stepped forward and smiled, holding out her hand. "It's a pleasure to meet you, Mr. Saunders."

Blake smiled. "A pleasure to meet you, too, I won't shake hands or you'll be wiping oil off your hands for days."

Rosa smiled and dropped her hand.

"I'm sorry we took Phil away for so long. If I can compensate...."

"I told you there isn't any question of that," Phil interrupted.

Blake watched the two women glare at one another but there was something else there as well. There was a spark that had nothing to do with hate. Interesting. "I think those children need to get inside. They look beat."

Rosa nodded. "It's all the excitement and we have been up a long time. Thank you for your concern, Mr. Saunders."

"Call me Blake. I can't have a beautiful young woman call me mister. I'll have them thinking I'm ready for my grave." He winked at her.

"Less of the courting, *old* man." Phil grinned. She took the twin's hands and Rosa followed suit with Tao. Bang managed to walk proudly alongside Phil.

"Aye and you'd know all about that, my friend." Blake slapped Phil on the back playfully. "Have you arranged where your friends are staying?"

"Kind of, but I guess...not really." Phil frowned.

"Okay, let me make a few calls. I know someone who will help." Blake ushered them inside the building.

"It isn't cozy, but it is home. Well, I spend most of my time here," Blake muttered. He walked to the bench that held a kettle and switched it on.

"Anyone for a cuppa?"

"Oh, I'd love one, thank you, Mr....Blake," Rosa said.

"Do we have any coffee left or has Jamie snaffled it all in my absence," Phil asked.

"The boy dare not touch his mentor's coffee for fear that he'll end up on worse runs than he already does." Blake chuckled. "What about the wee ones?"

"Water will be good." Rosa looked to the children.

Blake waved a hand toward a cupboard. "I think I can do a little better than that." He opened the cupboard doors and removed four bottles.

"Is it okay?" He showed Rosa the coke bottles.

Rosa shook her head. "I'm not sure about the children but I'd love one."

Phil chuckled. "Well, Blake, guess you have a way with the ladies."

"And you would know." Blake winked at Phil.

"Guess it's a cola all round then." Phil snatched a bottle from Blake's hand.

"I'll stick to tea. This stuff I'm sure isn't good for you, I bet they put weird things in the mixture," Blake said.

"And you offered this to children? Shame on you," Phil said.

"I'm probably wrong. Hey, they say it's the bestselling drink in the US. Can't be harmful then, can it?"

✝

Rosa settled against the doorjamb of the room the children had been given, which Blake had arranged for them. He called them Mrs. Randolph's special occasion rooms. It had once been a coach house for wealthy Europeans in the eighteen hundreds. It now had a similar purpose but wasn't as opulent as she suspected it may have been a hundred years ago. The facade was faded and needed a facelift and the roof looked like it was a patchwork quilt. Still it was very clean and the owner was friendly.

Now she watched as the children slept. It really had been a long and exciting day for them, and for her too.

Phil was downstairs talking to Mrs. Randolph, whilst she'd put the children to bed. They looked peaceful and the twins had been very quiet since leaving the aircraft hangar. Who could blame the poor mites? Only a few days ago they were fugitives in flight for their lives.

Satisfied they were in no danger and at rest, she closed the door, and wandered slowly back down the stairs. She smiled at the various, grotesque in her opinion, portraits hanging on the wall. One in particular caught her eye. It was of a man, Georgian in dress style, with a large carbuncle on his nose. She stifled her laughter at the portrait. He appeared so proud.

Nearing the bottom step, she stopped and gazed at a mural of Chinese children at play in a courtyard. It was on a four-foot piece of paper with gilded edges. The scene held so much that she was sure she could probably stare at it for hours and still find something new.

"Have you found something interesting?"

Rosa smiled at Phil, who was staring at her from the open doorway of the vestibule.

"Yes, don't you think it's beautiful?" She pointed to the mural.

Rosa watched as Phil turned to look in the direction her finger pointed. At this angle, she could see the strong jaw line. She figured he was probably smiling. When he turned, she was right.

"Wonderful. If you want one, I'm pretty sure I can source one for you in the market."

"Perhaps when I have somewhere permanent to live." Rosa glanced once more at the picture in front of her and then stepped down the last step. What she hadn't bargained for was a slight pile in the carpet that covered the step and she lost her balance.

The next thing she knew Phil was holding her close, their breath mingling.

"That was a close call," Rosa said as her eyes caught Phil's.

There was no reply from Phil, who locked his gaze with hers and didn't let go.

Phil's hand moved to touch her cheek and trailed a gentle finger down the plane of her face. "I can't have you injure yourself under my watch."

"I'll remember that," Rosa replied huskily.

Phil's head moved and seconds later, their lips touched.

It was a tentative motion until Rosa kissed Phil harder. As their lips locked, Rosa placed her hands in the soft hair at the back of Phil's head and moved their bodies closer. She wasn't sure what was happening to her but at this moment she didn't care. All that mattered was the surge of energy that rushed from her head through her body down to her toes.

Then Phil pulled them apart and stepped away. "I'm sorry."

Rosa frowned and shook her head, trying to understand what was happening. "You're sorry? Why?"

"Because." Phil dropped his gaze to the floor.

There was something more. There had to be. Perhaps Phil wasn't that interested in her. Though he had instigated the kiss on both occasions. Surely, that meant there was some attraction on his side.

"Because, isn't an answer, Phil. I know a kiss might not mean that much to you, but to me it's important. I don't go around kissing just any man."

Phil turned away and then back. "I'm not the person you think I am. You deserve more."

"How do you know what I deserve?" Rosa demanded. "I think I'm entitled to make my own mind up on the type of person you are." Rosa rubbed a finger over lips that still tingled from the kiss. She wanted more.

"Take my word for it. When you know exactly the type of person I am, you might well regret this action." Phil looked toward the room. "Mrs. Randolph was making tea and should be finished now."

Rosa placed her hands on her hips. "Why did you kiss me...twice now?"

She gazed at Phil and noted the red stain mark his cheeks. Did that mean he was embarrassed? Could that be the reason? From what Prudence told her, she knew some men were hesitant when it came to discussing their feelings. But this man? No, it didn't seem to fit.

"I don't know." Phil muttered.

"You don't know? What kind of answer is that? Are you attracted to me and too shy to say?"

Phil shook his head. "That's ridiculous. No one would ever call me shy."

"I thought not, so...."

"What on earth are you both doing here in the drafty hallway?" Mrs. Randolph asked. "Come inside by the fire. The tea is all mashed."

149

Rosa glared at Phil before turning a sweet smile toward the elderly lady. "Thank you, Mrs. Randolph. I'm dying for a cup of tea."

"Then you'll love this, my dear. It's oolong and I only use it for special occasions."

Rosa's eyes flew open. "Mrs. Randolph, that's the most expensive tea in the world. I've never actually had any before."

"Then you will remember having tea with this old woman long after I'm gone. Come or it will be cold."

Rosa turned to Phil. "This isn't over."

She pushed past him and entered the parlor.

†

Tea had been set out on a polished mahogany table. A silver teapot stood at attention in the middle, flanked by three floral-patterned china cups and saucers. A plate of dainty sandwiches that would make even the Ritz happy accompanied the tea.

"Oh, this is too much, Mrs. Randolph," Rosa said. She held a hand to her mouth as her lips quivered.

"Call me Kitty. It's a pleasure to share my evening with younger folk. Now this isn't all charity. I want to know all about you. Gossiping keeps me young." Kitty chuckled and poured the tea. "Sit or I'll think you're going to bolt."

Rosa sat next to Kitty and discreetly watched Phil take a seat at the far end of the table. He was as far away as possible. Darn the man.

"Tell me, Rosa, you aren't related to David and Amelia Moran are you?"

"Yes, they were my parents. Did you know them?"

Kitty nodded. "I thought so. You have your mother's hair and your father's eyes. They were very special people. Now this is going to be very interesting gossip."

My goodness, she knows my parents! Rosa thought. How in a country as large as China could I be so fortunate as to meet her? I can finally find something out about them.

"I have so many questions," Rosa said.

Kitty sipped her tea and then smiled. "I'm sure you have. First, please tell me how you are here at this place now. I heard on the grapevine that your grandfather took you back to England."

"My goodness, you do know me or at least of me. Were you and my parents very good friends?" Rosa's excitement at the prospect of finding out more than the sparse information the missionaries had on her parents' exploits was thrilling.

Kitty chuckled. "Oh, yes."

Ten minutes later Phil stood up.

"Thanks, Kitty, for the tea but I need to go. I have things to discuss with Blake."

"Happy to help. Any of Blake's friends are welcome here. He is a very good man."

Rosa wasn't sure if she should see Phil out. A part of her wanted to, but another part was irritated at his attitude. "Goodnight, Phil."

Phil nodded. "Goodnight, Rosa. I'll be around tomorrow afternoon with the next step for the twins."

"Thank you."

"Night." Phil left the room and Rosa clenched her hands together under the table, desperately wanting to follow him.

Rosa stared at the fragile china cup in front of her. She thought of how relationships could be that fragile, too.

"Now, as I was saying, your mother was eight months pregnant when your father decided it was time they remained in the city, at least until you were born."

Rosa turned her attention to Kitty's meanderings of her parents' past. *I want to hear this but why are you being so difficult, Phil.*

"Was that when they ended up in trouble?"

Rosa saw tears well up in Kitty's eyes. "I'm sorry if that was the wrong thing to ask."

Kitty wiped away her tears on a silk handkerchief. "Not wrong, Rosa. No, it was just a very sad time."

Rosa leaned and touched Kitty's hand. "I'm glad there is someone who can tell me all about them—the good and the bad. I know so little and sometimes I feel that I was a burden to them."

"Oh, my dear, Rosa, you were never that. My goodness, no. They loved you so much. I want to show you something." Kitty stood and shuffled to a writing table and unlocked a drawer. She retrieved a small wooden box and brought it back to the table.

Kitty opened the box and withdrew two photographs. "The quality isn't what it was, I'm afraid. This one was taken a week before you were born. Right here in this very parlor."

Rosa gingerly took the photograph and stared at the picture. A tall, dark haired man in a smart suit stood beside a heavily pregnant woman. She radiated happiness, sitting there with her arms over her extended belly. "These are my parents?"

"Yes, indeed. They were a very handsome couple. Your mother had a gentle soul. Never had a bad word for anyone, even those that deserved it." Kitty smiled. "Your father was quiet but took everything in. Very deep your mother used to say of him and that was true." Kitty passed along the second photo.

Rosa stared at it for a long time before she found any words. "That's me."

"Yes, and now do you believe me when I say they loved you very much?"

A sepia image reflected back at Rosa and she now believed for the first time in her life that her parents had loved her and she hadn't been a burden at all. She so wished she could have known them. "My father looks happy."

"He loved to hold you. You were very precious to them both." Kitty blinked back her tears but several trickled down her cheek.

"Thank you, Kitty, for sharing these with me." Rosa handed back the photo, which Kitty placed back in the box.

Then Kitty handed her the box. "This belongs to you. We could salvage very little of their possessions...except the most important." Kitty gave a watery smile. "I always hoped one day that we would meet and now this old woman's prayers have been answered."

Rosa took the box and held it to her breast. "I'm so sorry it's taken me this long to find you. If it hadn't been for Mr. Saunders, we never would have met."

"I've found during the years that God works in mysterious ways. Shall we have more tea?" Kitty said.

Rosa nodded. Indeed He does. If only He could lead her down the path that would help with her relationship with Phil, then all would be well in her world.

"Will you tell me please what happened in their last days, Kitty?" Rosa implored.

Kitty frowned.

"Please, Kitty, it will give me final closure." Rosa took the cup offered to her from a shaking hand.

"You are right. It may give us all closure." Kitty drew in a deep breath. "There was a protest taking place in the square. You were six months old...."

✝

A thin mist hung in the air as Phil left Kitty Randolph's home. It covered her in a cold damp shroud as she trudged down the cobbled street leading to the main gate out of the city. It was still reasonably early in the evening but already there was a crowd on the main street she entered. The throng of people and the smells of life lifted her spirits. It never ceased to amaze her what effect the sheer volume of people coming and going had on her. Kitty's memories had her recalling the last time she visited her uncle.

"You're going to do this, squirt, with or without my permission, am I right?"

"Yep, I am, Uncle Ralph." Phil crossed her arms.

"Give me one good reason why I shouldn't tan your hide and stop you?"

Phil laughed. "The last time you tanned my hide, I was seven and that was only because Mrs. Whittaker was watching."

"True. That woman was hard. She'd have made a great general on the front line. Still you aren't old enough without my permission, so I figure that's a plus to me."

Phil stared at her uncle, his face covered in stubble. No matter how often he shaved and he did every day, that beard was persistent.

"Yep. But you taught me that once I'd outgrown something, I had to move on, no matter how hard it was, and who might be hurt." Phil caught her uncle's gaze.

154

"I taught you too well. Why do you want to go to Chicago anyway? It's full of gangsters." Ralph shook his head.

Phil chuckled. "It is not. Anyway, how do you know? You've never left Charlottesville?"

Ralph Casters grinned and shook a finger at her. "I did leave my home town once. I was conscripted."

"Did you leave the US? I thought you hadn't been abroad?" Phil frowned.

Ralph stood and the rocking chair he had been sitting in rocked for several seconds afterwards.

"I'm a dark horse, young woman. I left this good land of ours and ended up in England before the war. That's where I learned to fly. I think I was more a pilot for the English than the US at that time in the war." Ralph moved to the balustrade of the decking and leaned on it. "I love the vibrancy of city life, young Phil, but there comes a time in your life when you have to choose what is more important."

"I don't understand. How does city life and what you did in the war move in the same time frame."

"It doesn't. When I say I was conscripted, I meant that my heart was. To the love of my life, Laney Smith. She was from London and we met at her aunt's farm—Jameson farm." Ralph stopped speaking

As Phil gazed at him, he seemed lost in a world of his own. "What happened to Laney? You obviously didn't marry."

Ralph looked at Phil with tears in his eyes. "No, we didn't marry. She loved the bright lights of the city and I followed her much against my father's wishes. He wanted me to take control of the farm."

"Okay, but you came back and Laney didn't."

155

"We traveled around England and she loved to fly. It was the new thing for the rich folk back then. I decided that I needed to learn and she paid for the lessons. We had a wonderful time, not that anyone knew we were having a romance. I took a job as chauffeur for her father at first. He was a shipping merchant."

Phil leaned against the wooden rail next to her uncle. "You were the hired hand in love with the daughter of the house? How come I'm only hearing this story now?"

"Old news." Ralph moved away from the rail.

"The war came and I was more than a chauffeur, I was an exalted fly boy." Ralph sighed. "My father died and I didn't know for a year. Your father eventually caught up with me and begged me to come home. By then of course, I'd sustained my leg injury. He looked down at the false leg. "I knew I had to choose at that moment—the city life with Laney with an uncertain future or my family and a certain future."

Phil felt sorry for her uncle because he had obviously chosen the safe route. "Was she mad when you left her?"

Ralph shook his head. "When I told her, she laughed and said I should go back to Dullsville. There was no way she was going to marry a cripple. She married some rich titled guy from Europe six months later."

"Wow. That must have hurt?"

"I was a dalliance for her and it broke my heart or so I thought at the time." Ralph smiled and walked back to the rocker.

Phil stared at her uncle. "I'm sorry."

"No need to say that. When I came home, I found the real love of my life. She just appeared on the doorstep the day I came home and wanted to sell me some cookies for the local orphanage. Didn't know it then but she stole my heart that day and I never regretted a second of my life. From that moment on she was the one."

"Aunt Daisy was wonderful, I wish...."

"No wishing on the dead, Phil. Only concentrate on the living."

"Do you know what happened to Laney?"

"Yes, she died on the Titanic. Life has an interesting symmetry. Don't you ever forget that, Phil."

"I won't. I promise."

"Good. Now remind me, what was it that I had to tan you for back then?"

Phil laughed. "Johnnie, Mrs. Whittaker's youngest, fell out of a tree when we were *testing* Joe Storm's newest apple crop. I swear it wasn't me who led him up the tree."

Ralph placed an arm around her and hugged her close. "Even at seven you were precocious. So tell me. Why Chicago?"

Phil stopped walking and looked around. Zongnan had so many cultures thriving inside its walls that she doubted anyone could say, for certain, who could be labeled a true daughter or son of the city. The smell of food assailed her, spices and burning oil, pungent and at the same time delicious. She could see the edges of a market stall at the top of a street and headed toward it. As she looked down the narrow street, she smiled. Wall to wall stalls selling everything under the sun. The noise was deafening as voices of all pitches screamed for notice. Down the center, people wandered from one market trader to another. She began to wander down the street and cheerful vendors accosted her, wanting to sell her anything from a paper dragon to a salted dumpling. The mist that had hung in the air dissipated with the heat of the fires and the number of people around. Lanterns filled the street with enough light to inspect a prospective purchase.

"You want dinner?"

Phil looked at the woman, though she could barely call her that. The vendor wore cast off European clothes, and she held out a sheet of paper.

"I'm not sure I'm hungry."

"Hungry, yes hungry, Englisie. We have best food here."

The broken English was good for a street seller. Had to be, Phil guessed. Money made the world go round. Foreigners were everywhere in China's bigger cities. Phil looked at the menu, which actually was appealing. Her stomach rumbled and it reminded her of another occasion and of Rosa.

"Okay." The vendor shared a bright smile and pointed to a wooden bench. A long table that could house at least ten people was virtually empty. An old couple at the far end were drinking soup.

"You want drink?"

Phil scratched the side of her head. She certainly needed one. "A beer."

The girl nodded and rushed off to the stall.

Phil looked up to the sky and closed her eyes. "Why on earth didn't I just say I wasn't a man? What kind of coward am I?" she whispered. Then she opened her eyes and gazed at the star filled sky, deep in thought.

✝

Rosa collapsed on the bed in the room next to the children. Tonight had been enlightening and certainly miraculous. In this world, how fortunate was she that Kitty had known her parents, even had a memento for her. She reached to the small wooden bedside table and picked up the small box Kitty had given her. She rolled it around in her hands. It had simple markings—of birds carved into the wood. Tears filled her eyes as she recalled Kitty's emotional explanation of the last days of her parents. Life could and was very cruel—the proof was in her parent's demise.

She opened up the box and once more looked at the photographs. "They look so happy and in love. One day I'm going to have that, I know it in my heart."

Rosa looked at the other trinkets inside, a small black bead bracelet, earrings to match, and a jade dragon. It wasn't big, barely half a finger's length, but it had jeweled eyes of green. She plucked it out of the box and held it tightly.

"You believed," Rosa breathed out.

All her life she had felt a connection to China far beyond her parents and the trinket proved it. The symbol of the dragon was the most important of all the symbols in China. Rosa spied a scrap of paper tucked into the very bottom of the box. She fished it out.

Unfolding the page, she read it voraciously.

Dear Kitty,

This may be the last time I can smuggle a communication to you and I beg you to make contact with my father and ask him to care for Rosa. He has not answered any of my mail in the past but perhaps in this dire circumstance he might put his pride behind him. Tell him I loved him unconditionally no matter how he lied to mother and me. Life as I have found in China has a symmetry quite beyond any imagination. Moments before our arrest, David arranged for Rosa's care. She will know nothing of us other than we are dead. It is for the best, David said. Yet, Kitty, I want my father to find her and bring her up in the knowledge of what we did and why we did it. Life brings decisions that cause hardship. I do not want our baby girl to live in the darkness of not knowing that we loved her. Sometimes life takes on a mantle of its own and we are just journeymen with the hope that when we die we have done the right thing. With this note, I know I have done the right thing.

God bless you, Kitty.

Your ever-faithful friend, Amelia Moran.

Rosa sucked in a breath and choked on it before coughing for several minutes. Then she read the note again and wept.

Chapter Fifteen

Blake Saunders stared down at the bedraggled pilot who he considered not only a business partner but also a friend. Right now, it looked like she needed one. He kicked the cot she was laying on.

"Go away."

Phil covered her head with a mixed wool blanket and curled into a ball.

"Aye, and you'd like that, wouldn't you? Well, I'm not letting you off that easy. You owe me an explanation for your days away and all the fuel bills you've accumulated in your travels." Blake kicked the cot again and Phil groaned.

"I'll have coffee ready in five minutes so get yourself up."

Blake left Phil bleary eyed and frowning.

As Blake poured the coffee, he saw Phil gingerly making her way toward him out of the corner of his eye.

"Good timing."

"Yeah," Phil responded lethargically.

Blake handed Phil a tin mug of coffee. She took it with shaky hands. "A heavy night then. What was it in aid of Ming or the new girl, Rosa?"

Phil curled her lips in what Blake could only decipher as distaste. He guessed he hit a nerve.

"Drink the damn coffee and tell me what happened." He saw the raised eyebrows. "You owe me since we're partners."

"Yeah." Phil gulped down the coffee and grimaced.

"That bad, is it? Well, you could have made it."

"Not that bad. Thank you." Phil closed her hands on the mug and hugged it to her.

"You are welcome."

There was a short silence.

"It wasn't Ming," Phil said.

Blake smiled. "Didn't think so. I have to admit, seeing you arrive yesterday with a woman and four kids in tow was quite something."

"Yeah, me too. Who would have thought I'd be a sucker."

"Are you?"

"What do you mean?" Phil replied.

"A sucker? Rosa Moran looks like a very nice woman. Not sure how the four Chinese kids enter into it but I can imagine with her pedigree." Blake took a mouthful of his coffee.

Phil looked up. "Her pedigree? That signifies you know something about her background. She doesn't even know, or so she said."

Blake shook his head and poured another cup of coffee.

"I do, at least a little of it. Mrs. Randolph was a great friend of her parents."

"I figured that out last night. Still, how do you know so much?" Phil said.

Blake sipped on the coffee. Then walked to his desk and opened a drawer. He took out a wallet. Then walked to Phil.

"Look at these."

He watched Phil flick through the various photos he had given her. "And these mean something to me?"

Blake shrugged. "No. I was a good looking guy back then though, don't you think?" He pointed to one of several people in the photo.

"Wow, that's you."

"Hey, I haven't changed that much."

Phil laughed. "A double chin, balding, a little wider. No, you haven't changed at all."

"Sarcasm doesn't become you. I was only twenty-three at the time. Wet behind the ears but I made great friends." Blake took the photo and stared at it. "Sometimes people cross your path and you think hell, what am I doing with this crowd."

He pointed to a woman who was sitting. "That's Rosa Moran's mother. Amelia was a fine woman, so strong in everything she did, yet gentle, too. I did have a crush on her, in an awestruck way."

"You did?" Phil's eyes widened.

"Amelia loved her husband." Blake pointed to a very proper looking gentleman. "She loved him so much she couldn't just say what the authorities wanted when they arrested them. That is all it would have taken for her to be free and return to their baby. I never understood that." Blake dropped the photo on the bench.

"They say that's true love," Phil said quietly.

"Do you think you could love someone that much you'd give your life?" Blake asked softly.

"I'm not sure," Phil responded.

Blake nodded. "Jamie is overdue by an hour. If he doesn't arrive by mid-afternoon you know what that means."

"I do and I will. I'm taking Rosa to meet Donna at midday. Send me a message if you need me," Phil said.

"The Moran's were good people, fearless, and determined. If you like their daughter, more than like her, be honest with her. If she's anything like her folks, she will only trust the truth."

"Yeah." Phil frowned.

"I know that look. Give."

Phil sighed heavily. "I can't really explain it. Somehow or another, she thinks I'm a man."

Blake blinked twice and then looked at Phil. Shorter hair than normal, guess you could call it a man's style. Slim body, flat chested and an attitude—yep, he understood. "I noticed your style and figured it was the heat."

"Ming mentioned that she liked short hair."

"Ah, Ming. Have you contacted her since you've been back?"

"Hardly. I haven't been here twenty-four hours yet and I have other commitments right now. Afterwards…maybe. What does that have to do with anything?" Phil asked.

"You look like a man. Short hair, thin frame, hardly any breasts." Blake shrugged at Phil's evil eye. "Hey, just saying. You wear trousers and a leather jacket as your staple fashion statement. I can understand the confusion."

Phil didn't say anything.

"I'm game. Why does it bother you so much? By the end of the day she isn't your problem right?" Blake watched several emotions flicker across Phil's visage. "Is there something more to this that I'm missing?"

Phil moved to the grimy window that couldn't possibly show the true nature of what was happening outside. "I kissed her."

The bald explanation echoed around the room.

"You kissed her?" Blake was surprised. Phil was one of the few honest people he had come across in this country during the years. He respected her and her lifestyle—but this was out of character.

"I kissed her. No big deal. Right?"

"No big deal except she thinks you're a man. I hope it was only once. I respect you, Phil, but deceiving a person that way isn't the done thing. You know that, right?"

"I know that. I wanted to tell her. I thought about telling her several times and either it wasn't convenient or...."

Blake looked at Phil's face. To him there was no doubt that she was upset and holding back her emotions.

"Or?"

"I was scared, Blake. She scares me in a good way. I don't have a compass for what I feel about her but all I know is that it's right. She fits so right for me that I want her to be happy and safe no matter the sacrifice. What does that mean, Blake?"

Blake smiled and walked to Phil, placing a hand on her shoulder. "Tell her the truth. Life has a way of working it out if you are honest. At least that's what I believe. As old as I am, I think it will work out for me, too."

Phil turned and smiled. "You like Mrs. Randolph, don't you?"

"Maybe."

"God, I hope it doesn't take me that long to work it out. No offense meant."

Blake grinned. "What the hell. The worse-case scenario is that we are stuck together."

Phil laughed. "Yeah, right. Now I know why you and I are together."

"Finish your coffee and go tell the girl."

Blake smiled and walked back to the bench where he was working on a stripped down motor.

†

Phil rapped on the door of the boarding house and waited. The side street was busy, filled with laughing children, women washing their clothes and others gossiping. An odd, old man trundled a cart by with an array of items. She deduced from the pungent aroma that it was mostly spices.

The door opened and a beaming Kitty Randolph stood in the doorway. "Why, Phil, you are earlier than Rosa expected. She's taken the children to a play area run by a friend of mine a few streets away. I'm getting too old to run after youngsters, I'm afraid."

Phil smiled. She liked the woman. She seemed genuine. Not to mention the fact that Blake more than liked her, even if he didn't admit it. That sold it for her. "I will come back. How does an hour sound?"

"Sounds like a good idea, though you can come inside and wait. I don't mind at all." Kitty volunteered.

"I have a few errands to do but I'll be back." Phil waved and headed away from the house. She didn't have any pressing errands to run. In fact, she had nothing at all to do, except wait.

Exiting the street, she crossed the dusty road, almost colliding with a haphazard rickshaw driven by a man who looked at least eighty. The toothless man grinned and gave a hearty chuckle as the left wheel barely missed her feet.

She knew the street opposite had a small restaurant. It was barely a restaurant, really more a tea and dumpling place. It was where she had first met Ming. Trudging ahead a minute later, she opened the door to the shop and walked in. Several heads turned. Some stared at her in fascination, others merely with curiosity and then went back to what they were doing. She walked to the counter and smiled at the owner.

"您好马伊-马伊岭今天心情如何?" (Hello, Mai Ling, how are you today?)

"蛀蜢脚轮很好,很高兴再次看到你." (Missy Casters, very good, happy to see you again.)

"和您." (And you.)

Phil smiled and nodded toward the sweet apple dumplings Mai was renowned for.

"我将两个苹果吃饺子、茶请迈岭." (I'll take two apple dumplings and tea please, Mai Ling."

She walked to one of only two tables free and sat. Fortunately, it was one with a view of the street and she watched people walking by getting on with their own business. This was a good time to reflect.

Two things kept circling around in her head. Dare I pursue Rosa, tell her the truth, and hope against hope that she feels the tangible force that keeps us moving closer together? The other thought—Ming and how she felt about her.

If anyone had questioned her interest in Ming prior to this last trip, she'd have blackened his eye. Now she was questioning it big time. What did it mean? Was she that fickle to cast off someone she professed to love for a complete stranger? One that she didn't even know would accept her as she was.

A smiling waitress deposited a steaming pot of tea and a cup on the table. Seconds later, the dumplings arrived.

For a few seconds, she was lost in the smell of apple and cinnamon. Placing a forkful of the dessert in her mouth, she smiled at the burst of flavor on her taste buds.

Then her mind went back to the problem at hand.

Even if I...no, when I tell Rosa, she might reject me. The odds were heavily stacked in that favor for lots of reasons, not the least of which is that I lied to her. I could play the game at both ends by not telling Ming anything until I know Rosa's reaction. It was what any cad would do.

I'm not a cad.

Phil reached inside her jacket and withdrew a notebook and pen. She scribbled a note. It was brief and to the point but Ming would understand. It was the same note she had been expecting from Ming for months. Folding the paper into fourths, she stood, and went to Mai Ling. She gave her the message and handed her a few coins before going back to her tea.

She had time to work out exactly what to say to Rosa but she couldn't think of the words. Maybe the soothing tea would help.

†

Phil once more rapped on the door of the boarding house and waited. Within thirty seconds, the door opened.

"Kitty said you came earlier," Rosa said in a decidedly snippy tone. *She's not happy to see me.*

"Yes, I was a little earlier than planned. I might have to go on a retrieval run this afternoon. Figured going a few hours earlier wouldn't be a problem. Is it?"

"No. No, the sooner the better." Rosa looked behind her. "I'll just inform Kitty we are going. Be right back."

Rosa left the door open and Phil watched her go back to the parlor where they'd had tea the previous evening.

Guess she doesn't want me to come in. Rather impolite of an English woman—Kitty would be devastated. Phil chuckled softly and looked down the street. No sign of the old man and his wares and the throng of women washing clothes had now disappeared. It was eerily quiet. China was never quiet. Not in the city, at least.

"Right, let's see your friend and hopefully reunite the twins with their mother," Rosa said briskly as she shut the door behind her.

"Absolutely. The twins are the most important right now."

"Yes, they are, Mr. Casters."

Darn, there it was again. Phil schooled her features and smiled slightly. "It's about half a mile away. We will know the outcome very soon and all this can be done."

Rosa glared at her. "Yes. Done."

Okay I'm not her lover, but dang, right now I feel like she's treating me like an errant one, Phil thought, frowning.

"Let's go then." Phil walked quickly away and heard Rosa mutter.

Ten minutes later, they entered a poorer part of the city. This was evident by the rundown houses and signs everywhere touting bars and massage parlors. Now, it was relatively quiet. In the evening, it changed to a vibrant life comprised of sex, drugs, and just about anything you wanted if you had the money.

"The twins' mother lives here?"

Phil rolled her eyes at the naïve question. She didn't know any different. How could she?

"No, a friend of their mother and mine is the go-between. She is the only one I would trust in this. If she says it's good then it will be." Phil knew in her heart that Donna would not betray the woman she loved and that extended to her children.

"I have to say, I don't like this area." Rosa moved closer to Phil.

Phil laughed. "It's an acquired taste."

"You have obviously acquired it."

"Sure, I have. During the years you come to know all the warts in the area."

Rosa stopped.

"I'm a naive fool to you, aren't I? My experience can't possibly match...." Rosa waved her hand around. "All of this."

Phil heard a tremor in the voice and bit her lip.

"After we talk with Donna, will you have lunch with me so we can talk? I need to explain some things to you. What do you say? Will you?"

"Yes. We so need to talk."

"Great. Donna's bar is right ahead."

Rosa chuckled, "I can see that, the sign is very prominent."

"Yep, she's a big personality around here." Phil winked. "To her friends she is one of the gentlest people alive."

Phil walked toward the entrance of the bar and opened the door.

✝

Rosa followed Phil inside. What was unexpected was the rush of footsteps toward them and a woman with long, black hair pulling Phil into a tight embrace.

Rosa was further shocked at the kiss they shared—it wasn't chaste by any means. Could this woman be why Phil hadn't wanted to explain?

Rosa held her breath at the startling welcome, wondering what else was to come. When it did, she almost choked.

"Well, I can't believe you managed to get here so quickly. You are one wonderful woman."

Rosa stared blatantly at the woman, certain her mouth was like a guppy. Phil's averted face didn't allow Rosa to see her expression. No, it couldn't be. Phil a woman? It just can't be. She would have known.

"Who have you brought with you, Philly?"

There was a distinct clearing of the throat as Phil turned slowly to face Rosa. "This is Rosa Moran. She was going to take care of the children. In fact, she did until we received your message."

Rosa was unable to speak. Shock more than anger was taking precedent. *I have every right to be angry, yet I'm not. How odd is that?*

"Rosa, thank you."

Rosa gave the woman a half smile—it was all she could muster.

"I'm Donna Poillucci. I own this." She waved a hand around the bar. "If there is anything I can get you whilst you are in town, please, my door is always open to you."

Rosa nodded and murmured gratitude, at least she thought she did. Donna appeared nice. But what did this all mean? They were kissing like lovers, not friends. At least not the friends she had ever known. A chaste kiss on the cheek was the usual greeting. That had been a full-blown kiss.

"She doesn't need help, Donna. Now I want the story from you. What's happening? The twins will be confused because I sure am," Phil said. She walked to a chair on top of a table and placed it on the ground. She did this with two more chairs. "Let's sit and talk about this."

"You have brought the children though, haven't you, Philly? I made a promise and I don't want to break it," Donna implored.

"We brought the children." Rosa finally found her voice,

Donna gave her a bright smile. "Yeah."

They all sat and Donna sighed.

171

"When I asked you to take the children, I thought they would be safe at the mission. I heard on the grapevine the next afternoon that there was trouble in the area and was frightened for the twins' safety."

Phil narrowed her eyes. "You were frightened for the twins' safety...what about the rest of us? Are we chopped liver?"

"No. No, of course not." Donna vigorously shook her head. "Look, I told you it was quite sensitive when you took the twins. Well, it got complicated, once Nang, my friend, knew the children were gone and where, she decided to bare her soul to her father-in-law. Apparently, he wasn't that impressed with his own son and had taken a liking to Nang when she married into the family."

"We didn't come here for a history lesson, Donna," Phil burst out.

"Let her speak, Phil. I want to know the background. It may explain how the children will cope with this situation." Rosa didn't make eye contact with Phil. She was looking at the wooden bar straight ahead of her.

Phil grumbled and sat back in the chair.

"Thanks, Rosa." She winked at Phil. "Nang knew something that would incriminate her husband in a fraud and she told the old man. He's a senior official in the government and this would cause him to lose face if others found out. He called out his son, who tried to kill Nang. Once restrained, he was sent indefinitely to a mental institution. The action to make the children fugitives is void now and Nang wanted them home. She came to see me a day after you left and we managed, by the skin of our teeth, to find out where you had potentially gone. Prudence sends her well wishes."

"Thank God they are safe," Rosa breathed out. Her heart had been on overload with all kinds of horrible images when Donna had said there was trouble.

"There were some casualties. I'm sorry I don't have the details." Donna shrugged.

Rosa drew in a deep breath. When this was all sorted out, she would find out more. Even if it meant that she needed to go back there to find out.

"Okay, but how do we know that next week things might shift in the husband's favor? It's China and we both know about family ties here don't we, Donna," Phil said.

Donna stood and walked to the bar. "Nang is leaving with me. I've booked a passage for the twins and us from Shanghai to London. The ship sails in five days' time."

Phil's chair rocked

The action amused Rosa.

"You are doing what? What about this place?" Phil screeched.

"Enough of the histrionics, Philly. You know I'd do anything for her and this place is just that—bricks and mortar, nothing more. Nang is my heart and soul. She always has been since the first day she walked into my life. I can't expect you to understand." Donna sighed.

The air filled with electricity, the only sound a dripping tap.

Rosa had to admit that this was the weirdest conversation she had ever encountered. Again, the surprising thing was she felt comfortable about it all and that got her thinking.

"Nang is arriving tonight. Will you bring the children?" Donna asked.

Phil stood and walked to the window. "Not here. It isn't a suitable place."

"Then where?"

"I can ask Mrs. Randolph if she will permit the meeting at her home," Rosa said. Her eyes moved to Phil and she saw the softness in the gaze that had attracted her previously. *Whoa, attracted? I can't be attracted. She's a woman.* A little devil in her mind said, *you were attracted before, why not now? It is the same person.*

"Wonderful, what time?"

Chapter Sixteen

"We need to talk," Phil and Rosa said in unison.

Rosa and Phil looked at one another as they exited the bar.

Phil shrugged. "I'm sorry."

"You should be. How could you deceive me that way?" Rosa shook her head and began walking down the dusty street. As she bypassed several puddles, she hitched up her skirt.

Phil caught up to her. "Look, I never meant for you to think I was a man. It just happened."

"It just happened! You kissed me. Twice. You didn't think that was a good time to tell me you were a woman," Rosa blasted.

"I'm sorry. I figured it would be better in the beginning if you thought I was a man." At Rosa's raised eyebrows, Phil continued. "Most women want a man at their side in difficult times."

Rosa moved ahead with her head held high, blustering forward. Then Phil's hand seconds later dragged her back before a rickshaw almost cut her down.

An old man with tobacco-stained teeth grinned and chuckled as he went on his way.

Rosa wiped her hands down her skirt and then, with as much decorum as she could, looked at Phil. "Thank you," she said, through gritted teeth.

"That guy has a death wish for foreigners. He nearly got me earlier," Phil admitted with a half-smile.

It was that smile that was Rosa's undoing. She smiled back.

"Hey, that's a start. You smiled."

"Don't for one moment think, Mister....Miss Casters, that I have forgiven this untruth. I want to know why and that guff about it just happened doesn't wash with me." Rosa crossed her arms and gave Phil a glare.

Phil laughed.

Rosa pouted. The laugh was a soft sound that was familiar and made her heart swell.

Darn, why do I go all mushy every time Phil smiles, or laughs or, talks? Oh, I'm a lost cause.

"How about I take you to this great place to eat? I'll pay for lunch and we can talk properly."

Rosa looked up at the sky. It was darkening and the rain wasn't far away.

"I'd like that."

Phil grinned. "Great."

Ten minutes later, Rosa felt sure Phil was taking her on a hike. Their trek was becoming quite a trip to the mountains. "I was hungry before, now I'm starving."

Phil grinned. "Sorry. I found this place quite by chance last night after leaving you and Mrs. Randolph. Sometimes the unexpected reaps rewards. It's down the next street."

Rosa contemplated Phil's statement. Yes, the unexpected can reap rewards. *I just hope I'm not making a major mistake,* she thought. *Alfred would be proud of me.*

When they finally reached the place, Rosa laughed. She couldn't help herself. Before her was a long wooden bench with the requisite seating and nothing else. "This is the place?"

"Yeah." Phil smiled.

Once more, that was enough for Rosa and she sat at the bench. *I'm really going to have to find an antidote to that smile,* she told herself.

A grinning young woman arrived, spoke in pigeon English directly to Phil, and thrust the menu in her hands.

"Sorry, she remembers me from last night," Phil said.

They both ordered remarkably the same things and laughed about it as the waitress left.

"Are you going to tell me why you lied to me?" Rosa asked quietly.

Phil, sitting opposite, appeared uncomfortable.

Rosa refused to give her any more rope to hang herself. "The truth, I have always found, will set you free."

Phil gave her a quizzical stare. "If I said I didn't know, would that help?"

"No."

Phil shrugged. "I had to try."

Rosa sighed. "Look, we are relative strangers. I owe you nothing and you owe me nothing. I think that about sums it up."

"That isn't it. I do owe you. I owe you big time and I'm really sorry I was such a jerk." Phil replied. Her cheeks grew red.

"Why?"

"Because you gave me an opportunity that I never could have envisioned. I'm a woman in a man's world, yet I own a part share in a business. My uncle would be proud of me," Phil replied.

"You loved your uncle a lot. Wasn't he proud of you before?"

"Sure."

"So how much more could he be proud? Owning a business is success. Well, maybe." Rosa smiled.

"Maybe? What do you mean?" Phil frowned.

"The business might not be."

"True. You've obviously been speaking with Blake." Phil gazed at Rosa.

Rosa felt that usual electricity draw her to this woman. Had her heart taken leave of its senses and was it about to tumble her into a situation she frankly had no experience of? Or had she.

"You look deep in thought," Phil said.

Rosa blinked rapidly, clearing her mind. "Perhaps."

She looked around. The area was typical of any traditional street in a bustling city. Houses lined the street and some had converted from dwellings to businesses. This was the place to visit for any manner of purchase, from a broom to the best eateries. Stalls, many of them closed, were dotted along the path, allowing traffic to flow. She suspected that in the evening they would open.

"I love China. It's in my blood. I cannot envisage it not being part of my life. How did you come to be here?" Rosa turned her attention back to Phil.

Phil ran a hand through her hair.

Rosa watched in fascination. It was very short. On Phil, it was not unattractive.

"I worked in Europe for a few years, traveling through several countries. You could almost call me a gypsy." Phil chuckled. "I'm not. Not now at least. There was an opportunity and I took it about five years ago."

"Mr. Saunders?"

"Nope, Major Johnson's organization. When he knew I was a woman, he pulled the job."

Rosa's eyes flew open wide. "He did? How atrocious."

Phil shrugged. "He was honest. Said he didn't want to be jinxed."

"Jinxed? I don't understand?"

Phil chuckled. "You don't understand and you're almost a native. The Chinese are very structured and in their own way, a superstitious people. Besides, he did me a favor. I joined Blake and the rest, as they say, is history." Phil held out her hands.

Rosa wondered what Phil made of her. "I must be rather dull with regard to the people you have met."

Phil reached across the table and touched Rosa's hand.

She did not move it, since the touch was comforting and warmed her.

"You are not dull. I have so much respect for you and what you have done with your life and it's barely begun."

"Barely begun? I'm twenty-nine. My grandfather believes I should be married with several children by now."

"Is that why he wanted you to leave here six months ago?"

Rosa sighed and gazed at several passersby. No, that was not the reason. In a strange way Phil was probably the only person it now appeared that she could tell, even if she might not approve.

"Look, you don't have to tell me. I understand."

"Actually, you don't. Yet you are the one person who, if not approving of my decision, would understand it. At least I think." Rosa bowed her head.

At that moment, the waitress appeared with their steaming bowls of rice and within a few minutes, the table was laden with sizzling beef, peppers, garlic, and onions.

"You were saying," Phil said.

"Let's eat, I'm starving." Rosa picked up her chopsticks and delved into the food.

Phil nodded. "Sure."

Phil ate and at the same time was watching the expressions that crossed Rosa's features. She was not a chocolate box beauty by any standards. Her nose was too long for that. Yet she was so much more beautiful with those wonderful lights in her eyes when she enjoyed something and the brilliant smile she portrayed when she was happy. Not to mention her compassion for people, especially the orphans. Phil had learned such a lot from being around her in such a short time. And she wanted to be a much better person when around her.

"Phil, aren't you hungry?" Rosa asked.

My, if you knew just what I was hungry for, you'd run a mile.

"Just resting up a little." She picked up her chopsticks and speared a piece of beef.

"Are you planning on staying in China or moving on with the current unrest?" Rosa asked.

Phil stared at Rosa and felt like she was lost in a dreamscape that was never going to end.

"Depends."

"On what?"

Phil wiped her mouth and dropped her chopsticks. "On how difficult it is to do business. Things are changing in China—rapidly. Sometimes there is no option but to cut and run."

"I will not leave China. My parents' graves are here. Did you know that?"

Phil frowned. "I didn't know for sure, but figured they might be."

"You brought me to Kitty. I thought perhaps...." Rosa dropped her chopsticks.

"Nope, that was all Blake. What happened? What did she say when I left?"

Rosa was hesitant then shrugged. "She was my parents' friend. She told me how they died."

The horror in Rosa's voice had Phil clutching her hand. "Hey, I'm here. If she hurt you, I will...."

"No!"

"Okay, so what?"

"She gave me the love of my parents. Told me that I wasn't a burden to them. That they loved me," Rosa said softly.

Phil drew in a huge breath and expelled it before replying. "You know, between us we have major baggage. I want to clear ours before we delve into the past. What do you think?"

Rosa, tears filling her eyes, stared at Phil.

Phil bit down on her inner lip. *I so want to hug you and tell you that for the rest of your life you will be okay. I can't do that can I? Because you probably don't want me, like I want you, and my help would be a no no. I can stand the not loving me but not the not wanting my help.*

She closed her eyes.

"Please, Phil, help me understand...it all."

Phil squeezed Rosa's hand.

"I've loved women seemingly forever. I was a six year old with a crush on my best friend, Sadie Radcliffe. I always blame her, actually." Phil smiled "She did a truth or dare and I ended up kissing her. It worked for me but not her—she was grossed out."

"You lost your best friend?"

"Nope, not really. It took time, but Sadie waited a few years and by the time we were sixteen, she was on the lookout for a score for me. I swear she lived vicariously through me for a few years." Phil laughed.

"She sounds rather shallow."

Phil smiled. "Not shallow, but practical. She is still my number one fan. I get a letter from her every six months or so. She's married with four kids and happy in her little world. I wanted a much bigger picture."

"So do I."

Phil stroked Rosa's palm and didn't feel any withdrawal. "I'm sorry. I mean that. I kissed you and you didn't know the truth."

Rosa clutched Phil's hand.

"You were wrong to not tell me. I was developing feelings for you," Rosa said.

Phil's heart plummeted to her toes and she drew in a shallow breath. "I know and I'm the worse cad in the world, but I never ever meant any hurt to you."

Rosa shrugged. "Life is never simple, is it?"

A messenger stopped at their table and interrupted them.

"Mr. Saunders say flight up in an hour."

Phil growled and nodded at the messenger.

"You have to go," Rosa said.

"I'm sorry. One of our pilots hasn't returned after a scheduled flight and I need to retrieve him."

Rosa nodded. "Perhaps we can have dinner when you return and continue our conversation?"

Phil drew in a deep sigh of relief. "Sure. I'll be back by nine latest."

"Then we have a date."

Phil's heart swelled at the words.

"You most certainly have a date. I look forward to it."

"Take care."

"I will. Can I walk you home?"

Rosa smiled.

"I know the way home. Just make sure you do."

Phil grew a couple of inches with that remark. *I think I love this woman,* she thought.

†

Kitty shook her head slowly as she watched Rosa pace the parlor for at least the hundredth time.

"What time did you say your dinner engagement was for, my dear?"

Rosa glanced at the gilded clock on the mantle. "Phil said no later than nine and it is now twenty past that."

"No need to be worried, dear. I'm sure if there was a major problem, Blake would have informed us." Kitty picked up her knitting and continued her labors.

"That may be, but what if he is just busy?" Rosa paced the floor again.

"You will wear my carpet out at the rate you are going. It isn't as if it's a date now, is it? Philomena may just have had to land elsewhere, earlier than planned. The weather can spring surprises."

Rosa stopped pacing and slumped into the chair next to Kitty.

"She's called Philomena? I've only ever known her as Phil."

Kitty smiled. "That girl, she has a beautiful name, why she shortens it in that fashion is a mystery to me. I've only met her twice before she brought you to me. I think she likes being more with the boys, if you know what I mean."

"To blend in, probably."

"She blends in well enough. I think there is more man in her than woman. I have heard rumors, of course. I would never pay heed to gossip. She's a very likable woman." Kitty dropped a stitch and gathered it up again. The click of the needles was the only sound in the room for a while.

"I know she likes women, if that's what you were talking about. She has made no secret of it since we have been here," Rosa said softly.

Kitty pursed her lips. "So, are you worried because this is a date?"

Rosa dropped her gaze to her hands. "Would it be a problem if I said yes?"

Kitty dropped her knitting, took one of Rosa's hands in hers, and held it gently. "Rosa, my dear, life can be very complicated. Please don't confuse your gratefulness for a silly romantic notion. I would not want you to be hurt and you probably would be hurt by being with Philomena."

Rosa clutched Kitty's hand tighter. "Why? If she likes me as well, would it be such a wrong thing to want?"

The vehemence in the tone took Kitty aback. "Her choice of a partner in this area has been somewhat unwise and I would not want you embroiled in such affairs."

"She has a partner as in," Rosa hesitated. "A lover?"

There was a knock on the door and Rosa quickly rose and headed for the door.

Kitty bit her lower lip. This was not good, not good at all. She would have to talk with Blake.

From the doorway, she heard women's voices and suspected the errant Philomena Casters had arrived.

Rosa popped her head around the door. "It's Phil. Thank you, Kitty, for taking care of the children for me. I promise not to be too late."

Kitty smiled. "Have a good time, that's all that matters."

Rosa grinned and left.

Kitty picked up her knitting but stared off into oblivion as the front door closed.

✝

The opulent Mighty Dragon restaurant was in marked contrast to the lunch venue. It had several tables covered with white linen and silver utensils and other than the prevalence of chopsticks, it was a totally different experience. The staff was dressed in a clean uniform and everyone smiled. The smell from the kitchen was to die for, as the aroma of various spices and foods assailed Rosa.

"Isn't this a rather expensive place, Phil?"

Phil grinned. "Sure, but you are worth it. Blake said it's the best westernized restaurant this side of the city."

Rosa's heartbeat increased when Phil said she was worth it.

"I'm told they do a mean steak. I think that's on my list."

Rosa chuckled, as they sat at a table in the window. "Did you ask for a window seat?"

"Nope, if you want to move, I can—"

"No, I love watching people go by," Rosa admitted.

Phil nodded. "Sorry I'm really late."

"You already said that when you arrived. You are here now and that's all that matters."

Phil gave Rosa a serious stare.

"Is anything wrong?" Rosa asked.

"No, I'm just...to tell the truth I'm amazed at how well you are taking my deception and what I am," Phil said.

"We discussed the deception, if it doesn't happen again, we will be fine. What you are...well, a woman comes to mind. How can that be a problem?" Rosa smiled and reached out a hand to place it on Phil's arm.

The waiter came toward them with a wide grin. He gave them each a menu and then placed a drinks menu beside Phil.

"Be back in five minutes." The waiter scurried away.

"I guess you must look like the person in charge." Rosa giggled.

Phil winked and cocked her head from side to side. "It must be this swanky hair cut I have."

They both laughed and several pairs of eyes watched them—most with indulgence.

"Kitty told me that your full name is Philomena."

"Ah, you've been talking about me behind my back. What else did she say? I confess I didn't think she knew me that well." Phil looked at the drinks menu.

"We weren't gossiping. She was worried I was going to walk a hole in her carpet."

Phil chuckled. "Go on."

"I was worried about you. Anyway, she said it wasn't a date so why was I worried so much. She intimated that she knew of your personal preferences." Rosa paused. "She said you had a partner."

Phil stared at her, remaining silent until the waiter arrived.

"You ready to order drinks?"

"I was thinking wine, what do you think?" Phil asked.

Rosa shrugged. "You choose. I'm not very experienced in wine. Mostly what I've had was in church." Rosa confessed with a slight smile.

"Well, we definitely have to change that experience." Phil summarily ordered something with a French sounding name and the waiter disappeared again.

"I'm impressed that you spoke the name almost faultlessly." Rosa said.

Phil shook her head. "Don't be. I know a smattering of French, German, and Spanish. Just enough to get by."

"Except for English and Chinese, I don't know any other. When I was in school in England, the teachers said I was too old to teach and didn't have an ear for languages. I suspect you have though." Rosa smiled.

"When you have the choice between eating or not, you learn fast. I think those teachers were wrong, Chinese is a hard language to learn and I bet you know more than one dialect?" Phil grinned and they locked gazes.

Rosa dropped hers first. "Well, the seven main ones I guess, Putonghua, Gan, Kejia, Min, Wu, Xiang and Yue. I'm more fluent in Putonghua and Yue. What about you?"

"Wow, you have just blown me away. Cantonese and a little Mandarin for me. Are you sure you weren't Chinese in a past life?" Phil asked.

Rosa shook her head. "According to the Grand Master perhaps."

"I have to admit that the old man resonated in me somehow. Can't figure it, but he did. Sounds a bit odd, I guess."

"Not really. If I wasn't a Catholic born and brought up, I'd seriously consider the Taoism teachings. I quite like the concept that we all go back to the The One. Don't you think it makes everything more comforting? Perhaps I'm odd too."

"Then we can be odd together. I think that would work out just fine for me." Phil grinned and pointed to the menu. "I guess we'd better at least look at the menu. He will want to take the order when he comes back with the wine."

"Then we should." Rosa opened the menu and was stunned at the dishes on offer. She was so used to basic Chinese fair. "Oh, my goodness, Phil, I don't even know what some of these are."

Phil winked. "Let me translate. I'm sure some place in my head, I'll have the right English term."

Several minutes later, and with the aid of the waiter who had arrived with their wine, they ordered their meals. Phil chose Beef Wellington for a main dish and Rosa decided on Lamb Cutlets a la Pondicherry. They had both agreed on

mock turtle soup and sardines as the first starters. The rest
they decided, as it was late, would be if they were still
hungry.

"Her name is Ming."

"I never asked," Rosa said.

"I know, but you need to know. We have been lovers for
almost two years. I thought I was in love with her. I told her
so, many times. She was…is married."

Rosa swallowed hard. What did you say to such a
confession?

"It's over now."

That final disclosure sounded genuine, heartfelt even.

"Hey, that's my news. What about you? Are there any
old lovers lurking in the background?" Phil gave a half smile.

Rosa's heart warmed anew. *It's incredible the reaction I
have to Phil. How do I prevent myself from being sucked in?
Do I really care if I am?*

"When did it end? You talk as if it might not be?" Rosa
asked tentatively.

Phil's cheeks paled.

Rosa wanted to take back her question.

"Yesterday."

Rosa's eyes flared at the admission. The question on her
lips if she dare ask, was *why*.

"I found that what I thought was love wasn't." Phil
sipped her wine. "What do you think of the wine?"

Rosa automatically took a sip and allowed it to swirl in
her mouth before she replied. "Fruity and light."

"You like it?"

"I do. It was a good choice, Phil. Thank you."

"It was my pleasure. I hope that there are other things
that I can introduce you to that you will enjoy equally if not
more so."

Rosa smiled. The words didn't sound like they had a hidden agenda. "I'm looking forward to that."

"A toast then—to the future and our continued friendship."

"I will certainly drink to that." Rosa raised her glass and they clinked them together.

The waiter arrived with their soup and they settled down to enjoy the meal.

✝

The boarding house doorway was within feet of them as they walked slowly toward it.

"I had a wonderful time, Phil. The meal was divine. I can't remember tasting such exquisite lamb, and the trifle, it was delicious." Rosa exclaimed rubbing her tummy.

Phil laughed. "Well, now I know how to make you happy—a quart of trifle. They will never forget you at that restaurant."

"I wasn't that bad. Was I?"

"Ordering two portions...yep, going to remember you forever. It was kind of cute though." Phil grinned. Her body was tingling with happiness. Somehow, out of all the lies and the Ming situation, Rosa wanted her company. She wasn't going to kid herself that it was love. But friendship with Rosa would be enough, for now at least.

"Oh."

Phil laughed and pulled Rosa into a hug. "I'm joking. Except that I now know that trifle tickles your fancy."

Rosa gazed into Phil's eyes with such innocence. There was no way she was going to demean that. Pulling away, she pointed to the door. "You are home."

189

"I am. Thank you for a wonderful evening." Rosa didn't walk to the door, she remained at Phil's side.

"Sorry it's so late. You'll be up early with the kids, I'm sure." Phil felt her heart race at the continued proximity.

"Tomorrow we will have a conclusion for the twins. I do hope it will all work out for your friend and their mother."

"It will. In the years that I've known Donna, she hasn't done anything that there can't be a happy ending attached to. They will all be happy and safe." Phil knew that in her heart that was the truth.

"Is that your philosophy, too, Phil?"

"If I can, I will. I never guarantee. Life is too complicated."

"Kitty said the same," Rosa said and then looked heavenward.

Phil looked up at the sky filled with stars. Mother Nature was certainly surpassing herself this night.

"Good night, Phil, and thank you." Rosa encompassed Phil in a hold that didn't allow her to prevent the kiss that followed.

The kiss was slow and deep and every nerve strummed at the sensation. When they broke apart, Rosa quickly left her and entered the house.

Phil stood in the same spot for a while. One thought went through her head before she eventually turned for home.

Rosa kissed me!

Chapter Seventeen

Phil rigidly sat at the table in Kitty's parlor. Rosa had taken the twins along with Bang and Tao to the school for a short time and hadn't arrived back. There was a knock on the door and Phil stood to answer.

"I will open the door, Phil." Kitty levered herself out of the rocking chair and left the room.

Phil frowned. She'd wanted so badly to see Rosa again and had arrived half an hour before the assigned time to meet with Donna and talk with her. That hadn't happened.

I'm a darn fool, she agonized. She only kissed me because she had a great night…or it might be payback. What the hell am I supposed to think?

"Phil." Donna walked into the room and smiled before beckoning behind her. "I want you to meet Nang Peng, the twins' mother."

The diminutive woman gave Phil a grave stare. She was well dressed in an emerald green silk tunic and black silk pants with the motif of a dragon embossed on the tunic's left breast. She was one of the most attractive Chinese women Phil had ever encountered.

"Nang Peng, it is a pleasure to meet you." Phil held out her hand.

Nang Peng moved forward. Her smaller stature did not give the impression of weakness, in fact just the opposite.

191

She held herself twice as tall—confidence clearly a big part of the woman's makeup.

"Donna has spoken of you. May I see my children?" Nang asked abruptly.

Phil cringed, turned away, and looked at the clock on the mantle. *Fuck you.* She dropped her hand. *Where are you, Rosa?*

As if Rosa was reading her mind, the front door opened.

"Sorry I'm late, Kitty. Has Phil arrived yet?" Rosa's voice sounded breathless.

There was a squeal from children.

Phil smiled. "Just on time," she whispered.

Rosa walked into the room and grinned at Phil then smiled at the other women in the room.

"Oh, forgive me. I didn't realize the time. What must you think of my manners," Rosa said. Her hands clutched the twins who didn't move.

That was a bit odd. One would think they would be pleased to see their mother. Phil creased her brow.

"儿童是您要说你好你的母亲吗?" Nang clipped out. (Children, are you going to say hello to your mother?)

Rosa's face dropped and her bright smile watered down considerably.

Phil felt much the same way. Who talks to kids like that?

Obediently, the children dropped Rosa's hands and walked to their mother. They bowed politely.

"母亲您好!" They said simultaneously. (Hello, Mother.)

Phil looked at Rosa who gave her a pained look.

"Great, now we can make plans." Donna said enthusiastically.

"Hold on a minute. Don't get ahead of yourself. Rosa in particular needs to know that the twins are going to be safe.

192

After all, she's technically their guardian." Phil said watching Donna and Nang's expressions carefully.

"They are my children." Nang's jaw tightened.

"Quite so, but you gave them away to Donna, me, and then Rosa. They are not parcels we can foist on just anyone. I'm not impressed with their life so far, are you?" Phil asked

"Phil!" Donna's hand went to her mouth.

"What? Just because you want her in your bed doesn't mean what she did was right. From what I see she isn't making up for it, in my humble opinion." Phil crossed her arms. "Don't give me that look either, Donna. You know I'm right."

"I think I'd better take the children to Kitty until we've sorted things out," Rosa said. "Come children, Mrs. Kitty will have a treat for you." She smiled at the children and motioned them toward her.

Mai and Ziong didn't move.

Phil watched a smirk cross Nang's lips.

I hate you, Phil thought angrily. And I don't even know you. Whatever do you see in her, Donna? Are you blind, woman?

"孩子们与罗萨." (Kids, go with Rosa now.) Phil winked at them and they grinned.)

The children moved toward Rosa and she shot Phil a grateful look as she left the room.

"You had no right," Nang said imperiously.

"Oh, yeah, I do. More to the point, what right do you have abandoning your children to complete strangers and then swan in here all royal like. Any mother with a heart would have hugged and kissed her children, but not you." Phil curled her lip.

"Phil, please, you know the circumstances. It wasn't Nang's fault," Donna pleaded.

"Prove to me she's a fit mother and the twins can go with you."

Nang glared at Phil. "I don't need to explain myself to you or any of them. If you do not give me my children, then I will bring back people to help me retrieve them."

"You think that scares me? Well, think again." Phil smiled. Inside she was shaking like a leaf. *Damn what have I done? I'm no match for her contacts. She sure as hell will have them. But those kids deserve more out of life than that cold bitch.*

"You should be scared. Come, Donna, we will return later." Nang stepped toward the doorway.

Rosa, standing in her way, frowned. "Tell me why Phil is wrong and you are right?"

"This is ridiculous. I gave them life, that should be enough," Nang announced.

"It isn't though, is it? What you did to keep them safe tells me more than you are admitting now. Why not just say it." Rosa smiled.

Nang lowered her head.

Confused by the gentle manner Rosa was taking in this situation, Phil frowned. Surely Rosa understood her stand on behalf of the twins.

Nang raised her head, looked at Phil, and then narrowed her eyes. She turned to Donna and there was an immediate softening of her features.

"I love my children. I will and have done things I am not proud of to keep them safe. We will have a better life and so will they when we leave China. Until we do, I have to maintain my distance to avoid suspicion." Nang's expression dissolved to one of apprehension.

"The first decent thing you've said since you came in here," Phil muttered.

Rosa took Phil's hand. "Then we can discuss how best that can be managed. Don't you think so, Phil?"

Phil was lost in the look Rosa gave her and nodded obediently.

"Kitty wanted to know if English tea would suit everyone," Rosa said.

Donna and Nang nodded.

"I'll pass," Phil said.

Rosa pursed her lips. "That wouldn't be polite, Phil."

"Fine." Phil rolled her eyes and smiled as Rosa left the room again.

"My, she's got you under her thumb." Donna chuckled.

"She has not," Phil mumbled and sat down. "Take a seat. Kitty loves to entertain."

✝

Rosa discreetly watched Phil say goodbye to her friend and the twins' mother. Tomorrow the twins would be with their mother on the eve of them leaving for Shanghai. Donna was definitely a gentle woman with a heart of gold, much as Phil had described her. The twins' mother was quite another proposition. However, that did not make her some evil queen out of a storybook drama as Phil appeared to be making her out to be. No, Nang Peng was a very strong woman because she needed to be.

"Are you going to tell me what's going on in that wonderful head of yours?" Phil asked.

Rosa grinned. "I was thinking about Nang."

"You know, I'm still not sure we are doing the right thing. She reminds me of the wicked witch of the west." Phil slumped down in the closest chair.

Rosa gazed at Phil and her heart swelled with pride. She had been right all along to trust this woman even if she thought her a man at first. At the end of the day, it was the heart of a person that mattered, not their gender. "Thank you."

Phil frowned, "For what? Being belligerent and fanciful?"

Rosa laughed then sat next to Phil. "It wasn't until today that I discovered something very important and it makes me ashamed."

"Ashamed. Why?" Phil sat bolt upright in the chair.

Rosa gazed at Phil and then dropped her gaze. "Do you remember the reason we first met?"

"Sure, I brought you a letter. How could I forget? That day changed my life."

"I suppose in a way, it changed mine too. Alfred will be smiling in heaven at the irony," Rosa softly said as she felt the prick of tears as she vividly recalled Alfred's face.

"Okay, lost me. Who is Alfred?"

"There are things you need to know about me, Philomena Casters."

"Wow. Am I in trouble? No one uses my full name unless I'm in deep trouble," Phil said.

Rosa smiled.

You have entered my heart, Philomena Casters, and I wonder what will happen next.

"You are not in trouble." Rosa could hear the children beginning to get loud with excitement. Kitty was good but she tired easily. "I need to rescue Kitty from the children and I know you must work. How about we have dinner this evening and I will explain?"

"Dinner you say. Is it your treat?"

Rosa giggled. "Yes, but I'm afraid not as elaborate as your dinner. I do not have the ready funds."

"I'll take anything…even a simple bowl of rice. What time?" Phil grinned.

"Seven. Kitty is very accommodating regarding the children but I think I am taking advantage of her."

"Then don't. How about we meet up at four and take the kids and Kitty out to dinner. Bang and Tao will like it, especially if they will be losing their best buddies tomorrow. Do they know that the twins are leaving?"

"I will explain when Bang and Tao arrive home this afternoon. Thank you for thinking about them." Rosa felt an overwhelming connection to Phil. It was like the other half of her soul. "We may not be able to talk frankly."

"No problem. There will always be another time—I know there will be." Phil grinned and pointed to her heart then stood. "Guess I'd better do some work today even if it is only the paper stuff."

"Later then?" Rosa asked softly.

"You have a date." Phil grinned. She leaned down and kissed Rosa on the cheek. "See you at four sharp."

As Phil left her alone, Rosa closed her eyes and allowed the emotional connection she had with the woman wash over her. It really was quite earth shattering.

†

The food market Phil found was the perfect place for the family to be together. As Rosa looked around the table, she felt very blessed. There was Bang and Tao who had captured her heart many years ago, laughing with the twins. Phil, who had strayed into her world on a perfectly innocent errand, had turned her world upside down. Then there was sweet Kitty Randolph, who had known her parents and had been present at her birth. What was it the Grand Master had said? We all go back to the beginning. It is a never-ending circle. How true the old man's words had been.

"You look lost in thought, my dear, are you all right?" Kitty asked.

Rosa looked at the lined face of the older woman that she had known for just days. Rosa felt in every fiber of her being that the woman was family in a way that her family at the mission had never been. Well, perhaps Prudence. She smiled, thinking of the older woman.

"I'm sorry, Kitty, I'm well. Thank you for asking. You did not have to tell the children about the twins. However, I'm grateful you did. They took it very well. I'm not sure I could have done as good a job. Thank you."

"You don't have to thank me, Rosa. I knew it would be difficult for you. You have such a tender heart—like your mama. I wish you could have known her. Silly me. No use in wishing. That's for children." Kitty sighed. "I have never been here but I do know the young woman who is serving us."

"You do? How?" Rosa asked.

Kitty looked in the direction of the stall where their food was being prepared and smiled. "She's the granddaughter of my late husband's assistant. Her grandfather was a very clever man and well connected."

"Really." Rosa smiled as the young woman grinned at them. "Why then does she waitress if the family has good connections?"

Kitty chuckled. "Not every connection leads to powerful government jobs or old royal houses. No, they had connections that were much more powerful in times of need."

"Missy, Rosa."

"Yes, Bang?" Rosa turned her attention to the boy.

"Will we fly away soon?" Bang's eyes moved to Phil who was talking to Tao. Rosa felt tenderness as she saw Phil's serious expression as she listened to the young girl.

"Fly away to where, Bang?" Rosa smiled.

"Mr. Casters here now with us. I learn to fly." Bang's animated expression as he spoke made Rosa smile. Ah, yes. Phil and that promise.

"Well, we shall have to see, Bang. Ah, our food is arriving." Rosa was thankful. Its arrival solved two things. Explaining that Phil wasn't a *Mr.* Casters and that flying was not on the agenda.

Plates were loaded on the table and everyone tucked in with gusto.

"So, Mrs. Randolph, how long have you been here?" Phil asked after they had consumed half the mountain of food.

"My, it seems forever, and I suppose to you young folk it would be. My husband came here as a commerce attaché to the British consulate in 1895. I was twenty. Harry and I had been married a mere six months when he whisked me to foreign parts, as my parents called it. Quite the adventure." Kitty's voice held wonder.

"Wow, more than forty years. Have you been back to England?" Phil asked.

"Of course. Twice. My father died ten years after we arrived and my mother followed a week later." Kitty nodded. "They always were such a devoted couple. When Harry died in 1920, he wanted to be buried in his home town."

"Did you want to stay in England then?" Rosa asked, fascinated by this new information.

Kitty laughed. "My family may be British and I'm proud of it. But my heart...no, my heart belongs to China. I fell in love with the country and the people from almost the first

199

day I set foot on this land. I shall see out my days here. That is what I want."

Rosa was awed at the statement. "I feel the same way, Kitty. I love the culture, the country, and most importantly of all, the people." Rosa's eyes moved to the four children talking animatedly together.

"Can't say I have the same mojo about the place. I'll be moving on soon. I've heard rumors that the Japs are reaching their tentacles farther into China than expected. Might be months away, but it will not be years before there is an all-out war," Phil said.

Rosa was aghast. "This rumor, how truthful is it?"

"Pretty good intel I'd say."

Rosa frowned.

"From an honest source," Phil reiterated.

"How long have you been in China, Phil?" Kitty asked.

"Sometimes too long. Okay it's not that bad. Five years. Can't compete with you two ladies, that's for sure." Phil shrugged.

Kitty smiled. "It isn't about the years, Phil. It is the magic of being. You obviously have not found that yet. Someday, my dear, I hope you do."

"Magic of being? Hey, have you been talking to a Taoist priest recently?" Phil winked at Rosa. "The only thing that will make me stay in a place that doesn't appeal to me will be a *someone*. I guess I have never found that," Phil stated.

Rosa felt deflated upon hearing Phil's responses.

"Let's eat this feast. After all I'm paying." Rosa listlessly picked up her chopsticks and moved food around in her bowl.

†

Phil stared up at the stars, taking in the clear night and the twinkling heavens. She wondered if there really was a place out there in the Universe, which accepts humans back when they were finished. Maybe she needed to study a little of what the Grand Master taught. It sounded mighty interesting and more up her street than any Christian religious mumbo jumbo. She stumped out her cigarette and sighed.

"That was a heavy sigh. How was dinner?" Blake said. He was sitting in a cane chair on the decking.

Phil tapped her stomach. "Filled to the brim. Do you know the Kia Stall on Feng Street?"

Blake laughed and shook his head. "Who doesn't? It's the best place in town for a feast without the trimmings. The Kia's are respected."

"Well, I have to say I found it by accident a couple of nights ago." Phil laughed. "I've been there three times since. It must have made an impression."

Blake puffed on his pipe. "What's going on, Phil?"

"What do you mean?" Phil stared at Blake, engaging him in eye contact.

Blake didn't flinch. "You know. In all the years I've known you, passengers were a big no no. Then you end up ferrying them around the country and then bringing them here. You've spent more time and energy on Rosa Moran and her orphans than anything or anyone else—even flying. What about Ming? I thought you loved the woman." Blake spoke quietly and puffed on his pipe.

Phil watched the plume of smoke rise into the air and she withdrew a packet of cigarettes out of her jacket. She levered back the lid of her steel lighter, rolled the flint, and a flame appeared. She placed it against the cigarette and drew in the first drag of smoke. As it filled her lungs, she felt the nicotine begin its insidious path into her system.

"I owe her."

Blake frowned. "Why, because of this?" He waved a hand around the hanger. "Not worth losing your heart over, kid. Believe me, there are better reasons."

"Who said I have lost my heart." Phil sucked in too much smoke and exhaled it rapidly.

"Oh, Phil, it isn't so bad losing your heart. But, you have very different circumstances than the usual romance. Does she know?"

"Yes," Phil bit out.

"Good. That's one obstacle out of the way. Have you asked her on a date?"

"Not exactly. We had dinner last night, lunch today, and dinner, her treat, tonight." Phil thought long and hard then muttered. "She kissed me."

Blake stood and walked to Phil and grinned. "Good for you and her. There still is one problem though."

"That is?"

"Ming." Blake looked upward.

Phil narrowed her eyes as she considered Ming. She was now irrelevant. "Ming and I are through. I communicated such when I arrived back. Ming won't care. She will move on to someone else."

"Ming Xian is from a very powerful family, Phil. Are you sure she won't care?"

"Why would she? She has a husband, a good standing in the community, and if she makes waves then I will do the same. She won't want her reputation sullied. I know that much about her." Phil crushed the cigarette underfoot, barely smoking half of it.

"People with her kind of connections are apt to go underground to solve any problems. Besides, you really think that the family doesn't already know about a two-year long sexual encounter. Are you that naïve, Phil? I know damn well you aren't." Blake sat back in the chair.

Phil shuffled her feet. Ming said she had always been discreet. "How can you know that?"

Blake shrugged. "I've been here longer than you. I know how it works."

"Do you know the Xian family?"

"Thirty years ago I encountered Ming's father-in-law. He was a punk with money and a respected family name. He thought he could do anything. The worse thing was, he could," Blake said.

"What happened?" Phil sat on the wooden floorboards of the decking.

"He took a fancy to a friend's daughter, Lulia. She was a bright young woman and her family had ideas that she might be educated beyond the norm. Genghis Xian had other ideas. He wooed her and told her he loved her. That he would eventually marry her. Of course, she believed it all. I can still recall today the lost innocence and bitterness that rained fire when he took her and discarded her without regret." Blake went silent.

"I guess that goes on a lot but it doesn't mean the same thing." Phil wasn't sure where this story was leading, other than being of the same family—it certainly had no other parallel.

"The Xian family had Genghis followed so they knew his every move. Genghis killed her."

"What? What the hell! He killed her? Why?" Phil was aghast.

Blake had a faraway look in his eyes. "She'd told her family the truth. They had connections with the British embassy and that was a powerful ally back then. It still is today in most places."

"And the outcome, Blake? It can't have been that good a connection. She died, for God's sake."

"That's the trouble. It was. The Xian family was in hot water with the authorities and the only way out was to silence the woman. Genghis killed her, threw her body in the river, and moved to another province. No one could pin the murder on him because his family moved so fast. No one ever came to justice for Lulia's murder though we all knew that he killed her. That family is evil, Phil, please don't underestimate them."

Phil balled her fists. She wanted to seek out Genghis Xian and see him in hell for what he had done.

"Why didn't the British consulate do something?"

"Politics is a very cruel game and it wasn't expedient for them to help."

"Expedience be damned. The darned British can't be trusted," Phil blasted.

Blake chuckled. "Says she who is smitten by an English woman."

"Yeah, well, she's more a child of China then Britain," Phil replied dogmatically.

"The Randolph's employed Lulia's father. It was their action instigating any kind of recompense to the family and it was large. What Harry and Kitty couldn't do to bring Genghis to justice, they fought to make the Xian's pay for their misdeeds."

"Kitty was part of this?" Phil shook her head.

Blake laughed. "You sound surprised. Kitty, Harry, and several others were very active in helping the poorer Chinese to better things. In her day, Kitty taught English to poor kids. Secretly, she still funds younger folks to carry on the movement."

Phil liked Kitty more and more. "What did you do?"

Blake feigned surprise and then chuckled. "Got me. There were times when people needed relocating. In the early days, it was by boat or horse. When I bought my first plane, it had its uses."

Tears pricked Phil's eyes at the man's admission. You could know someone but never really know them.

"A knight in shining armor, Blake. I'm proud of you."

"Hardly that, Phil. Besides, look at yourself. I'd call you that with no qualm. The Moran girl is very lucky to have you."

"You were coerced?"

Blake stood, tapped his pipe on the arm of the chair, and grinned. "I most certainly was. Kitty Randolph has been my heart's desire for a long time now and it's the real thing. You aren't the only one who would stay in a place for someone."

Phil was shocked, amazed, and filled with tenderness for the man. She'd learned more in half an hour than in the five years she had been working for him. "I'm honored. I think we should celebrate with a beer."

"Grand call."

Chapter Eighteen

Phil looked in the mirror and smiled. Her blonde hair was slicked back. It might look manly but she really didn't care because apparently it didn't matter to the only woman that was important in her life—Rosa. Maybe Rosa liked her masculine appearance. It probably was the reason she considered her company in the first place. No, forget that. She liked Phil and Phil knew it. Though she did wonder why Rosa wasn't more disturbed by the fact that Phil was a lesbian. Most women would be. And who was she talking about when she mentioned Alfred? Rosa might come across as the naïve Catholic teacher of orphans with a mission in life but it appeared she was certainly far from that image.

Pulling at the deep blue silk jacket collar, she straightened it into a respectable style. She then smoothed down the black trousers, also of silk, that flared at the bottom showing perfectly polished black boots. She grinned at the mirror and winked at herself. "Yep, I look good."

She opened the door of her room at the Chinese boarding house and locked the door. As she stepped toward the stairs, a figure appeared from around a pillar.

"You look very dashing. Is it for your new paramour?"

Phil recognized the voice immediately. "What are you doing here, Ming?"

Ming Xian moved to stand within inches of Phil.

The scent of her body was increasing Phil's heart rate.

Ming placed a finger on Phil's chest—the extraordinarily long lacquered nail could very easily rip the silk of the jacket she wore. "Why, my love, to see you, of course."

Phil closed her eyes for a second as the soft notes of Ming's voice drew her toward the woman. "I sent you a message. Didn't you receive it?" She knew Ming had as her earlier question indicated.

Ming's finger trailed to the opening of the jacket and she slipped her finger inside, cruising slowly across the skin to reach the top of Phil's breast. "I received your tawdry message. You dare not see me in person to deliver such a blow. I had not realized you were a coward?"

Phil's pulse went into overdrive as the finger touched her nipple and she drew in a deep breath. A part of her wanted Ming still. Resisting a beautiful woman had never been easy for her, especially when one was being thrown at her. Phil placed her hands on Ming's arm desperately wanting space between them. When Ming tugged on her nipple, she pulled Ming close and kissed her ferociously. Her tongue slipping into the open mouth and tangling with Ming's. All sense of propriety went out of the window as she moved her hands over Ming's bottom and squeezed the cheeks until Ming moaned into her mouth.

Ming scooted up and wrapped her legs around Phil's waist. Her lose fitting tunic wafted the scent of Ming's arousal and Phil was not immune. She growled and with Ming in her arms, she moved back to the door. "I need to unlock the door," she whispered, releasing their lips.

"Let me." Ming placed her free hand in the left pocket of the jacket and found nothing, then she dexterously searched the right and took out the key. "I want you so much, Philly, you cannot leave me." Phil's mouth captured Ming's and she sucked on her tongue. The door opened and Phil pushed it wide and carried Ming to the bed. She threw the woman down and looked at her.

Ming spread her legs and the tunic left little to the imagination as Phil spied the dark hair that covered Ming's mound.

"Come to me. Make love to me now."

Phil's lust for the woman had taken control and she was powerless to resist. She pulled her jacket off and threw it on the floor her pants followed then she climbed onto the bed and covered Ming with her body.

"This is the last time," Phil growled then kissed Ming again.

†

Rosa twirled and Kitty nodded approvingly.

"You look lovely, Rosa. That shade of red suits you."

Rosa shrugged. "I have to admit, spending money on frivolous clothes has never been something I've done before. However, when I saw fabric in the shop, I couldn't resist. Thank you Kitty for helping me make the dress." She smoothed the red silk across her curves and was happy at the reflection in the mirror.

"Philomena better know what she's got in you, my dear," Kitty said with a wink.

Rosa's cheeks grew warm. "You are happy with my choice then, Kitty?"

"Of dress? Of course, my dear."

"No, I meant Phil. Most people would not be as tolerant," Rosa said. Her eyes never left the older woman.

"I've seen many things in this life, my dear. One thing I know for sure is that if you care for someone, might even love them, you should follow your heart." Kitty stared off into a place only she knew.

"I'm not so sure I'd go for the stronger version of love at this time. I certainly do care for Phil. I believe she cares for me too. She told me she had broken off her relationship with her...friend. I do not want to complicate matters by being a rebound. Besides, it might be a moot point in a few days." Rosa held up her head accentuating the words. The action was more for her benefit than Kitty's.

"Then you are being very sensible, my dear. What time is Philomena due?"

Rosa glanced at the mantle and the clock. "She said seven but as it's five after I guess she must be one of those people who are always late."

Kitty chuckled. "Being late might become the fashion one day, but in my day, as I'm still here, it is very rude to keep a lady waiting."

Rosa smiled and hugged Kitty. "You are a blessing in my life, Kitty. I'm sure she will be here soon."

Kitty hugged Rosa back. "You are a blessing in mine too, Rosa. Your presence in my life has shown that there is still time for happiness."

Rosa wasn't sure what Kitty meant. It sounded personal and she left the exploration of it for another time.

"I'll just check on Bang and Tao, before I go. They miss the twins. Do you think they arrived at the port in time for the steamer?"

"I have received a note from a friend who was watching out for them. They are aboard the ship and safe," Kitty said.

Rosa glanced at Kitty. What pies doesn't this woman have her fingers in? She was amazing. "I have never met anyone like you before, Kitty. Thank you."

209

"No thanks necessary, my dear. There are just some things in life that need a helping a hand. Whilst I can no longer physically do so, I do so via others."

Rosa bent and kissed Kitty's cheek. "I'll be but a moment." She left the room and marveled at her fortune in meeting Kitty.

"Now where are you, Phil? You promised not to be late tonight."

She climbed the stairs heading for the children's bedroom.

✝

Phil's body was soaked in sweat.

She got up from the bed and looked at her reflection in the long mirror on the wall. There were bites on her neck and breasts. Claw marks covered half of her torso and her arms had taken a battering. Ming had made her pay the price for pulling away. What were her words?

"If I can't have you, she won't want soiled goods and I'm going to mark you so much that she'll go running to the hills."

She walked to the washing area and emptied a jug of cold water into the porcelain bowl. She washed the spittle from her face. The temperature sobered her to the events that had occurred in the last half hour.

She drew her hands through her hair and cradled her head.

Lust. You nearly gave into lust! Are you stupid? Sure you are. What else could be the explanation? You have fallen in love for the first time in your life and you nearly lost it, might still, for a few hours of sex! Grow up. Life isn't about who excites your libido for a shady session. Life is about meeting that someone—The One. Rosa is my One.

For what seemed like hours, she remained in that position then dragged herself into the real world again. She looked at the fancy clothes on the floor and shook her head.

"I made the right choice."

She glanced at the time—it was seven-thirty. She would be late but she still might salvage the night.

With a fresh course of action, she walked to the bed and from under it, she pulled out the duffel she kept there. Inside she withdrew a clean white shirt, underwear, and a pair of faded brown trousers. *I won't look a prize package but I will be clean.* She tied a royal blue silk scarf around her neck to hide the bites as the final accessory.

With a speed she was proud of, she dressed and left the room. This time she took the stairs ten to the dozen and with a sigh of relief left the building. In ten minutes, she'd be at Kitty's. What excuse could she use this time?

✝

Rosa pursed her lips as she considered the menu. Her mind was most assuredly not on the contents.

Phil cleared her throat and Rosa looked at her.

"Have you made up your mind, Rosa?"

A young waitress hovered with a smile that almost split her face.

"Sorry," Rosa smiled at the woman. "I'll have spring rolls and Cantonese chicken with fried rice. Thank you," Rosa said. She gave the menu to the waitress and dropped her gaze to the white paper table napkin perched on the plate in front of her.

"Do you want something to drink or shall I order for us."

Rosa gave Phil a sharp glance.

"Water, please," Rosa replied.

"Me, too," Phil said.

There was silence then Phil spoke. "I know I was late again and I'm really sorry." Phil twiddled with the scarf at her neck.

"You said."

"But you're mad. I can hear it in your voice and you won't look at me."

Rosa drew in a shallow breath and stared at Phil. She wore that half smile that under normal circumstances dissolved any predilection to anger she held toward the woman. It wasn't working this time.

"Why were you late?"

Phil shuffled in her seat. "I told you. I got caught up in paperwork."

The sheepish way Phil said that for the second time didn't wash with Rosa. Phil had made no effort to dress for the occasion looking just like she did at her workplace. Except for the fancy scarf that kept slipping down her neck. She hadn't even noticed Rosa's new dress.

"I don't believe you. If you didn't want to take me out again, all you need do was say so. Now that the twins are no longer in danger and are safe, your obligation is finished."

"How can you know that they are safe?"

"Kitty said so and I believe her." Rosa narrowed her eyes. She had begun to feel the ice forming on their relationship from the moment Phil had arrived at Kitty's.

What had happened in such a short time to do such a thing? Was she too much a country girl for Phil? She probably wanted someone with more experience, now that she was back in a thriving city.

"I believe her, too, and that's great news," Phil said.

The waitress arrived and poured water into two glasses.

Silence once again cocooned them.

"Look, I want to be here, Rosa. I want to be with you," Phil shouted. Several pairs of eyes turned to them and then turned away as quickly. Phil reached for Rosa's left hand, which rested on the table.

Rosa watched Phil take her hand in what seemed like slow motion. She didn't want her touch because she was mad. There was something not right about tonight and it all had to do with Phil. She jerked her hand away.

"Please tell me what's wrong because it sure is more than me being late?"

"The twins have gone. You no longer need bother yourself with Bang, Tao, and me. They are my responsibility. I thank you for all your help. We are indebted to you," Rosa said.

"That's bullshit!"

Rosa glared at Phil.

"Sorry. I'm not here for any other reason other than I want to be with you. I like you. I care about you."

"You have a strange way of doing so."

"How so? I invited you to dinner. Isn't that good enough?" Phil pleaded.

Rosa wondered if she was being paranoid and then Phil's scarf slipped to show red marks. "Yes, however...." She hoped her voice didn't sound wobbly.

"However?" Phil raised her eyebrows.

"You dress like you are going to work. You didn't notice my dress." There she'd said it and it made her feel better. She watched Phil pale at her words.

"I...it's beautiful and I'm sorry isn't hardly enough for my not saying so. I do have extenuating circumstances."

"And they are?" Rosa lifted her chin.

"I don't notice what you wear, because you, Rosa Moran, are a beautiful soul. Everything else pales in

213

comparison. I'm sorry I didn't notice and say something. Now that I have been admonished for my oversight, may I say that the color particularly suits you?"

Rosa closed her eyes for a split second as the praise washed across her. She had been wrong earlier. Yes, she cared for this woman, but deep inside she knew she loved her and that was why it hurt so much.

"Thank you. That still does not answer your dress. Unless..." Rosa frowned. "You have to fly out tonight?" The red welts on Phil's neck were noticeable now and they looked like bite marks. Damn. She was playing her for a fool.

"Well, I didn't want to spoil our evening. Jamie is still jittery about a long distance flight. Blake has put me on the red eye shift for the next week," Phil remarked.

"You never did say what happened to him."

Phil shrugged. "He's a young guy, barely out of diapers. Worldly wise, I mean." She grinned. "He got in over his head in a poker game with the guys who run the airstrip."

"Did they hurt him?" Rosa asked, concerned.

"His pride maybe. I managed to smooth the ruffled feathers."

Rosa melted anew at that smile.

"You are good person, Phil Casters. I'm glad to have you in my life. However I have news, too."

Phil frowned.

"It isn't so bad in some ways. My Grandfather is sick and needs me. This is one message I cannot ignore. I will leave with Bang and Tao as soon as arrangements can be made." Rosa dropped her gaze.

"You're leaving?"

Rosa smiled. "Yes. I have an appointment at the British embassy tomorrow to work through the paperwork on the children. I will not leave without them."

"When did you know?"

"A letter arrived last night after you left. I have not kept anything from you. We promised, remember."

Rosa saw Phil hesitate.

"I remember."

"I know you are not telling me everything, Phil, and that is your prerogative. We are, after all, people who met in special circumstances. It does not necessarily mean that a relationship will last." Rosa pointed to the scarf.

Phil's eyes bulged. "It will. Ours will. I promise you. I can explain this." Phil placed a finger on her neck.

Rosa heard the desperation in the words and her heart leapt to answer it—her head refused. "Kitty has contacts. She assures me that we can be on our way within a couple of days if there is transport."

"That's impossible."

"Apparently not. Kitty has very influential contacts. This will probably be the last time we see one another. We can start again when I return if that is what you want. Be very sure it is, Phil. I will not allow you to break my heart." Rosa whispered her last words and by Phil's expression, she heard them.

Phil drew in a deep breath. "I might not see you again?"

"I will come back, Phil. This is my country. It is in my blood," Rosa said.

Phil grabbed her hand. "It's a good thing. England is safer. China is in a volatile position right now. When you come back, everything will be resolved. I'll be here waiting for that start."

"Than that gives me more reason to return."

"I'll drink to that." Phil lifted her glass of water.

They toasted and the food arrived.

✝

215

Phil leaned against the railing of the pier and rested her head on her arms. There appeared to be a thousand people milling around the area. That didn't matter, in her heart she knew that Rosa and the children would look in her direction when they boarded the ship destined for England.

"Relative going home?"

Phil frowned and looked at the person who had spoken. "Something like that. You?"

"Yes, the wife. She does not like China. She's taking the three young ones with her. Doubt I'll ever see them again."

Phil straightened and looked at the man who she figured was in his late twenties. "So, why aren't you with them?"

"I have a great job here working for a mining operation. Can't get the work in England."

"That doesn't mean you won't see them again?" Phil bit her bottom lip. Didn't make any sense.

"She's going home, familiar territory. Before you know it, she'll want a divorce. Cannot blame her really, it has been difficult making friends and settling in. I'll miss them desperately."

Phil's stomach double somersaulted. "Can't you go home and see her and the children, make it work if you love her?"

The man laughed and then vigorously waved.

Phil looked in the direction of the wave and saw a thin woman dressed in black with three children the eldest barely at school age.

The children waved back and then bright blue eyes pierced first her and then the man at her side.

"If you love her, forget the job and join her. Love is never easy but damn it, it is worth having if you get the chance," Phil said quietly.

The young man looked at her and frowned. "Is that what you would do?"

Phil drew in a shallow breath. "If I had the chance, that's what I would do."

The sound of the whistle on the ship indicated that the last passengers were aboard and caused Phil's stomach to churn, her eyes glancing in all directions.

She never saw Rosa embark but knew she would be safe. If Rosa wrote her and asked for her to join her, she would be there in a heartbeat.

Phil tapped the young man on the shoulder. "Want a drink? I'll buy."

"Thank you." The stranger grinned.

Chapter Nineteen

"Bang, be careful, darling." Rosa shook her head and smiled at the boy. He was intelligent in many ways but rather uncoordinated. How Phil ever thought that he could be a pilot was a mystery. Still it was a strange country for the boy and every second glance was one of curiosity as they went about their business in Shackleforth.

"Missy Rosa, can I?" Bang asked and pointed to a nearby park.

"Yes, but be very careful." Rosa grinned as he dropped the shopping packages at her feet and sped off to the children's playground.

Rosa picked up the discarded items and made her way to a bench so she could see the entire park. She sat and smiled as Bang climbed up the wooden fortress and waved at her. He was happy. She surveyed her surroundings and nodded. It was a good place to bring up Bang and Tao. Indeed, if she said to Tao that they were leaving, she would not be happy.

"My quiet, reserved Tao has been my grandfather's savior." Rosa said aloud and looked up at the sky. It was blue with a light cloud skirting the sun's profile, much like a fan. "So much so if I took her away, he would most certainly die," she whispered to the breeze.

"May I sit?"

Rosa looked up. A young man, her age, with a cheerful countenance stood in front of her. "Yes, by all means."

"It's a beautiful day."

"Yes, it is," Rosa replied amiably.

"I have seen you here before, many times with the Chinese boy and sometimes a girl. Are they orphans from the war there?"

Rosa balled her fists. "No, they are my children."

Gentle brown eyes caught her volatile ones. "I apologize. Even so, it is good they are not in China now. The news is not good there."

"No apology needed. I'm sure things will settle down. China is a sleeping giant, she will rally. I'm sure of it." Rosa didn't want to talk about China. She knew it was difficult there from the last letter she had received from Kitty.

The man turned to her, smiled, and held out his hand. "I'm Lionel Black. I live in Walcott Avenue. Who might I have the pleasure of addressing?"

Rosa almost laughed aloud at the polite introduction but held herself in decorum. "Rosa Moran. I'm living in Shackleforth Manor at the moment." A distinct freeze appeared in the air as she finished.

"John St Philip's home?"

Yes, definitely icy.

"Yes, he is my grandfather. Do you know him?"

"I know of him. I offer my condolences." Lionel stood.

Rosa placed her head to one side and felt the very devil tempt her. *Prudence would be proud.* "Condolences? Why? He is not deceased."

Lionel's sharp nose appeared to get even pointier to Rosa as he narrowed his gaze.

"The likes of him should be. You would be better off if he was."

Rosa stood. She was five inches shorter than this man, but it did not matter. "That is an insult, Mr. Black. Just who are you to say such things?"

"A concerned citizen. He destroyed his wife and his only child left. If indeed you are his granddaughter, I pity you." He strode off.

Rosa felt spent when he'd left. She had been ready for a fight, yet thwarted. She absolutely hated people like that!

Bang appeared.

"Missy Rosa, good?"

Rosa saw the concern etched on the young boy's face and wept inside at his innocence. Life outside of what *people* called the norm were freaks or worse—wished dead.

"I'm very well, Bang. Shall we go and find Tao and Grandpa."

"Yes, I love Grandpa's stories."

Rosa smiled as they took up their packages. "As do I, Bang, as do I."

†

They approached the small manor house on the outskirts of town and were greeted by a wonderful array of flora. Snapdragons, Geraniums, poppies, and foxgloves danced in the light breeze, as pollen floated around the flower heads. A peacock butterfly wandered from one flower to another its legs covered in bright yellow pollen.

Bang giggled as he chased a starling that, in turn, was bullying a blackbird. The whole scene reminded Rosa of her first visit to England as a teenager when everything she encountered was new. The children had taken to England far better than she ever had, even as a child.

Bang ran up to her and offered her a daisy, which she took before smiling at the boy.

"Why not run up to the house and tell Grandfather and Tao we are back." She ruffled Bang's pitch-black hair. "Take a few of the small packages." She handed Bang several. He grinned and ran to the gate, opened it and rushed toward the house.

Rosa stopped and looked at the eighteenth century building. It wasn't of opulent proportions, five bedrooms in all, sufficient for a family. It was part of the dowry that her grandmother had brought to the marriage. There was ivy growing up the walls, giving it a majestic presence along with the sashed windows. It gave the appearance of comfort rather than of excessive wealth.

The house had always appeared sad to her when she had lived there the first time. Now it had a satisfied smile on its facade. Perhaps it enjoyed the children's laughter. Yes, that must be it. Happy children.

She began a slow walk toward the gate and opened it. The perfectly manicured lawns stretched on either side of a small fountain. The sun's rays glistened as they hit the water pouring from the angel spout.

Her feet crunched on the gravel and moments later, she reached the double entry door. She clasped the iron handle and heard the loud click as she slid it open. As soon as she deposited her packages on the hall table, Tao ran to her and hugged her tight. Her usually shy features were now wreathed in happiness. Her huge smile looked like there was a cherry on top.

"Why, Tao, you almost took me off my feet." Rosa chuckled as she hugged the girl tightly.

Large almond shaped eyes looked at her and Tao giggled.

"Tell me why you are so happy?"

"Pappy say we stay here," Tao said with an expectant face.

Rosa chewed on the inside of her lip for a few seconds. Now why did her grandfather say that? He knew they intended to return to China. "Well, shall we go speak with Pappy about this?" She took the girl's hand and they headed for the study. Knocking on the door, Rosa heard a faint call to enter.

They opened the door.

"Grandfather, sorry to disturb you. Tao imparted some interesting news," Rosa said. She had never been one for prevarication.

"About staying I presume."

She must have inherited the trait from him—he didn't prevaricate either. Spit it out child, he had always told her.

Rosa nodded. Then turned to Tao. "Why don't you find Bang and check what time dinner is? If it isn't for a few more hours perhaps Edith will allow you a biscuit."

Tao squealed in delight and headed for the door.

"Only one." Rosa tried a stern voice, knowing full well that Edith would give them at least three.

The door shut behind Tao.

Rosa moved to sit opposite her grandfather. He had never had much color in his cheeks in all the time she had lived with him. Yet, these days a rosy hue grazed his upper cheeks.

"I'm sorry, Rosa."

Rosa nodded and pursed her lips. "I know you enjoy the children's company, Grandfather, but this is not their country."

"And China is yours?"

"Yes. I was born there. Spent my formative years there and although I respect the opportunity of the education you gave me here, I do not belong and we both know that." Rosa sighed and locked her fingers together.

John St Philip stood, walked to the window and looked out.

Rosa saw by his body stance that he wasn't happy.

"You always belonged here, Rosa. Alfred may well have been the one to convey that we would miss you. I so very much wanted to say the same and more. It was like a breath of fresh air into a stagnant space when you arrived here, breathing life into our hearts and the walls of this house. When you left so did that life."

Rosa heard a tremor in the voice and in a way, she was grateful her grandfather wasn't looking at her. She had been right. The house was sad.

"I…I never knew. At least not to that extent." Rosa frowned. "We have been here six months. I have to go back."

"There is too much trouble in China, Rosa. It will be dangerous. I read in the newspapers and have letters from friends in Hong Kong that it is not safe with the Japanese moving farther into the country." John spun around.

Rosa saw genuine fear in his face. "More reason that I should be there. I can help," Rosa said.

"Help? How? Can you protect yourself if a Japanese soldier decided you were fair game? No, my dear, I cannot allow it in all good conscience. I permitted my daughter to die in that country when I might have been able to help. I refuse to do the same with my granddaughter. What of the children? They would be easy pickings and please don't insult my intelligence that they would come to no harm. You had to save them once from their own people."

"You can't tell me what to do or how I bring up the children," Rosa shouted. She knew losing her temper wasn't the answer. But she'd made promises and she wanted to go back. For China and...for Phil.

"Then leave the children behind and you go off on your folly. When you are settled and sure that they will be safe, they can travel back. You know they will be safe with me." John strode to his desk and flipped open the ink well. "I will pay for you to return forthwith, if that is your choice."

Rosa narrowed her eyes at the bribery. She had money, but not enough for all three of them. Her allowance would take another three months before she could pay for passage for all of them.

"The children love you, Grandfather. Tao adores you."

"As I do her. She is my chance of being a proper grandparent and to do things better. I want better things for you all, Rosa. My wish is that, if years ago I had been more forthcoming, perhaps then your mother might not have left on such a hare-brained journey. One that cost her life. I regret that more than any other choice I have made in my life. Please, let me do this."

Rosa stood and walked to the desk. She placed a hand on his arm and was surprised when he did not shrug it off. Instead, her surprise increased as he took her hands in his.

"I love you. I might not have had the opportunity to tell your mother such, as circumstance dictated otherwise, but all I have ever wanted to do was the right thing."

"I understand, Grandfather. My mother loved you, regardless."

"You cannot say that, child. She hated me. If she had loved me, she would not have eloped with that missionary. He wasn't good enough for her, you know. I'm sorry to say that, as he was your father." John sighed.

Rosa gave a half smile. "I bet everyone said that about Alfred."

Rosa's heart lurched as she saw tears fill the aged eyes.

"I miss him every single moment. He was the best part of me. So full of life and yet, when it mattered, gentle as a gossamer wing."

"I loved him too, Grandfather. I'm sorry I wasn't here when he died. You understand why I didn't return when you sent the letter, don't you?"

John sniffed hard and wiped a hand across his eyes. "He told me not to contact you when he became sick. He wasted away for almost a year and he wanted you to remember him as he was—typical Alfred—always the martyr."

Rosa clutched his hand tightly. "I would have come back. I loved Alfred. I love you, Grandfather. Not making the journey for a funeral that would be long finished was something that pained me but he would have understood."

"I know, Rosa, and I'm so very happy that we are together again." He bowed his head. "Even if you want to leave."

Rosa softly chuckled. "In truth, it isn't just China I want to return for."

"Really. And who pray is this young man?"

In for a penny or a pound. "Phil Casters, she's a pilot."

"She?"

Rosa laughed. "She. Guess it must be a family trait."

"Does she know you like her like that and is she...."

"She most definitely is and she most definitely does not, at this moment." Rosa smiled.

"You are very like your mother—gentle with deep undercurrents."

Rosa laughed. "Then you must tell me why. Except first we need to find the children or Edith will fill them up with biscuits and they won't eat any dinner."

"Good idea." John closed the lid of the inkpot. "Oh, you have a letter from London." He handed Rosa the letter.

She gave it a cursory look and dropped it in her pocket.

†

Rosa smiled as she watched through the window as Donna Poillucci and Nang Peng walked up the drive to the front door. The twins followed them closely. Seeing them in European clothes made them look strange somehow, yet she had never thought that about Bang and Tao in the same way.

The bell rang out and Rosa rushed to the door and opened it.

"Donna, Nang, how wonderful to see friendly faces." Rosa grinned and ushered them inside. Once they entered, Rosa hugged the twins who were excited to see her again.

"Ziong and Mai, it is so lovely to see you again and my, how well you are looking." The twins remained silent as they looked at Nang. Some things never change.

Then footsteps on the stairs heralded the arrival of Bang and Tao. Where there had been reticence, now there was joy as the children met again.

"Children, why don't you go and play outside in the garden? We will call you for lunch," Rosa said.

There wasn't any hesitation as the children ran off in the direction Bang took them.

"I'm not sure…." Nang said.

"Yes, Nang, it is the right thing," Donna replied and placed a hand on Nang's arm.

Rosa wasn't sure what was going on, but it looked familiar, heralding back to when they'd first met in China.

"I can assure you, Nang, that no harm will come to the children other than playing with other Chinese children. I suspect that since you've arrived that has been limited."

Nang stared at Rosa, her gaze, haughty initially, changing significantly. "None at all. My children have not been received well in London."

"It isn't quite that bad, Nang," Donna said.

"It doesn't matter here. They have friends…true friends." Rosa smiled and indicated they move to another room.

They entered the parlor and sat down.

"I have to say, I wasn't expecting you to invite us here, Rosa," Donna said.

"When I received your letter, it indicated that you did not find London to your taste and that of the children."

"How could you know that?" Donna asked.

Rosa smiled. "I remembered when I was a child and came here. It was never easy. I did not have friends who understood my problems." Rosa shook her head. "I believe I do now."

Donna nodded. "It hasn't been easy, that's for sure. I was thinking that we might try America. They still have relatively open borders for immigrants."

Rosa nodded. "I was thinking that you might like to stay here."

"Here?"

"Why?" Nang asked.

"Long story, but I want you to think about it. I will introduce you to my grandfather. He owns the house."

"Why would you want us to live here?"

Rosa smiled.

"I want to go back to Phil."

Donna grinned. "Good enough reason for me. Have you heard from her lately? Last communication I had was three months ago. That pilot monkey was never good at keeping in touch."

Rosa drew a shallow breath. "I have heard nothing. How was she?"

"Oh." Donna frowned. "I just figured that you and she...well, it was dated a month prior to my receipt. She said the Japs hadn't entered the province but were on the borders. Blake was being awkward about leaving and she was trying to persuade him."

Rosa felt her heart clench, realizing that Phil might be in danger. The Japanese had been gaining significant territory when last there was a report in the *Daily Telegraph*. Perhaps her Grandfather was right. China was too dangerous right now. Then her heart responded to her head. How more dangerous is life without the person you love, be it for a second, minute, hour, or the rest of your life.

"Blake has a reason for staying that far outweighs his respect for his own safety and possibly that of others," Rosa replied sagely.

Rosa was surprised when Nang spoke up.

"Mrs. Randolph."

"Why, yes, I didn't think it was common knowledge."

Nang's nostrils flared. "I am not common."

"No...no, of course. I never meant any disrespect. I was just...surprised." Rosa knew her cheeks were red since her fingers heated as she touched a cheek. "I didn't realize that it was well known."

"It isn't. I didn't have a clue," Donna said. "How do you know, Nang? I didn't think you had even met the woman until we saw them together that first time."

Nang lifted her head high and appeared to Rosa to look down on her and Donna. How did Donna love this woman? She was so frigid.

"The Chinese power brokers in the main provinces are very well-informed. My father-in-law had information."

"Yeah, but that doesn't mean he'd tell you, right?" Donna asked.

Nang shook her head.

Rosa felt that Donna's question was one she would have asked and wanted to know.

"Donna, I always knew you were naive." Nang stretched her hand to touch Donna's lips. Rosa saw the gentle caress and her heart finally warmed to Nang. "When I told my father-in-law that the children may be in danger, he mentioned Mrs. Randolph as a possible ally. I, of course, did not know this woman and frankly decided to take my chance with the only person I knew in my heart that I could trust." Nang smiled at Donna.

Donna took her hand and touched her lips to the slim fingers.

"That doesn't ratify why you would know about Blake's attachment to Kitty," Rosa said.

"When I needed to leave, Mrs. Randolph's name was mentioned again. My father-in-law gave me more details."

"You never said, Nang," Donna replied.

Rosa noted the heightened color in Donna's cheeks.

Nang nodded. "I did not, that is true. What would it have helped in the circumstances?"

"That Kitty Randolph was a good person, not someone to be wary of," Donna exclaimed.

"I did not know this. All I knew were the details I had been given. I may have trusted my father-in-law with my life. But my children…that was another matter."

"I understand that perfectly," Rosa said. "Nang, do you still have contact with your husband's family?"

"No, she doesn't," Donna replied.

229

Nang stared at Rosa. "Yes." Then she turned to Donna. "He is an old man. I love him like my own father. I abandoned so much, my love. I could not do so to him."

Rosa watched the reaction of Donna. It was much as one would expect—disbelief.

"We agreed that there would be no contact, for all our safety."

"I know. I'm sorry. Do you forgive me?" Nang asked.

Donna's face clouded and she looked away toward the window that showed the well-manicured lawn in front of the house.

Rosa felt sorry for her. Lied to by one you trust and loved must be hard. She knew it so well.

"We'll talk about it later," Donna mumbled.

"Why don't we seek out my grandfather?" Rosa said.

Chapter Twenty

The pier was thriving with bodies and with shipping. Every way one looked, there were people talking, shouting, or chasing down a person. Rosa allowed the sights and smells of China to immerse her once more.

I have missed this so much, she thought. China is my home. There can be no other.

A thin Chinese man who appeared to be in an immense hurry jostled her. He didn't even acknowledge that he had been rude. Rosa smiled. It was just as she remembered it. Now she needed to find transport to take her to the hotel. She scanned the area as best she could through the wall of people for any sight of a taxi or rickshaw. After several passes of the surroundings, she sighed.

"Darn, I can't walk with all my baggage."

"That won't be necessary."

That voice sent tingles down her back and through every nerve ending. She composed her smile, which had widened and turned to the owner of the voice.

"Is that so?"

"Yep, unless you *want* to carry your belongings to your lodgings."

Rosa narrowed her eyes and schooled her features. She refused to allow the overload of her emotions at seeing Phil again after so long overtake her.

231

"How have you been?" Rosa asked.

"All the better for seeing you again," Phil answered with a smile.

Rosa was lost, as always, when Phil smiled at her. Then she noticed the longer hair tied up harshly into a ponytail. It still gave her that semi-masculine appearance with her strong jaw and square face. Brilliant blue eyes stared at her and she knew that they were embodied together—China and Phil. Each held her ransom and she didn't care.

"I thought you may have forgotten me by now."

Phil laughed and shook her head. "Not a chance. Besides, we get to start again right?"

Rosa swallowed hard. More than nine months had separated them and it felt like mere hours as she looked at Phil. "Yes."

"Great, now how many trunks have you? And which hotel have you booked?" Phil looked behind Rosa.

"I travel light, two suitcases, and my personal handbag." Rosa declared. She then waved toward her belongings a few feet away.

"And the hotel?"

"I booked a night at the Emperor."

"Wow, you are splashing out. I'm surprised they didn't send a taxi for you." Phil whistled before she walked to the cases.

"Just how are we getting there?" Rosa asked. Phil grinned and Rosa's heart flipped.

Phil pointed to a rickshaw. "Your transport, my lady."

Rosa laughed. "Well, I guess I couldn't expect the plane?"

"Nope, not enough runway." Phil looked around. "None at all. Let's go. I bet you want to freshen up."

"Oh, yes. One of the reasons for this choice of hotel. They have showers," Rosa said. "I will help." She held out a hand to take one of the suitcases.

"Not today. Today I just want to welcome you back home," Phil said as she strode toward the rickshaw.

"Now I know I'm home," Rosa whispered and increased her step to catch up to Phil.

✝

Phil paced the foyer of the Emperor hotel and then flicked a glance at the time. It was ten after six. Darn, where was she? She said six prompt and not to be late.

Walking to the mirror by the reception desk, she looked at her image—clean and well presented. She smoothed her hands down the black silk trousers and admired the fit. She glanced at the tunic she wore, bright turquoise, with gold braid holding it together. There were even a couple of dragons embroidered on the lapels. Kitty had been right—this was her style.

She smoothed the bang that fell over her left eye and frowned, this never happened when she had short hair. Phil gazed at her face. Even she had to admit she was aging rapidly. Where had those lines come from? She was pretty darn sure they weren't there six months ago.

"Do you like what you see?"

Phil grinned. Then turned to Rosa, holding her breath at the sight of the woman she loved, looking absolutely perfect. "Well, yeah. What's not to like, right?"

Rosa laughed. "Americans, where do you get your confidence from?"

"State secret. You'd have to live there to find out." Phil winked at her.

Rosa smiled. "Right now I'd rather eat. I'm rather peckish."

"Peckish? I guess you mean hungry. You've been in England way too long."

Rosa grinned and nodded.

"I'm hungry too. Then, me lady, let's go. I have a table booked," Phil said.

"Here?"

Phil frowned. "Is that a problem?"

"No. No, of course not. I just thought...."

Phil's mood decreased somewhat at the reply. Crap, she should have taken her to a swankier restaurant. "I can cancel and take you to a better restaurant."

Rosa took Phil's arm. "No, let's see if this swanky hotel can provide a decent meal. Because I have to admit that they have a lot to live up to."

Phil loved Rosa even more as she compared this hotel restaurant with the lowly stalls and regional restaurants where they had previously shared a meal together.

"Kitty said we should give it a score. Five out of ten, that kind of thing."

"You have been keeping in contact with Kitty?"

"Yeah. How else was I to know when you would arrive? You never wrote me." Phil felt a twinge of pain hit her heart.

Why didn't you write me? You knew where I was? I never knew where you were.

Rosa frowned as she looked at Phil and stopped at the entrance of the restaurant.

"It wasn't that I didn't care."

Phil shrugged.

"I remember it all. Casual is what you said. Casual friendships don't necessarily mean you write. I get it," Phil said.

"It wasn't like that. I wanted to write to you but I didn't."

"Yep, got that. Look, you are here now, and we don't need the pen and paper." Phil began to walk forward.

"I am, Phil," Rosa said, not moving.

"Sure you are. Let's go or we might end up with a line behind us." Phil took Rosa's hand, pulled them to the door, and entered.

"Do you have a reservation?" the man at the door to the restaurant asked.

Phil ground her teeth at the supercilious way the man looked at them. She thrust her head high. "Yep, Casters for two," she answered.

The man was a European for sure but was not English. Maybe German. He looked at them with distaste in his eyes.

"Yes, of course." The man clicked his fingers and a Chinese waiter arrived almost immediately.

采取这些人表0 (Table Thirteen.)

The Chinese waiter nodded and waved his hand for them to follow.

"This is ridiculous. We are nearer the kitchen than the chef," Phil announced. She glared at the waiter who seemed to shrink before her eyes.

"I ordered a window table. There are damn well no windows for the next hundred feet!"

"It's okay, Phil. I'm sure they will change if we ask the head waiter."

Phil pursed her lips. "He's a damn German, no leeway with him. Wouldn't surprise me if they didn't entice the Japs to conquer China. I never liked the Germans."

"You can't say that for not everyone is tarred with the same brush." Rosa giggled. "You do sound like my grandfather though."

235

Phil shook her head. "Damn, that's why I love you. You think the best of people even when they act like scum."

Rosa's mouth fell open and she stared at her.

Phil cocked her head to one side. *What had she said?* "Want us to go elsewhere?"

Rosa shook her head.

Phil breathed in deeply before turning her attention to the nervous waiter.

"0告诉你的老板是好运气我们爱表中." (Great choice of table, thank you.)

The waiter grinned and scurried off.

"You hate the table," Rosa said.

"I know but he doesn't and that damned German can wipe the smirk off his face."

Rosa grinned. "I missed you, Phil."

"No more than I missed you, Rosa. So tell me how our kids are?"

Rosa chuckled.

Phil leaned her hand on her chin and simply watched the animated expression. She had missed Rosa— more than she would ever know.

"You are staring. Do I have a smudge on my nose?"

Phil grinned. "Absolutely not." She reached a hand out and touched the object of their discussion. "Now, if Blake had done that, you most definitely would have a smudge on your nose."

Rosa laughed.

"I am still not sure I did the right thing in leaving the children in my grandfather and Donna's care. However, I said it was only temporary. When we have a secure base for them to live they will come home as I have."

Phil's left cheek twitched at the mention of *we*. She was pretty darn sure Rosa said that without knowing what it could mean. Or maybe she did know. "In the circumstances here, you did the right thing." Phil drew in a deep breath. "I wish you'd remained in England. I think it's a safer bet than here right now."

"It can't be that bad, Phil. I saw no evidence of the Japanese invasion that everyone says is happening. By some of the things I've read during the past three months, I was expecting the invading force to overrun me. I see only what I remember as a glorious chaos of people." Rosa looked around the room.

Phil did the same. The patronage was what she would have expected. Influential Europeans and the elite of the Chinese society were sitting and amicably enjoying a meal. There appeared no evidence that the country was in turmoil, though she knew it most certainly was. "Believe me, looks can be deceiving."

"You sound bitter. Have you had problems with the Japanese?" Rosa asked.

"One or two skirmishes on the border," Phil said. She settled back in the chair as the waiter finally arrived with the menus. They ordered drinks and looked at the offerings.

"Wow, I'm going to have the Chinese banquet," Rosa exclaimed.

Phil saw pure joy in Rosa's eyes and she laughed. "All for yourself? Didn't they feed you in England?"

"Oh, I'm sorry, Phil, they did but I missed my Chinese cuisine. I'm sure one day someone will package it and it won't matter. No matter where in the world we are, we can still enjoy the food."

"Well, maybe that's your new goal in life. Not a bad idea." Phil grinned. "The Chinese banquet it is."

"Oh, Phil, I'm sorry. You probably wanted something European. I can change my mind. I saw shrimp and fried rice."

"No way. This is my treat to you for returning. I thought you might not." Phil dropped her gaze to the white linen tablecloth.

Rosa's hand reached across the small table and settled on Phil's arm.

Phil looked up and smiled.

"I would have come back. I will always come back."

"Yeah, I know. China is in your blood."

Rosa hesitated.

Phil gave her a quizzical look.

"It isn't just China, Phil." Green eyes bored into pale blue.

They remained in a trance like state, simply staring at one another. Then the waiter disturbed the moment by plonking down two glasses of water and a bottle of red wine. The water splashed Phil's tunic.

"Hey, be more careful," she growled.

The waiter rushed away.

"Well, that broke the moment."

"Yes, it did." Rosa chuckled. "Why is it every special moment we have seems to be when we are eating or about to?" Rosa grinned.

"I heard that food was a way to the soul and I definitely want to win yours," Phil replied.

"You already have. Now, let's order and eat. I think we need to talk and here isn't the best place."

Phil was surprised but nodded. She waved for the waiter and they ordered the food.

✝

Rosa stood for a moment looking at the side profile of Phil's features. There was something arresting about her face, not necessarily beautiful but courageous.

Yes, that was the right term. Rosa could see how in the right circumstance, someone could take her for a man. But she did not see her gender. She saw the person within. Phil had proven so many times that her heart was definitely made of gold. Of course, Phil would laugh and say Rosa was being fanciful.

Narrowing her eyes, she noticed the lines at the side of Phil's eyes. If they had they been as pronounced before she left, she hadn't noticed.

"Rosa, are you—" Phil turned and stared at Rosa. "Okay, it's my turn now. Do I have a smudge on my nose?"

Rosa smiled. "I was watching you but not because of a smudge." Rosa walked the short distance to sit on the edge of the bed opposite Phil who was sitting in the only chair in the room. Her room had a large bed taking up most of the room. She had at first thought it rather opulent, but now she was glad.

"Should I be worried?" Phil winked.

"I hope not." Rosa placed a hand on Phil's knee and was pleased that Phil didn't remove it.

"Good to hear." Phil replied huskily.

"You haven't said much about Donna and Nang going to live with my grandfather?"

Rosa was surprised at the change of subject when she had mentioned it at dinner.

Phil shuffled a bit then she sighed.

"You knew?" Rosa asked.

"Well, yeah. Donna and I were tight for a while and she's been keeping in contact. I received all the gory details

239

yesterday. I think she figured that you would arrive before the communication."

Rosa hesitated and frowned.

"Hey, look, Rosa, it wasn't gory. That was just a figure of speech." Phil spread her hands

"What did she say?" Rosa quietly asked.

"Oh, just that you invited them to stay indefinitely to help with Bang and Tao. Do you know how immensely grateful they are for your kindness? She couldn't say enough about how good you and John had been to them. I take it John is your grandfather?"

Rosa nodded.

"Donna wanted me to protect you at all costs."

"She said that?" Rosa asked.

"Scout's honor…okay. Guide's honor, then." Phil chuckled and Rosa joined her.

Their hands met and the bond that had been growing from the first time they had met now seemed to multiply a thousand fold.

"I want you to know that it wasn't just China I came back for." A river of tears floated by her vision.

"You said that earlier. Do you forgive me?" Phil quietly asked. She clutched Rosa's hands tighter.

"Is there anything to forgive?"

"Yes. A great deal, yes. Until I met you, I walked through relationships like a ghost. I know that now. No one had anything but my body and friendship. From the moment we met, you had my friendship, my protection, and later, as I knew you, my body and soul. I regret that last night in so many ways. It haunts my dreams."

Rosa tried to speak.

Phil stopped her. "I just want you to know that I didn't make love to Ming that night. I rejected her at the last minute and the scratches you saw were her retaliation. Of course, I blame myself for it. I should never have gone that far and—"

"Is it through?" Rosa held her breath.

"Yes. I haven't seen Ming since that night," Phil admitted.

Rosa nodded and sucked her bottom lip for a second. "I will not lie. I was upset. I was beginning to feel that we were more than friends."

"We were…are. I thought the same."

"Yet you allowed her to be more that night and it made me think that my naivety in such things was a problem. I believe the months of absence have proven that point for us both."

"Yeah, but I promise it won't happen again," Phil quickly interjected.

"You are correct. It will not."

Phil stared at Rosa and she could see the fear in her eyes.

"Because we won't ever be lovers. I can see how you would think that and maybe you are right—since it seems I can't be trusted."

Rosa's heart swelled at Phil's genuine remorse for the situation. She moved forward, captured Phil's chin, and lowered her head to kiss the recalcitrant lips.

"You trust me?" Phil asked breathlessly, when the kiss broke.

"With my life, my body, my soul, and my love. Now please stop talking and kiss me," Rosa said.

Seconds later, Phil was pushing her gently back onto the bed.

†

As they both crashed onto the soft mattress, Phil gently kissed every crevice and inch of skin on Rosa's face, only allowing Rosa time to breath, before she began the onslaught on her mouth again. Rosa's murmurs had Phil's heart beating irregularly. As she pulled away slightly, she gazed into Rosa's eyes and saw a glazed expression. She carefully stretched out beside her. She traced a finger down the side of Rosa's left cheek, caressing her lips and then traveling lower to the button of the blouse she wore. She then slowly circled the ivory-collared blouse.

With her head close to Rosa's and snatching another long, satisfying kiss, Phil felt all the patience of waiting for this woman had paid off big time and she was grateful. Yet, was this the right thing to do? Carnal desire was one thing, but to take Rosa's love was another. Did she deserve it? Perhaps not now but in the future if she worked hard to erase her past indiscretions.

"Phil?"

Phil smiled. "Yeah?"

Rosa lifted a hand and pressed it against Phil's breast. "I want this, Phil. You are not taking advantage of me."

Phil cocked her head to one side and slowly smiled.

"You make me want to swoon when you do that."

"Do what? I'll do it all the time," Phil replied softly. She bent her head closer.

"Smile. That half smile you do. I have never suffered such a reaction before until I met you," Rosa admitted.

Phil pressed Rosa's hand closer to her breast. "I want to make love to you, Rosa, but I need to know that you won't regret this. Have you ever been with another woman?" Phil held her breath. She was ninety-nine percent sure that Rosa wasn't experienced but....

Rosa smiled and moved her hand to the opening of Phil's tunic. "You can be the judge. Now, stop talking and take action."

Phil laughed. "Hey, I gave you the chance." She moved to straddle Rosa and then captured her lips in a searing kiss.

Opening the buttons on the blouse Rosa wore, Phil feasted her eyes on the linen-covered bra that separated her from her goal. She circled the outer seam of the right breast and heard Rosa suck in a breath. Phil kissed her as she reached around Rosa and unclipped the bra, allowing her access to the white silky skin. Seconds later, her hands moved in slow motion over the breast and when it reached the nipple, she tugged gently. Rosa's hips moved upward at the touch.

Phil slowly kissed down Rosa's neck as her hand molded the small breast in her hand. Her body hummed as she heard Rosa's moans.

When her lips reached the breast, she moved her hand to the left breast and mimicked her earlier actions as her mouth captured the light brown nipple. Slowly she rolled it on her tongue and her juices began to build as Rosa gripped her hair in response.

"Please," Rosa ground out.

Phil had never experienced as much joy ministering to another woman in her life. The simple touch of Rosa's skin to hers was like magic. She moved to suck in the right nipple as her hand touched the skirt Rosa wore. It might be beautiful but right now, it was a barrier. Her hands went under the skirt and slid up lithe thighs to reach the apex of her legs, where the greatest prize lived.

Thank you, whoever. Phil's hands found the loose fitting knickers. She looked into Rosa's eyes and saw primal want in her love's eyes. Then her hand snaked under the cotton fabric and circled the hair she found there.

Rosa squashed her legs together in reaction.

"Do you want me to stop?" Phil asked huskily.

"No. Please, no. Phil, you are killing me," Rosa replied.

Phil took the lead and slowly traced her finger through the hair, which now, on reflection, was soaking wet. One finger traced the clitoris and this time Rosa moaned loudly. Phil smiled and kissed Rosa deeply as her fingers brushed across the sensitive nub. When Rosa began to moan incoherently, Phil knew it was time.

She sucked on Rosa's tongue and gently entered her with first one finger then, at Rosa's sigh, another.

Rosa was reacting to the intimate touch with enthusiasm as her hips lifted and ground back onto the bed.

Soon Phil found Rosa's rhythm and began to thrust in time with her. It wasn't long before Rosa screamed out in passion and gripped Phil's hand, which had stilled inside her.

"Let me." Rosa said hoarsely. She pushed her hand under the waistband of Phil's silk trousers.

To Phil's amazement Rosa's hand quickly entered her vagina and placed three fingers inside. Phil couldn't believe her immediate reaction, not to mention the speedy orgasm.

Phil gazed into Rosa's eyes and grinned. "I was going to say are you okay but you look great. I think I'm the one in shock."

"Why? Did I do something wrong?"

Phil shook her head and held Rosa close. "Nothing at all, in fact you were great. Better than great—wonderful."

"You do look somewhat bemused. I had a teacher."

"What?" Phil asked and she knew her face mirrored shock and surprise.

Rosa chuckled. "Don't worry. It was merely educational, nothing physical."

"Then who?"

Rosa blushed. "Your friend Donna."

"She taught you? Wow." Phil was in shock. How had that happened?

"Yes, she figured it might help our relationship. Did it?"

Phil chuckled, "My God, did it! Did she teach you much?"

Rosa grinned. "I consider that just the start."

Phil shook her head with the widest grin on her face. "Then, my love, why don't you show me."

Rosa pulled Phil closer, kissing her passionately. "Do you think we can dispense with the clothes?" she asked between breaths.

"Absolutely."

✝

Rosa's lips curled into a smirk. Her fingers were gently teasing the short pubic hairs of her lover. Phil moaned softly but remained sleeping. Their lovemaking had been incredible. Donna had told her so many things to help her through the first time. Was it the first time? It felt as though she and Phil had been making love for a lifetime because they were so in tune with one another.

She now had knowledge of why her grandfather had never abandoned Alfred. If he felt even half as much as she did for Phil, then she totally understood, now. She wished she had been a better granddaughter all those years ago. How useless it is to wish for something that is impossible to change? The past is the past. She wanted better for their family and understanding was the first priority.

Rosa kissed the top of Phil's head. She smiled as she moved her free hand to the longer tresses now free of their restraint. Now she did look like a woman and Rosa couldn't be more proud.

The sound of shouting from the street below had her reluctantly disengaging from Phil. Wrapping a coat around her naked body, she walked to the window and opened it a little to hear the skirmish.

There are times in one's life that you wish you hadn't done something. Rosa felt that as she listened to the voices.

"日本(Japs)正在日本(Japs)正在未来的未来." (Japs are coming. The Japs are coming.)

Rosa closed her eyes. Not now, not when she had found everything she wanted in the world.

"运行您的生活,使您的孩子安全是怪兽大战外星人》" (Run for your lives, keep your children safe. They are monsters.)

Rosa clasped her hands to her face and raised her eyes to the heavens. Thank God, Bang and Tao were not here.

When she opened her eyes, she saw the hotel concierge moving the young peasant away.

"There is no problem. Go home. No problem here," the concierge shouted.

He didn't sound convincing.

Rosa turned back and looked at Phil who was still sleeping peacefully. How did one do that with all that noise? She smiled. That was Phil—this was her Phil.

She padded to the bed, slipped back under the covers, and snuggled next to Phil, who simply fit against her body like a glove.

"I love you, Phil Casters," Rosa whispered.

"I preferred it when you were touching me and kissing me."

"What?" Rosa asked. "Have you been awake all this time?"

"Depends on what you mean by all this time. The last ten minutes…oh, yes. Hey, I have never had this much attention lavished on me ever."

Phil looked up and Rosa saw that hypnotic smile.

"Really?"

Phil pulled her head down slowly. "Really." She kissed Rosa deeply, their tongues meshing in a primal dance of the ages.

When they broke for air, Rosa sighed. "Did you hear what they said outside?"

Phil laced her fingers with Rosa's. "Yes."

"Perhaps we should leave?"

Phil winked. "Not a chance. I have the love of my life in my arms, who, by the way, knows more about pleasing me than I could even imagine. No war party is going to spoil this night. In the morning we shall make a hasty retreat to a safer place."

Rosa frowned. "Can there be a safer place in China for us, Phil?"

Phil smiled. "There is a place for us. Trust me."

Rosa considered the statement and relaxed. "I trust you."

"Great. Now, I believe…." She took Rosa's hand and placed it on her mound. "I think as I'm awake, we can be a little more active. What do you say?"

"I say…." Rosa captured her lips and began stroking between Phil's legs.

Chapter Twenty-one

Chaos abounded.

Rosa ran toward Gilda. She was in a line holding hands with six children under the age of six.

"Run, children, run. We are almost there."

One little girl dropped off the line and sank to the ground.

Rosa pointed to the plane. "Keep going children, keep running." She disengaged her hand from the line and ran back toward the fallen child.

Kneeling down in the dirt, she smiled at the girl. "您的姓名是什么?" (What is your name?)

"一个." (An.)

Rosa smiled.

"一个,借我的手我们要达到大金属的鸟,你明白吗?" (An, take my hand. We need to reach the big metal bird. Do you understand?)

Rosa smiled. "An, take my hand. We need to reach the big metal bird. Do you understand?"

An nodded and took Rosa's hand. She was barely four years old. Her eyes held a fear that Rosa had never known.

Scooping up An in her arms, she ran toward the security of Phil's plane.

In the background, she heard a foreign tongue she was not familiar with—it wasn't Chinese. The Japanese had invaded more territory in the past three months than anyone, even the Europeans, could have expected.

I don't understand, therefore I'm going to run. Run as fast as my legs can carry us. God help us.

Rosa stole a quick look behind her and she saw a soldier standing with a gun aimed at her.

"Stop."

I understand that. But if I do stop....

Rosa drew every single resource of energy in her body to speed up her progress. The soldier obviously wasn't happy as a close passing bullet, too close, went to the right of her. She stopped.

Reluctantly, she put An on the ground and turned to the soldier.

"Take me. Let the child go."

The soldier moved closer and gave her a cold look. His gun prodded her and then he turned to An.

"Leave her alone. She's a child, for God's sake," she screamed, seething inside.

The soldier gave a smirk and pulled out a knife and placed it at An's throat.

Rosa screamed.

A single shot rang out from behind Rosa.

The soldier dropped to the dirt.

Rosa instinctively clutched An to her and ran with the devil at her heels toward the plane.

As she reached the relative safety of the aircraft, she saw Phil with a rifle in her hands. She had a grim expression.

"Was it you?"

Phil remained silent and just stared at her. Then she pulled her into a vice like grip. "I will never lose you to this." Phil kissed her gently, defying the violence of the situation.

As they moved apart, Rosa smiled. "We have an audience."

"Sure we do. We always do, but that's what makes it even more interesting."

"You are crazy…I love you more." Rosa smirked and kissed Phil. "However, I do think that An might want to join her comrades. And we need to get out of here."

Phil laughed. "Spoil sport. Wheels up in five."

Rosa grinned then looked behind her. "Maybe right now would be good."

"Right now at your command." Phil kissed her and climbed into the cockpit as Rosa entered the cargo hold and drew up the door. Just as she did, bullets zinged off the metal.

"Good timing. Get us the hell out of here, Phil," Rosa shouted. She closed her eyes as the children huddled close.

"Hey, that's no way for a God fearing church goer to talk. But I hear you."

Rosa heard the throttle drawn back and the wheels screech. More bullets hit the metal and she moved to sit beside the children and speak.

"我记得第一次走过我的孩子在这个平面内,你想听到它吗?" (I remember the first time that my children traveled in this plane. Do you want to hear about it?)

Rosa watched each of the six children in turn. Some were so downright traumatized they kept their eyes closed while others gave her fearful glances. One child, who she'd not heard speak since meeting the children the day before, lifted her head, and spoke.

"它是一个真实的故事吗?" (Is it a true story?)

"It most certainly is." Rosa placed a hand against her cheek and whispered in a conspiratorial way, knowing that

Phil would hear every word. "The pilot was a little cranky back then. She didn't want her precious Gilda hurt by children's inquiring hands."

"Is Gilda your child?"

Rosa shook her head. "Gilda is the plane."

"Plane has a name?" Another child spoke up.

Before she knew it the children began to lose a little of their fear and participate in the story of Bang, Tao and Gilda.

†

Phil grinned as she heard Rosa begin to calm the children. It calmed her as well.

If that Jap had hurt either of them, she wouldn't have been able to forgive herself. Shooting the bastard was the right thing to do. She knew it was. She also knew Rosa would give her a hard time about it later but it would be worth it.

Phil looked at the ever-decreasing view of the town below. People, desperate to get away from the advancing Japanese army, were milling about. Some of the stories she'd heard were too horrific to imagine, never mind experience.

"Are you okay back there?"

"Yes, how long will it be before we reach Langshow?" Rosa asked.

"Weather permitting, six hours including the break to refuel," Phil replied. She turned her attention to the dials in the cockpit. The handling of Gilda wasn't as smooth as normal. If those bastards had hurt her, she'd be going back to finish them off.

"I'll conserve the supplies. You did fill up all the water canteens didn't you, Phil?"

Phil shifted her gaze to Rosa and winked. "Wouldn't dare do any other."

Rosa smiled and Phil's heart triple somersaulted.

If Rosa thinks that my smile sends her loopy, she thought. Well, it was a mutual thing. I still can't believe my good fortune.

She went back to her monitoring of the gauges and her thoughts drifted to several days after Rosa had arrived back in China...

"It's the perfect thing for us to do, Phil. Can't you see that?" Rosa asked.

Phil frowned. "Why can't we just leave like the rest of the European contingent and find a nice place for us to live and bring up the kids? I don't get all this do-good stuff. It's way too dangerous."

"Phil! You, of all people, can't say that. Look how you helped me and the children get to safety. Do you regret that?" Rosa pouted.

"No. It's different." Phil frowned. It was different, damned different back then. The Japanese weren't this close to taking control. *So tell her that, you idiot.*

"Kitty, will you help me?" Rosa turned to the older woman.

"That's a given, my dear, and a blessing for me to be useful again. We do need a base of operation though. This is no longer the place to be, as much as I regret saying that."

"Langshow," Phil and Rosa said at the same time.

"So you aren't as indifferent as you implied."

"I never said I was indifferent." Phil pursed her lips and wondered how to dig herself out of a hole.

"We can do much to help, Phil, we need you. The people of China, especially the children, need you," Rosa pleaded.

That's it. I'm in. No more dreaming of a life on a beach somewhere making out with the woman I love. Nope, I'm going to be embroiled in danger and hurt with the woman I love and I'll damn well cherish every second.

"Okay, is Blake part of the team?"

Phil looked at Kitty, who blushed. *Wow, that woman blushed. Good for you, Blake.*

"Blake has already made tentative arrangements about fuel for the plane in different territories." Kitty said.

"I didn't realize we had that much money." Phil laughed.

"He hasn't cheated you." Kitty frowned.

"I never thought that," Phil said.

"I used my money and…." Kitty stopped.

Phil noted that Rosa glanced sharply at Kitty. Hmm.

"When the shit hits the fan, pardon my frank appraisal ladies, we are going to need internal support as well. I know a few people who are champing at the bit to be part of scoring points against the Japs," Phil said. China's people were prideful and they would step up.

Rosa moved the few feet to Phil and wrapped her arms around her. "I love you."

Phil grinned and snuggled into Rosa's neck. "Promise me one thing. You will not get killed in this crusade you are about to undertake."

Rosa kissed Phil's neck. "Never going to happen because you will always watch my back."

"Always, no matter what I have to do." Phil gave Rosa a fleeting kiss.

"Do you want to eat?" Rosa asked.

Phil drew herself out of her memories and looked blankly at Rosa.

"Are you okay, Phil?"

The worried expression on Rosa's face gave her the energy to shrug off all the internal conflict.

"Great." Phil grasped Rosa's hand. "I love you. You are the most important person in my life. I don't live without you."

Rosa frowned then smiled.

"Thank you."

Puzzled Phil scratched her head. "For what?"

"Because you said the right thing."

There was a commotion in the back and Rosa left the cockpit.

"The right thing? What is that?"

†

Rosa found it hard to keep her eyes open as the plane began it's decent into Langshow. It had been the perfect sanctuary for them and an ideal base of operation for their adventures, as Phil called them. Especially since the Japanese had taken Zongnan a month after she arrived back in China. Her tired gaze went to the back of Phil's head. How Phil could keep focus after all they'd gone through in the past forty-eight hours amazed her.

She looked at the six children they had managed to extract from what was sure now to be a war zone. They slept. How easy it was for the young to sleep, even when turmoil surrounded them. China was in turmoil with, it appeared, no major ally to help them.

Rosa moved her gaze back to the cockpit. She smiled. They had Phil on their side and it would all work out. Even when Phil said she wanted out, she doesn't really. She was Rosa's beautiful adventure girl.

Her stomach lurched as they began the descent.

Home, they were going home. A new home, that was true but the people had generally welcomed them. One day Bang and Tao would arrive. Not yet. No, not yet. Phil said it wasn't safe. At least in England the children would be safe. Rosa missed the children every day.

She glanced at these new children. They moved but didn't wake. Keeping the children busy during the flight had subsequently allowed her to lock away her own terror of what had happened on the ground. Her gaze took in An, who remarkably hadn't seemed to be overly upset by the event. Rosa was a bloody nervous wreck inside. She was glad Phil didn't realize that or she'd put the plane down in the middle of nowhere to comfort her. They couldn't let that happen. Not yet. When they were on their own, she was going to hug her so close that an observer would think them joined at the hip. Her thoughts traveled to Chang. He was happy to see her return but not Phil. And when he realized that they were a couple....

"Hey, sleepy head, time to get the children up, there's been rain so the landing will be rougher than normal."

Rosa grinned. "For the record, I wasn't sleeping. I was thinking."

"Really, could have fooled me." Phil winked. "What were you thinking about?"

Rosa took a second to compose her reply then smiled. "You and me—always about you and me."

Phil laughed. "That's my girl. I'll have Gilda down in three minutes."

Rosa nodded to the back of Phil's head before gently proceeding to wake the children so they could hold the straps during landing.

†

The small house Rosa and Phil shared with Kitty and Blake had been a gift of sorts from the villagers of Langshow. At first, they were amazed at the generosity, but Blake let the cat out of the bag during their first meal there. Kitty was something of a well-known philanthropist outside the city she had made her home. Not that it surprised any of them really, but it helped when Chang was being difficult about her relationship with Phil. He'd made an incredible fuss about them living together alone when they'd sought refuge there.

"You look pensive, my dear, are you not feeling well?" Kitty placed a bony hand under Rosa's chin and lifted it so that their eyes met. "I cannot imagine what it must have been like facing death at the end of a gun."

"I'm fine. It didn't happen—death that is. I'm here, safe and sound." Rosa smiled. "How have you been?"

Kitty clucked like a mother hen as she walked to the rocking chair. She picked up her knitting and sat in the chair.

"Can't complain."

Rosa tiled her head a little and gave Kitty a long look. "You have never complained. That wasn't what I asked."

"My dear, you worry too much. I have the odd aches and pains as anyone my age does. Though...."

"Though?" Rosa smiled.

"I do not like that man Chang." Kitty sniffed the air.

Rosa wanted to laugh but refrained from doing so. She walked to her and settled on a stool next to Kitty. "You don't like Chang? Hmm, I'm surprised. I've always found him very affable."

"Affable" He's a chump!"

Rosa couldn't help herself and laughed aloud.

"Kitty, he isn't that bad."

Kitty frowned and then drew up her knitting needles, pointing them at Rosa. "He's a menace. How can someone not like Philomena?"

"Well, I have to say I'm biased. Chang and I grew up together in the early days at the mission. He means well. I know he may come across as a stuffed shirt but...."

"Stuffed shirt? I'd say more likely a taxidermist's next project. I hope he was happier as a boy, because he barely cracks his face now. Have you ever seen him smile as an adult?"

"Circumstances are a little strained between us."

"Tell me, has he ever been a happy person?" Kitty insisted as those needles twitched dangerously in Rosa's direction.

"Well...perhaps he was always a little reserved. Who wouldn't be? He had been taken from his family at an early age to live in a strange place with even stranger people."

"Stranger people?"

"Europeans, not Chinese." Rosa drew in a deep breath. She remembered the thin boy with the look of fear in his eyes when he'd arrived at the mission. "He was my best friend for a long time," Rosa said wistfully.

There was silence in the room and Rosa stood and walked to the door. "I'll make us some tea. Phil and Blake should be back soon."

Kitty nodded and began the click clack of her needles.

She wondered what was so important that Phil and Blake had needed to check it right away. Maybe Gilda?

✝

"Give it a rest, Blake," Phil said.

"I will not. You made a bad call and that's all there is to it," Blake replied.

Rosa heard the conversation in the tiny hall as the two entered the house.

"When I tell Rosa, she's not going to be happy."

"Then you won't tell her because my priority is keeping her happy," Phil hissed.

Rosa chose that moment to enter the fray.

"Good to know, but what's the problem?" Rosa asked.

"Hey, love, nothing. Absolutely nothing. Just guy talk."

"Really? And when did you become a guy?" Rosa raised her eyebrows.

Blake laughed.

"What isn't going to make me happy, Blake?"

Blake dropped his gaze.

"You know how it is…just work stuff," he muttered.

Rosa shook her head.

"Tea and sandwiches are being served in the front room."

Rosa turned and went back to the tiny kitchen area. She counted under her breath to twenty and Phil appeared in the doorway.

"It isn't anything to worry about," Phil said.

Rosa turned and faced Phil. "You said you'd never lie to me."

Rosa watched as Phil moved from one side of the door to the other before she replied. "I'm not."

"Okay, then what's the issue with you and Blake? He sounded upset."

"You shouldn't have been listening."

Rosa bristled at that and kept silent. "Keep your secrets then." She turned back to the task at hand and with a heavy tray, she moved toward Phil.

"Look, let's talk about this. I can explain," Phil said.

"You just did." Rosa moved passed Phil.

"Rosa, don't freeze me out."

Rosa heard the words and ignored them. After all, she shouldn't have been listening. She entered the parlor and shut the door behind her.

†

Phil stood in the passageway after she heard the click of the door closing behind Rosa. She dragged a hand across her face. "Will this nightmare of a day ever end?"

Taking a deep breath, she opened the parlor door and entered.

"Philomena! Lovely, now we can have tea," Kitty declared.

Phil smiled and sat crossed legged on the woven mat on the floor. She didn't look in Rosa's direction for fear that her lover was angry at her big time. She suspected neither of them could take much more overload today.

"Gilda's in a bad way," Phil said.

All eyes in the room turned to her.

"What do you mean?" Kitty was the first to ask.

Blake took Kitty's hand. "Don't worry, my dear, I shall fix her."

"Phil," Rosa said.

Phil settled her nerves. *Hell, this was worse than killing the Jap.*

"She took a few bullets too many. I knew she was sluggish but we needed to get the children to safety so I made a call. It was the right one. We got here safely, no drama."

"Drama!"

Phil refused to look at Rosa. Her one word reply was enough.

"Drama. Yeah, right, it was drama. I made the call. What's the problem? We arrived safely. I'm damned if I don't bring you home safe and damned if I do. What kind of odds are those?" Phil stood and paced to the window to look out on to the quiet street. There were a few people passing and an old man in a rocking chair outside the front door opposite.

"You put them all in jeopardy," Kitty said quietly.

"Sure I did and I would do it again. There is no decent protocol now, Kitty. It is kill or be killed. I wasn't leaving Rosa and the kids to that fate. I chose our own fate and I will every time. I'm proud of that," Phil said. She walked to the door. "I need a cigarette."

Chapter Twenty-two

"I'm proud of you."

Phil's heart pounded at the words. If there was one person in the world that she needed to be proud of her, it was Rosa. Stamping out the half-smoked cigarette, Phil gazed at Rosa. She stood on the only step of the front door with her hands clasped around her middle.

The elfin features that had attracted Phil in the first place seemed to glow in the candle light of the hanging lantern.

"I really am, Phil."

"I know you are." Phil moved the couple of feet separating them and pulled her into a hug.

"I needed that," Rosa said, settling her head against Phil's shoulder.

"Me too. I thought maybe I was in the doghouse."

Rosa sighed and then kissed Phil's neck. The chills that went down Phil's body had her desperately calming her clamoring desire to pick Rosa up and take her to bed.

"After what you did today, there wouldn't be a doghouse in the world that I'd put you in." Rosa gazed into Phil's eyes and smiled. "I love you, plain and simple."

"Plain and simple, huh. Well, I thought I was quite good-looking." Phil grinned.

"You are incorrigible."

"Oh, yes, Ma'am." Phil chuckled.

Rosa laughed and moving away a little, stroked the skin along Phil's cheeks. "It's going to be a long road, isn't it?"

Phil knew what Rosa was asking and she drew a deep breath before pulling Rosa closer. "However long it is, it doesn't matter as long as we are together. Our love will beat any odds."

"You say that so confidently," Rosa whispered.

"Don't you think so?" Phil asked. Furrowing her brow at what appeared to be Rosa's hesitation in the path they had chosen. "Look, if you want to go back to England, no one will think any less of you."

Rosa shook her head and lifted her chin. "It isn't about me."

"The kids I can see...."

Rosa shook her head.

"Okay, Kitty and Blake. They are old but...."

Once more Rosa gave a negative response.

Phil released Rosa and scratched her head. "I give in. Who?"

Rosa smiled.

Phil's heart fluttered.

"You. I feel I bamboozled you into this journey and I don't think I can live with myself if anything happened to you because of it."

Phil blinked rapidly at the sincere statement. She felt tears shimmering in her eyes as she took in the significance of the words. "No one except my uncle has ever cared about me in such a way. If I ever had any doubts about our relationship surviving the odds, they have dissipated right here and now."

She pulled Rosa close and kissed her head.

"If there was a situation that I've been bamboozled, as you say, into, this is one that I'll be forever grateful for being involved with. If I didn't love you with my heart and soul already, you could have what remained except there isn't anything. You have it all…warts and all."

Rosa smiled and lifted her head, kissing Phil lightly on the lips.

"I love the warts and all. Do you think it would be rude if we just went to bed," Rosa said.

Phil understood. It had been a traumatic couple of days and Rosa must be beat. "They will understand. It's been a long trip in many ways. I know I could do with the sleep. I'm beat."

Rosa frowned then took Phil's hand. "Who said anything about sleep? Unless you're really tired, that is."

"Me? No, it wasn't me who said that. Honest." Phil grinned, allowing Rosa to lead her back inside the house.

✝

Blake answered the door, calling out to Phil at the same time. "We promised to meet the ladies at the square in half an hour. Are you up yet?"

As the door swung open, Blake was astonished to see Chang standing there. His athletic body was taut and his face held an expression of distaste.

"Hello. Can I help you, Chang?"

"I'm here to see Casters."

The tone had Blake grimacing. *Hmm, this didn't sound promising.*

"Well, I'm not sure that…."

Phil gently thrust Blake out of the way. "Now, what can I do for you, Chang?"

"You have brought shame on Rosa's family name. I call you out to rectify that." Chang shouted.

Blake frowned.

"I don't fight in public, Chang."

Chang snorted. "Not even for one you profess to love. I call that a shallow person and not worthy of her affection."

Blake saw Phil puff out her chest before she answered.

"Rosa doesn't believe in violence, so I'll decline."

"Coward, hiding behind another woman's skirt." Chang turned away.

Phil moved like lightening and pushed at Chang's shoulder.

"Where and when?"

Chang sneered.

"The market in ten minutes." Chang walked away.

Phil turned to Blake and shrugged.

"She won't like it, Phil."

"I know but I'm not a coward and her name isn't shamed. I just can't let that go unchallenged. You can call me stupid."

Blake shook his head then placed a comforting arm on Phil's shoulder. "Not stupid but in love and we all do mad things when we are in love."

Phil smiled weakly.

"Right, let's get some fresh towels and water. Unfortunately, I think we are going need them."

†

The crowd in the center of the village was noisy but cheerfully so. Rosa glanced at Kitty. "Sounds like fun. Shall we watch?"

"Of course. It might be one of those Chinese theatres. They are very good puppeteers, you know."

They walked to the outer circle of the crowd and heard men and women cheering and saw others turning their faces away.

When Rosa politely asked the person next to her what was going on, he gave her a fearful look and moved aside.

As she edged closer to the center and the scene, she clutched Kitty's hand as the villagers were becoming more boisterous.

"I don't think it's a theatre. It sounds more like a sport or something along those lines." Rosa's jaw dropped when she could finally see what was going on.

"No!"

Her eyes bulged as she saw a shirtless Chang kick Phil, who was in a blood-splattered shirt. Phil dropped to the ground.

Rosa reeled at the violence and turned to Kitty. "You don't want to see this, Kitty, we need to go." She spoke the words but wanted the exact opposite.

"What is it, my dear?" Kitty snuck around. "My goodness. Philomena and your Chang."

"He's not *my Chang*," Rosa bristled. Then she spied Blake at the epicenter. He was obviously one of the referees of this barbaric fight. "Blake's there, too. What's going on?"

Kitty, without a further word, strode through the last wall of people and proceeded to Blake's side.

Rosa watched as Chang, who didn't appear injured in any way, pulverized her lover. Blood was seeping from the corner of Phil's left eye and her lip was split. A crunching kick to Phil's abdomen had her bent double and she dropped to her knees again. Rosa watched Chang move like a snake for a final attack. This had to stop.

Without regard for the whys and the wherefores, or protocol, she barged through the line and stood in the middle of the fight.

"What is the meaning of this?" Rosa wrapped her arms around her chest and glared at the two protagonists.

Both parties stared at her in surprise.

She could barely see Phil's eyes because they were swollen shut.

Phil dropped her gaze and touched her lip.

Rosa saw the painful expression on her face as she did so and wanted to run and comfort her—she did not.

Chang's expression was inscrutable.

"I want an answer for this," Rosa demanded.

Out of the corner of her eye, she saw that the people were disappearing, knowing that their impromptu entertainment was finished.

There was silence.

"I see."

Blake and Kitty came closer. Blake picked Phil up from the ground.

Something she should have done, except a part of her knew that Phil would hate that and call it a weakness. What was this? A death wish.

"Chang?"

Chang glared at her.

It was the first time he had ever looked at her with contempt.

"This is between me and—" Chang curled his lips. "The abomination."

Rosa frowned. "Abomination. What are you talking about?"

Chang sneered in Phil's direction.

Blake touched her arm.

"What?" Rosa said waspishly. She regretted her tone immediately when she saw his sad look. He looked so like a hound dog that you wanted to take him in your arms and cuddle him.

"Phil didn't have a choice. Glad you turned up though because our girl was losing ground."

"Losing ground? She could have been killed. Or badly injured if she isn't already. Why?"

Rosa closed her eyes. *You will not die on me in such a way. You will not.*

Blake shrugged. "You."

"Me?" Rosa blinked rapidly.

"Chang called her out about your relationship. Phil won't have any bad words said about you. Chang was adamant that only a fight would solve the problem," Blake said softly. "I think you should go speak with her."

They both looked at Phil who Kitty was ministering to, along with a couple of the villagers.

Rosa closed her eyes for a fraction and sighed.

Damn, you are one reckless person, Phil Casters, but I do love you. And even more so for defending my honor when you were so outclassed.

Rosa squared her shoulders and nodded at Blake. "You go to them. I will be there in a minute."

Blake shrugged and walked away.

Rosa held her head high as she stared at Chang. "You wanted to beat a woman to pulp for me? How does that work, Chang?"

Chang looked down at his hands then gave Rosa a glare.

"To teach her a lesson that it is wrong to pervert God's path for us."

"And that is?"

Chang dropped his gaze for a second then declared loudly. "A woman should be with a man."

Rosa wanted to laugh but didn't. It would obviously incite Chang more. "God's path is that we love, not hate. Each and every one of us deserves love. Life is tough enough without adding hatred into the mix," Rosa said softly.

"You are a hypocrite, Rosa. As a Catholic, you cannot wantonly go down this path. She has bewitched you," Chang replied.

Rosa smiled. "Yes, she has. Did so from the first moment I met her. Her heart is so great, Chang, in compassion and love. If you knew her as I...."

"No. I'm wasting my time here. You cannot stay. It isn't right." Chang began to walk away.

"The Grand Master wishes us to stay, Chang. We haven't a problem with anyone else in Langshow, not that we know of."

"You will."

"Is that a threat?"

Chang sneered and left.

Rosa watched him leave. He was not the man she thought he was. She turned and looked at the people she did care for and at one in particular. *Oh, Phil, I do love you, warts and all.*

†

"You haven't said much since we got back." Phil said, gingerly settling on their bed. Her eyes never left Rosa.

Rosa stood like a statue beside the closed door.

"In fact, you haven't said anything at all."

Rosa stepped forward before retreating to the door.

"Am I so far gone in your eyes that you won't speak with me? I didn't have much choice, Rosa. It was that or his insidious criticism every time we stepped out of the door," Phil declared.

"Perhaps this isn't the place for us," Rosa whispered.

"Nooo, don't say that, darling. You like it here and I frankly don't care about his views. He's not important, you are."

Rosa closed the gap between them and sat on the bed next to Phil.

"Will it always be like this?"

Phil sucked in a silent breath. *The truth. What could she say? Sure. Everyone is a gay basher. You might be spat at, called names, brought into fights that you didn't even know you had enemies with. I can't tell her that she might leave me.*

"You know it doesn't matter to me if people hate our lifestyle. I love you and that's the most important thing...except," Rosa whispered.

"Except?" Phil held her breath.

"Just stop being all macho. I don't need the worry. I need you. Will you promise?" Rosa caught Phil's glance.

"You don't like macho? And I do it so well," Phil replied flippantly. Her heart had stopped and started like someone switching on the electricity. The high was incredible.

"As I said before, incorrigible. Promise?"

Phil reached out and hugged Rosa close, clamping her teeth together at the pain. "I promise."

Rosa grinned and kissed her. When she touched her stomach, Phil involuntarily cried out at the pain. "Now we have to wait to make love. I guess that might consolidate the promise." Rosa grinned. Her fingers began a gentle massaging above the most painful part of Phil's body.

"Damn! I can make love to you in any condition. Want me to show you?"

Rosa chuckled. "Right now, I want you to tell me you love me. The rest...well, that's icing on the cake."

Phil looked into Rosa's eyes and saw the naked love for her embedded there. "I will love you until my dying breath and will be waiting for you until the end of time." Phil stroked a finger down Rosa's pale cheek. "I'm sorry I caused you to worry. I will not do that again."

Rosa nestled into her shoulder. "Don't give promises you can't possibly keep in this current environment."

"I didn't say anything about the environment. I'm talking about you and my love for you."

Phil heard Rosa sob and pulled her closer regardless of the pain she felt. "I meant every word."

"I know. I do, too." Rosa kissed the skin closest to her and Phil was lost. Who cared about a few bruises? They rolled onto the bed.

Epilogue

The sand was pearly white and sifted through their toes as they edged toward an area that was very private. Not that privacy was needed for there wasn't anyone in sight for miles. Phil had taken them on a trip to an area of desert for a day's rest before embarking on their next adventure.

Rosa almost dropped the pillows she carried as she stumbled in a dip in the sand.

"Okay?" Phil asked from behind Rosa.

"Yes, but watch your step. You have the provisions and I'm parched."

Phil laughed. "Thanks for the warning."

"Looks like a great place here. What do you think, Phil?"

Phil threw down the thick blanket she held. "Works for me."

Rosa knelt, straightened the blanket, and then fluffed the pillows they had brought. Now it looked like a cocoon made for them to snuggle into and forget the world.

"What do you think now?" Rosa asked.

Phil stood with arms crossed.

"You don't like it?" Rosa asked tentatively.

Phil grinned. "I love everything, especially you, but…."

"But?"

Phil rummaged in the over-sized bag she had insisted they bring with them. She removed three long stemmed roses and flourished them toward Rosa. "For you, for us, and for everyone we love."

Rosa's eyes watered and she struggled not to cry. "That's—" She shook her head and tried again. "That's perfect."

Phil dropped down and touched her face. "No, you are perfect and that's all that matters."

Rosa leaned into the caress and sighed. "I love you so very much."

"I know and the best of it is, I love you more."

"You do not." Rosa said, then shook her head at the smirk on Phil's face.

Phil moved closer and kissed Rosa passionately until they were both out of breath.

"Wow, you take my breath away."

Rosa smiled and dropped small kisses along Phil's jawline, satisfied when Phil groaned. "Good."

"Anything you want right now." Phil, lying flat on the blanket, drew Rosa over her.

"I know you will think this silly." Rosa knew her cheeks were coloring.

Phil leaned on one elbow and smiled.

"Never."

"It's Christmas and it's the first that I haven't spent with Bang and Tao since they arrived at the mission as babies. I hope they enjoy an English Christmas," Rosa said.

"Tell me what the English Christmas entails and I'll let you know. I'm a foreigner too, you know." Phil gave her a cheeky smile and a gentle kiss on the parted lips.

"Oh, log fires to keep out the cold. A turkey roasting from the early morning with the scent filling the house. I remember the first time I ever had a Christmas in England. It was …sumptuous. Alfred had a stocking hanging from the fireplace filled with presents. I'd never had that before." Rosa sighed.

"That was a happy sigh. I figured that you enjoyed some of your stay in England, contrary to some of the things you have said." Phil smiled.

"I loved Alfred. He was exactly what he purported to be. There was no falseness. My grandfather, in contrast, was cold and difficult to get to know."

"He changed when you were there this last time, right?"

"Yes, he changed. Tao was a lifesaver for my relationship with him. Who would have thought?" Rosa said.

Phil began to rummage in her rucksack and pulled out several parcels.

"Merry Christmas, my love." Phil handed Rosa a small package.

Rosa grinned and ripped at the gaudy paper. It was a snow globe with a snowman as the feature. She read the tag. "It's from Bang and Tao…how?" Rosa looked at Phil with tears in her eyes.

"You forget I have contacts. Donna sent the parcel and I received it by special courier two weeks ago.

"Carrington!" Rosa exclaimed.

"Yeah, handlebar moustache fly boy who wanted one last mission before he was stationed in Hong Kong."

"Phil, that's a terrible description of him. He was so kind to do this."

Phil chuckled.

"It describes him perfectly though, but he is as the British say, a very good chap."

Phil gave Rosa another parcel.

Rosa read the label from her grandfather. She ripped open the silver colored paper and gasped as she saw the contents.

"That's beautiful," Phil whispered.

They both gazed at the solid silver photo frame hinged in the middle. One side of the frame was a wedding photo depicting a couple who looked nervous but happily so—her parents. The second was a recent photo with her grandfather, Bang, Tao, Donna, Nang, the twins, and Edith.

Rosa began to cry.

"Hey, if I'd known that this was going to upset you, I never would have...."

"No. No, Phil, this is wonderful. I miss them but look at that photo, what does it tell you?"

Phil gazed at the images. "They look happy. Come to think of it, I've never seen Nang smile before. Now I know what Donna sees in her."

"Phil." Rosa laughed. "This makes not being with them easier. I could kiss your friend Carrington for bringing them to us."

"Hey, that's a bit too much. No one is going to kiss my girl but me."

Rosa giggled and withdrew a small package from the waistband that held her sarong together.

"This is for you."

Phil took the tiny box and studied it.

"It won't bite if you open it, Phil."

Phil smiled and opened the ornate box. It was a gold phoenix.

"Do you like it?" Rosa asked tentatively.

"It's beautiful," Phil said.

"I might once have called you a man but this, in Chinese tradition, definitely means you are a woman. One I love very deeply."

Rosa saw tears seep down the side of Phil's face and she stroked them away.

"I don't know what to say," Phil said as she wiped tears away.

"How about Merry Christmas."

Phil sniffled and nodded. "Merry Christmas, Rosa."

They shared a slow kiss that seemed to delay time.

"This is where I want to spend the rest of my life, with you, no matter what," Rosa declared softly.

Phil moved to a position where she looked into Rosa's eyes.

"I once thought that love…."

Rosa flashed a frown.

"Was never going to be lasting for me. You spun that one on the head the first time I saw you."

Rosa kissed her hard.

Phil continued. "I will, and have, gone out of my comfort zone for you, and do you know how I feel about that?"

Rosa's heart skipped a beat as she shook her head.

"Marvelous. You give my life meaning. How much more can I want? That isn't a question, just a rhetorical one. I, however, have one regret."

"You do?"

"Sure. Next time Chang gets all macho, I'm going to teach him a lesson he'll never forget."

Rosa giggled then stopped—it wasn't right—yeah, it was. She laughed. "Chang is a better Catholic than I am. Who would have known?"

"Pity you didn't or I might have known the beating I was going to sustain. Not that I'm complaining," Phil winked. "Your ministrations that night were worth every blow. In fact, if he calls me out again I might…."

"You might?" Rosa glared.

Phil smiled. "Okay. I'd decline and say talk it over with the missus."

Rosa shot up and gazed at Phil. *Missus, she had said missus. That meant...wow.*

"You look bemused," Phil said.

Rosa gazed at Phil. "Forget the picnic, forget the rest." She pushed Phil onto the blanket and began an exploration of her body that, if she remembered all Donna had told her, would ensure Phil was satisfied.

"You are The One," she whispered, before her lips covered Phil's.

About the Author

JM Dragon

Born in England JM Dragon is now a New Zealand citizen, living in the beautiful Canterbury countryside. JM Dragon loves to garden, travel, and has a love of animals. Her animals, many of them strays, including even the odd chicken, have proved a new focus in her life. Sharing her life with her family, four cats, two alpacas, and over eighty bantam chickens in differing breeds, she's found a totally different focus in her life than when she lived in England.

Her writing is a long cherished release for the characters that invade her mind on many an occasion. Always having written stories from a child, she found the Internet a place she could share her creative world with other readers. Having stumbled across venues on the net for her writing, she found new subjects to explore. She currently loves the creative, readership, and friendship genre she has comfortably taken residence in for the last fourteen years. She is also a keen reader of sci-fi, crime/mystery, classic, and romance, of course. She loves to explore different plot lines in her stories.

Other Books from Affinity eBook Press

The Chronicles of Ratha: Book 2 A Lion Among The Lambs—Erica Lawson It has been three years since Jordana Laren's path first crossed the Noorthi's—three years since she's had a drink, had sex, and a life of her own. Her only excitement has been spent keeping up with her two year-old daughter, Rice, who is definitely a chip off the old block. All has been peaceful until one of the colonists becomes sick. Bad news shifts to worse news when the disease spreads through their community. Unable to get proper medicine, Jordana is forced to rely on the Noorthi healers to come up with a cure. Soon the herbs run out, leaving her with no choice but to search for more on the Noorthi home planet. What is supposed to be a simple pick-up flight turns into a nightmare. Can Jordana believe in herself like her Noorthi sisters do? Only then can she fulfill her destiny as The Chosen One. Follow the colorful cast of characters in this action-packed adventure sequel as they traverse the galaxy. Of course, nothing ever goes smoothly when Jordana is involved.

Cowgirl Up—Ali Spooner When the new ranch hand, Coal Bryan, arrives at the MC2, the last thing she's looking for is love. Her co-workers are surprised when Coal turns out to be female. Coal, used to the reaction, quickly earns the respect of the crew with her work ethic and skill with horses. Coal uses the strenuous work and friendship of the ranch hands to try and forget her broken past. Melissa Conway, owner of MC2, offers Coal a place to live in her home. The both are shocked to find they are linked in a way neither of them imagined. Mary Leah, Melissa's sister, arrives at the ranch to recover from a recent tragedy. The attraction between Mary Leah and Coal is instant and mutual. Can the three women survive their personal dilemmas? The love and friendship they develop certainly helps but will it be enough to bring them together. Ride along with the crew of the MC2, for boot scootin', butt kickin', dirt eatin', rodeo adventures, with a love story thrown into the mix.

The Chronicles of Ratha: Book 1 Children of the Noorthi—Erica Lawson Jordana Laren is a hard-drinking, hard-fighting womanizer, who works as a freighter pilot in her spare time. Her latest customer drugs her, steals her ship, and abandons her on a desert hellhole called Rigeus, infamous penal planet for the worst women criminals. Her chances of survival aren't looking good. She has no food, water, or weapons, and the nearest bar is a million miles away. Just when she's ready to write her last will and testament, Jordana is rescued by a group of barely-clad women. Has she found nirvana? Her own personal harem seems like a possibility, until the intercession of their enemy, the Velkren. Their leader, Vel, remembers Jordana well, and not fondly. But why is Vel on this planet, surrounded by murderers, thieves, and bad-tempered bitches? Jordana knows Vel isn't a prisoner, so why is her nemesis on Rigeus mining mud, of all things? Jordana knows only one thing. She has to get off the planet before Vel kills her. Unfortunately, the women who saved her reveal themselves to be holy. They are the Noorthi, and Jordana's dream of endless debauchery becomes a nightmare of eternal servitude. The Noorthi make her one of them, marking her with a wrist tattoo, and leaving her no choice but to protect them with her life. The last thing Jordana wants is to become involved in galactic politics or heroic actions. But the tattoo ochre in her body is suddenly giving her morals and scruples, not to mention a better vocabulary! And she really can't pass up a chance to outwit Vel, whose megalomaniac plans are endangering not only the Noorthi, but the civilized galaxy itself. But Jordana is torn. Does she stop Vel at all costs, or does she get out from under the thumb of the Noorthi while she can? Some things were never meant to be easy…

If I Were a Boy—Erin O'Reilly Katie McGuire appears to have it all. A devoted husband, a job she loves, and a comfortable lifestyle. Helen Swenson is a successful financial director of a prominent investment firm, with an unfaithful husband, and few friends. Their husbands' annual trip to Padre Island National Seashore to reunite with their air force pilot squad becomes a pivotal point for the two women. Their lives take on a completely new meaning when an undeniable magnetism between them draws them together. Passion and secrecy becomes the norm, as they have no choice but to surrender to their attraction. Can the vacation love affair continue? When they leave for their respective homes, will they regret what happened? Life is not that easy to change and the people around them are the hardest to convince. There is no more powerful motivation than love. Except hate and there are plenty of people who want to see their relationship destroyed. Will Katie and Helen be able to make a life together work or succumb to doubts and the pressures of family? This story will fill you with the thrill of passion and the tenderness of love.

Nesting—Renee MacKenzie Macy Stokes, a divorced mother who is struggling with her sexual identity, jumps at a once-in-a-lifetime opportunity to help her friends. She doesn't foresee it will put her in jeopardy of losing her son, Jeremiah. Fresh out of high school, Cam Webber travels to Augusta, Georgia, to reconcile with her aunt. When she learns that's impossible, she determines to gain acceptance from her aunt's partner, Sharon. Meanwhile, Cam sets her sights on Macy, but Macy has other ideas. Kenny Brewer is a good old boy who loves his wife, Dorianne, even when he thinks she's gone totally off her rocker. Dorianne gets it in her head that a local woman is her long-lost half-sister. But soon, her obsession with that is eclipsed by medical problems that involve them all. Set in Augusta, Georgia, *Nesting* explores the age-old issues of guilt, regret, and redemption, and the part they play in driving people to create and protect family-at any cost.

Reece's Faith—TJ Vertigo In the return of the main characters from the bestselling novel *Private Dancer*, we see the blossoming relationship of bar owner, Reece Corbett and actress, Faith Ashford. The two women explore new, uncertain territory together, using sexual intimacy as a glue of comfort, helping them become strong and whole. A trusting Reece shares with Faith the sordid tale of how she became *The Animal* and Faith finds herself newly empowered by Reece's ongoing trust and support. Jealousy arises when Faith has to kiss a man on her TV show and two amorous women stalk Reece. When Faith is outed on her television show, things get crazy. With the arrival of her parents on the scene, the craziness escalates. As Faith tries to justify her lifestyle and defend her love for Reece, she discovers that nothing about her parents is as she once believed. This, not to be missed passionate and erotic romance, will have you begging for more.

Starting Over—Jen Silver Ellie Winters, a successful potter, is living on a remote hilltop farm inherited from her parents. Her well-ordered life is shaken apart when her past meets her present. Robin Fanshawe, Ellie's philandering long-term lover, has a fragile truce with Ellie. The arrival of women from Robin's present threatens to break that tentative pact. Charming Dr. Kathryn Moss, an archaeologist and an old lover of Ellie's, arrives on the farm searching for a new site to dig. When she discovers a previously unknown Roman settlement and ancient burial site on Ellie's farm, Ellie allows her to start an archaeological dig of the area. Will Ellie also allow the rekindling of an old romance or will she stay with Robin? Can that long term relationship, albeit tentative, recover from this collision or will an old romance trump everything she knows? Will Robin, seeing the interaction between Ellie and Kathryn, leave her womanising ways behind? Will she take a chance on giving herself wholly to the woman she loves? These questions and the mystery of whose royal resting place is disturbed at Starling Hill are answered in this classic romance of simmering passions, anguished loss, and the wonder of love.

Twisted Lives—Ali Spooner A twist of fate leaves Bet and her daughter Kylie stranded at the entrance of the home of Alex Graves, as she flees the control of an abusive husband. When custom–homebuilder Alex arrives to find steam boiling from Bet's car and a beautiful child asleep in the passenger seat, her heart goes out to them. Alex offers shelter to the pair setting off a chain of events that bring both mother and daughter close to her heart and danger to her door. A heartwarming story of true love that will keep you smiling long after you've finished the book.

Malodorous—Del Robertson Sequel to My Fair Maiden Something in Fairhaven stinks. Other than the mutton stew, that is. Gwen thought life after being a virgin sacrifice would be a bed of roses. Bodhi was just looking for a wench to bed. Neither less-than-dashing hero nor not-quite-so-pure maiden imagined they would meet again, much less be trapped together in a city the likes of the ill-named Fairhaven. There's a killer on the loose. Fairhaven's on lockdown, its citizens fearful for their lives. The local guards are corrupt. And, Bodhi's been accused of murder...

Desert Blooms—Dannie Marsden Luce's story continues in DESERT BLOOMS... When we last met Luce Velazquez in Desert Heat, she went through hell and back to salvage her soul and reputation. Hoping to get her life back on track with lover Beth Ryan, a woman who understands her pain and can relate on every level. Instead, Luce is in the hospital, and Beth in protective custody. Jessica Sullivan, Luce's friend and ex, has big doubts about the sincerity of Beth's love, and is in no hurry to release her from custody. Can Luce's new found happiness last, or is Jessica correct in her doubts? A heart stopping romance that will fill you with the wonder of friendship, anger of betrayal, and the everlasting vision of love.

Finding Her Way—Riley Jefferson Is it love or just great sex? After ending an abusive marriage, Jerrica Kerrison is finally alive and she's apologizing for nothing! She has a job with a financial firm in Boston, a townhouse in Newburyport, and a sports car she drives way too fast. Jerrica has everything except that indefinable emotion called love. Madison Jeffrey is a lost soul. A PR job in the south has always protected Madison from the pressures of her family. But one day, fate brings her back to New England, forcing Madison to face her long buried demons, and a sister who despises her. When a chance meeting brings Jerrica and Madison's separate worlds crashing together, the attraction is instantaneous. After one passionate night together, Jerrica retreats into the safety of her world, leaving Madison to figure out what happened. Will Jerrica open up her heart to the idea of love? Can Madison finally believe that she is worthy of unconditional love? Or will a devil hiding in the shadows tear them apart?

HER—Lisa Ron Fox has been looking for that one person who will make her feel complete-her perfect match. Together with her friends, Megan and Tree, Fox continues her quest while dodging exes and clingers, laughing a lot along the way. When she meets Madeline, she instantly knows that she has found HER. Madeline has her own problems-notably a domineering husband. Can Fox win her heart? Can they make a life together? This story will make you laugh, cry, and hold your breath as the story unfolds. With the right person love can conquer all.

Bayou Justice—Ali Spooner Hell hath no fury like a woman scorned. When Kara, Sasha's new lover is taken hostage as a diversionary tactic to allow the drug dealing Bellfontaine brothers to escape justice, Sasha springs into action. Kara is released physically unharmed, however her emotions and budding career in the District Attorney's office are left in shambles when she is held to blame for their release, Appalled by the failure of the criminal justice system, Sasha exacts her own brand of justice for the acts committed against her lover. From the Bayous of Louisiana to the jungles of South America, Sasha plots her revenge.

Out of Retirement—Erica Lawson Melanie Stokes was a doctor—a very good one, or so she hoped. She was calm and cool under pressure, and very little fazed her. Until…Caitlin Joseph ran a small retirement home for older women in need. The fact that everyone in the house was gay was a coincidence, although it did cut down the number of women agreeing to live there. Mel took up an offer to do some relief work for a local community center when their regular doctor was away on holidays. As soon as she arrived at the home she knew something was different about the place. Was it the little old lady chasing the paper boy down the street or the sign saying "Dykes Retirement Home"? But there was something about the place that also appealed to her. Sure, Caitlin was cute as a button, but it was more the fact that she took very good care of her charges despite their rather bizarre behavior. The older women seized the opportunity to introduce a woman into Caitlin's lonely life, using any means possible to keep Mel coming back. Their plans were boosted by the introduction of another woman into the house, who set hearts a fluttering and blood pressure rising. Now if she was a lesbian it would have been perfect…

Letting Go—JM Dragon A failed relationship puts Stella Hawke's life on the brink of chaos. When her grandmother falls gravely ill in Ashville, Stella ends her army career to take care of the woman during her last weeks. Little does she know that an old army comrade, socialite Reggie Stockton, whose family owns the local newspaper, also lives in Ashville. Will she allow herself to accept Reggie's help to turn her life around and let go of the past? This is a journey where both women re-evaluate what they want out of life. Will that path lead to happiness or to a parting of the ways?

Through the Darkness—Erin O'Reilly Becca Cameron is a loner—by choice. She lives in a hundred year old farmhouse built by her great grandfather. A tragic accident in her home a year earlier drove away her lover, and Becca tries to accept what she cannot change and hang on to the belief that love can conquer all. Chase Hunter had a meteoric rise in the Eastman Corporation and was, at thirty-four, the youngest vice-president. To Chase, her work was all consuming leaving little time for friends or lovers. There was simply no place in her life for anything but her job. When Becca and Chase meet at their work place, the attraction is spontaneous. Life begins to look brighter for both women as work takes a second seat to romance. Unknown to either woman, someone is watching their every move... Will passion outweigh doubt? Can love conquer fear?

Beginning of the End—Alane Hotchkin What happens when life doesn't go exactly as you planned and you must protect others from your own fate? Escaping a horrific childhood, Nikki longed to find happily ever after in adulthood. What she found was Hell. Or did it find her? Finding the courage to break the cycle of betrayal, she opens her heart one last time. Alex lived a childhood others dreamed of. Her father never once denied the young rebel a thing. All her life she dreamed of protecting others; to follow in her father's footsteps. Soon though she learned sex and fists made the most powerful of weapons. Alex controls the women in her life through fear and sex, will breaking the cycle be too much to overcome? Will loving Nikki be enough to change her, or is Alex beyond help? Alex would give Nikki the world, but at what price? When a person's tightly controlled reality snaps, what then...? This is the Beginning of the End for one of them and the ultimate sacrifice for the other. But who is who in this game of life?

Galveston 1900: Swept Away—Linda Crist On September 7-8, 1900, the island of Galveston, Texas, was destroyed by a hurricane, or 'tropical cyclone' as it was called in those days. This story is a fictional account of Mattie and Rachel, two women who lived there, and their lives during the time of the 'great storm'. Forced to flee from her family at a young age, Rachel Travis finds a home and livelihood on the island of Galveston. Independent, friendly, and yet often lonely, only one other person knows the dark secret that haunts her. Madeline "Mattie" Crockett is trapped in a loveless marriage, convinced that her fate is sealed. She never dares to dream of true happiness, until Rachel Travis comes walking into her life. As emotions come to light, the storm of Mattie's marriage converges with the very real hurricane. Can they survive, and build the life they both dream of? This second edition of one of Linda Crist's best-loved novels maintains the original story, while incorporating some reader-pleasing passages that were cut from the first edition. As an added bonus, the short story "Something to Celebrate" is included at the end of the novel, detailing further adventures of Rachel and Mattie.

Rapture: Sins of the Sinners—A. C. Henley & Fran Heckrotte   A serial killer is targeting young lesbians throughout the state of Texas. Texas Ranger Cochetta Lovejoy is assigned to the case. Convinced she knows who is committing the murders, Ranger Lovejoy is willing to do whatever it takes to put the perpetrator behind bars--even if it means stretching the limits of the law by manipulating the judicial system. Detective Agnes Kelly-Elliott is one of Ft. Worth Police Department's finest investigators. When Ranger Lovejoy appears on the crime scene of a recent murder, Agnes fears a dark secret that, if revealed, could destroy her family ties and end her career. This is a dark, gritty, graphic tale of desire gone awry, and flawed characters looking for redemption in all the wrong places.

Absolution—S. Anne Gardner Games of the rich and famous, love, lust, and forbidden passions weave this tale that play out through decades and the world. The close ties the Alcalas have to the royal house of Spain provide them with an unspoken untouchable policy. Their passions and their secrets are about to come to light with a force that cannot be stopped. In this whirlwind is Cristina Uraca Alacala who is searching for a truth that has been denied to her most of her life and she must find. She is not unlike her family; Cristina does not stop until she gets what she wants. In the fog lies the truth that she must travel through to find. In this tale wealthy socialite Annais Francesca D'Autremond is a pivotal person of interest in Cristina's search for the truth. When these two women meet they find themselves drawn together by something greater than themselves. As the truth of a hidden past becomes clearer their passions grow beyond the realm of the no return instead of a status quo. Both tied together by destiny; will both survive the onslaught of past and present passions?

Denial—Jackie Kennedy Time spent in Somalia has Doctor Celeste Cameron accustomed to living and working in a war zone. Coming back home to America, Celeste is glad to see the end of the peril she has been in—or so she thinks. Danger seems to follow Celeste and she finds it in the shape of Amy. What Celeste feels for Amy scares her more than anything she has faced in war zones. Amy has the same feelings, but is in denial and vows to marry Josh, Celeste's twin brother, no matter what. When fate brings them together again, will they give in to their mutual attraction or will they once again deny what they feel?

Taming the Wolff—Del Robertson ONLY ONE WOMAN... As devastatingly beautiful as she is headstrong, noble-born Alexis DeVale abruptly finds her preordained life in upheaval. Abducted at sword-point, held for ransom, thrust into a maelstrom of lawlessness and piracy... HAS THE POWER... The strength of her passion, the depth of her love... TO TAME THE WOLFF... Mayhem. Brutality. Murder. These are the tools of the trade - and Kris Wolff is the master of her profession. Captain of the high seas, a roguish pirate, her heart hardened by life, her passion tightly controlled by the secret she's forced to keep. Faced with a new danger, The Wolff finds herself unable to guard her heart from the tumultuous desires that Alexis DeVale has awakened.

Private Dancer—TJ Vertigo Reece Corbett grew up on the mean streets on New York City, abused, used and in trouble with the law. Faith Ashford grew up wealthy, with all the creature comforts that money provides. When they meet fireworks begin.

E-Books, Print, Free e-books

Visit our website for more publications available online.

www.affinityebooks.com

Published by Affinity E-Book Press NZ LTD
Canterbury, New Zealand

Registered Company 2517228